Sale $32.00 4/17

I LIKED MY LIFE

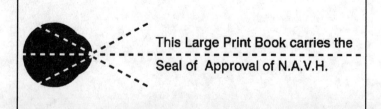

This Large Print Book carries the
Seal of Approval of N.A.V.H.

LIBRARY OF CONGRESS CIP DATA ON FILE.
CATALOGUING IN PUBLICATION FOR THIS BOOK
IS AVAILABLE FROM THE LIBRARY OF CONGRESS

ISBN-13: 978-1-4104-9847-2 (hardcover)
ISBN-10: 1-4104-9847-6 (hardcover)

Published in 2017 by arrangement with St. Martin's Press, LLC

Printed in the United States of America
1 2 3 4 5 6 7 21 20 19 18 17

I Liked My Life

Abby Fabiaschi

THORNDIKE PRESS
A part of Gale, Cengage Learning

LP FIC FABIASCHI

GALE
CENGAGE Learning·

Farmington Hills, Mich • San Francisco • New York • Waterville, Maine
Meriden, Conn • Mason, Ohio • Chicago

For my father,
Michael Anthony Fabiaschi
1955–2008

He had the gift of stopping time and
listening well so that it was easy to hear
who we could become.

— Brian Andreas

Twenty percent of the author's proceeds support women and children's charities around the globe. *Learn more at www.abbyfabiaschi.com.*

Chapter One

MADELINE

I found the perfect wife for my husband. She won't be as traditional as I was, which is good. She won't be as intelligent either, but Brady endured twenty years of my unending intelligence. Under my tutelage he learned that kale lowers cholesterol, a little girl wanting to marry her daddy is normal, and no matter how many times you look up at the road, emailing while driving is no safer than drinking and driving. These insights were valuable at the time, but useless given our present circumstance.

It's humbling, really. I spent my life hellbent on not turning weak like my mother, who let jugs of Gallo wine make most of her decisions, and yet what Brady needs now is someone softer than me. Not fluffy, not gooey — he'd never fall for a ditzy or fickle woman — but not so damn right all the time either. Someone who won't be ir-

9

ritated by the intermittent pauses he takes in the middle of a sentence. A good listener, a sleeper-inner, a nonscorekeeping woman naturally inclined to nurture our daughter Eve.

Recruitment is the least I can do.

I focused on elementary teachers, knowing it takes the unique combination of enthusiasm and patience to choose a profession where you spend most of the day reasoning with six-year-olds. The demoralized state of my family won't be a turn-on to the easily deterred. I was at first disheartened to find almost every teacher accessorized with a wedding ring. It's as though men know how tiresome they are and set out to marry women proficient at putting up with baloney. The available pool was so picked over that the few remaining were bitter about it, but as I readied to move on to nurses, I spotted Rory. She was on bus duty, sporting large, circular sunglasses and rhinestone-studded flip-flops. She somehow managed to look cool at forty, hopefully by not having kids. Brady and Eve have no room for additional baggage; there can be no *blending of families* in their future. Rory's brown hair was pulled back in a loose braid, every inch of exposed skin covered in freckles. She remained all smiles, even when a shot of snot from a passing boy landed on her skirt.

She's in the grocery store now. I'm taking in particulars to make sure my instinct is correct. You'd think intuitive faculties heighten after death, a sort of cosmic prize for crossing the finish line, but so far they have not. The Last World sits unceremoniously like a movie screen below me. There's no spirit offering guidance. I'm not gracefully soaring above in white satin gleaning insight on the existential questions that once kept me awake at night. People think of ghosts as haunting, but it's the other way around. You all haunt me. My life is now a delicious dessert just out of reach.

Perhaps I'm in purgatory. If I had known I'd cross the finish line in my forties, I might have given formal religion more consideration. Brady's parents were big into it, and there were a couple years during adolescence when my mom dropped Meg and me off at catechism, leveraging the church as a sort of free babysitting. She got the idea at an AA meeting, which I assumed was where one went to learn new places to hide booze, since after she came home from AA she always relocated her stash.

What did that young nun tell us? I strain to recall the details. Evil souls go to hell, pure

Catholics go to heaven, and souls destined for heaven but in time-out for reasons that are now a blur go to purgatory. I'm certain she said one couldn't go from purgatory to hell or stay in purgatory forever, because I remember finding it odd there were such defined, well-documented rules. Did someone have a direct line with God and, if so, could we kindly request more willpower for our mother?

I do sense there's more to the spiritual world than my current purview detects but see no path to get there. For me, there's nothing but space and time. That I put myself here makes it that much more agonizing. I won't find peace until I make things right for my family.

It pleases me when Rory selects a beautiful cut of veal. Brady would never fall for a vegetarian. Her choices suggest she's a good cook — pancetta, scallions, artichokes, capers — ingredients you'd avoid if you didn't know what you were doing. My replacement needs to know her way around a kitchen. Growing up, my mother leveraged the same ten ingredients for breakfast, lunch, and dinner. Our menu recycled like the school cafeteria's. Steak and potatoes from the night before became steak and hash browns for breakfast, steak sandwiches for lunch, and beef stew for dinner. Mayonnaise was duct tape in her kitchen; there was nothing it couldn't fix. Too dry? Spicy? Soupy? Thank God for Hellmann's. By the time I had my own kitchen I was desperate for variety, leaving Brady spoiled. With me gone he's lost weight, too much weight. I notice it especially in his face, where his skin suddenly hangs to his cheekbones for dear life.

Dinners were a big event in our house. We ate late to accommodate Brady's work schedule. I gave Eve a sizable after-school snack and she never complained. We all looked forward to the hour together. Every night, I set the table with clean linens and our gold-rimmed wedding china. The china was mostly to tease my sister, Meghan, who claimed registering for it was a waste. "You'll never use it, Maddy," she warned. "No one ever does." I'd call her sometimes as I set out the plates and we'd laugh.

"Who knew you'd become such a domestic diva?" she said one night. "I thought the ambition of a Wellesley College valedictorian would shatter glass ceilings." Right before I thought to be offended, she added, "Somehow you were blessed with perspective most intelligent people lack."

That's Meg for you.

When Brady got home he'd go straight for the stereo. Hellos and everything else commenced only after the music started. Harry Connick Jr. is Brady's favorite. I joked it was because people say they look alike, with their brown flowing hair and eyes set wide apart, but really, Brady loves anything that relies heavily on the piano. Music floated through the house as I put the finishing touches on dinner. We'd often sit at the table long after we finished eating, announcing our roses and thorns of the day, making plans for the upcoming weekend, laughing, occasionally debating. I'd advertise the book that had my attention, and Eve and Brady would rattle off all the reasons they were too busy to borrow it when I finished.

Eve came out with some doozies during these meals, often putting her raging hormonal perspective out there to digest with dinner. One night, when her usual vivacity didn't return with her from school, she said, "My thorn today was realizing that I have nothing to do with who I am. I'm whatever you've made me." I choked on my wine and stared at my Freudian thirteen-year-old, recognizing it was a deep thought. But on a Wednesday night with no context it was also a little over my head. A scary moment for any mother.

Brady recovered more gracefully, laughing off her drama. "Whoa there. Mom and I aren't signing up for that responsibility. You own who you are." It still sounded strange to hear Brady call me Mom. We swore we'd never be that couple, but when Eve's first word was *Maddy* we abandoned our adult identities without much discussion.

Eve looked down at her plate and let out a practiced sigh. "I knew you'd say something like that."

"It's true; I'm predictable," Brady said. "But my parents didn't make me that way. It's who I am." Eve gave a half smile at his cleverness and I beamed at the impressive level of communication from my highly functional family. There was always plenty to talk about then. Now our house, which used to be inviting with its oversized wooden door and broken-in welcome mat, is so dark and silent that passersby assume it's empty.

"Miss Murray," a girl shrieks, approaching Rory and ending my reverie.

"Well hello, Annie." Rory abandons a sweet pepper mid-inspection to crouch down and squarely meet the girl's eager eyes.

"Mom's taking me to Boston tomorrow."

"That's wonderful. You'll have to tell the

class about it Monday."

"Okay," Annie agrees, the trip now more exciting. "See ya."

She runs away but Rory remains caught in the moment. Her expression saddens. I need to know why. There must be a way to intuit underpinnings and have impact on the world I left behind. Why else would I be stuck here watching? I keep perfectly still, focusing all my energy on Rory. She clearly craves something, or maybe someone, but I can't discern what.

I'm impatient as she walks to the parking lot. Without the ability to intervene, I can't repair the damage done. My attention drifts as I recall Brady dutifully leaning in for a kiss good night. Sometimes a peck, but sometimes so much more. I linger there until my mind catches the impossibility and substitutes me with Rory. It's a wrenching thought. During those nutty hypothetical conversations married people have I always claimed I'd want Brady to remarry if I died first. I pictured him in his late sixties, needing a partner to tackle aging with. I hadn't realized how cruel afterlife would be, that I'd have to personally select my replacement because Brady would be disoriented and Eve would need support, that I'd have to watch the whole thing from this front-row seat.

I stay with Rory as she loads the trunk of her light-blue Volkswagen Bug. Everything about her is adorable. I struggle to think of the single adjective that would have described me. I come up with *reliable,* maybe *charismatic* on a good day. Certainly not adorable. My face was too angular and my opinions too sharp for a word like that. Rory shuffles around for the bag with eggs in it, moving the delicate goods to the floor. A planner.

Her cell phone rings as the engine starts. The noises compete, so Rory doesn't hear the call until the second ring. The car is in drive as she rakes through her bag. She grabs the phone, looks over her shoulder, and releases the brake in one motion, not realizing the car is moving forward until she hears the crunch of metal. The collision is with a pristine Audi A7.

"Augh," she says, tapping a palm to her forehead in an exaggerated gesture I've never seen anyone do without an audience. That was it — *Augh* — before answering the call on the fifth ring. "Hello?" She stretches her neck to assess the damage.

"Glad I caught you, honey. Your mother is having a tough go of it. Any chance you can get home early? She could use your magic touch."

"I'm about to drop off groceries, but then I'm supposed to tutor. Did Brian show? He promised he'd grace you with his presence at lunch." She laughs uncomfortably at the spite in her words.

"No, but he called. Said work was crazy. I'm sorry." The woman sighs. "I hate to add to your plate, but I can't fork over more meds without something in her stomach."

Tears well in Rory's eyes but don't spill over. "It's no problem, Greta."

"Thanks, sweetheart. I wish everyone I cared for was as lucky as your mother."

Rory cringes at the inaccuracy of that statement. "I'll be home in a bit."

It's borderline superhuman to me that Rory didn't share the news of her fender bender with Greta. Her self-control reminds me of an old deodorant ad from the nineties that featured a woman maintaining total confidence in any situation. The ad ended with a jingle that went, "She stays cool, soft, and dry." I never related to that ad. I would've retold every detail of THE AC-CIDENT. It may have even made the Christmas letter. For Rory, it wasn't worth a mention. This quiet calm is exactly what Brady needs to counter the resurgence of

18

his temper.

I know from often-exaggerated tales at Fourth of July barbecues that Brady was a hothead growing up. His college nickname was The Fireman from some drunken night when he yanked the fire alarm to evacuate a fraternity pledge who'd made a move on his girlfriend, then punched the guy as he exited the building. For as many times as I heard the story, I could never picture Brady in it. Sure, he could be a jackass, but he was my jackass and his temper was never a source of concern. Until now.

Rory walks around to gauge the damage. Her fender is dented but the A7 is unscathed, exposing the fifty-thousand-dollar price difference between the two cars. Still, she leaves a note: *Guilty of an accidental tap . . . Don't see any marks, but here is my name and number in case.* It's the perfect response. The Fireman is no match for this level of serenity.

Rory hops back in the car and again digs through her bag. She grabs a red leather book with a Buddha imprint on the cover. It takes me a moment to realize it's a genuine, tab-for-each-letter, impossible-to-change-when-someone-moves, pages-falling-out-of-the-binding address book. A lost art. I can hear Brady ribbing her already: *1984 called and wants its address book back.* Perhaps Rory will come up with a good retort. Over the years I came to think of Brady's iPhone as physically attached to his hand.

Rory finds the number she needs and musters up a good mood voice while it rings. "Hi, Nancy, it's Rory. I'm terribly sorry to cancel last minute, but can we reschedule tutoring for tomorrow?"

With her calendar now out, a separate leather-bound book, she scrawls an arrow toward the following day, gets off the phone, and immediately dials another number. This one she knows without consulting the Buddha. Before the voice on the other end has an opportunity to greet her, Rory starts in.

"Where the hell were you?" Her teacher's voice has turned aggressive and hollow, almost daring.

"I know. I'm sorry."

"If you were sorry we wouldn't be having this conversation. *Again.*"

"I'm expected to all but sleep here."

Rory holds the phone away from her ear and talks loudly into the receiver. "She is your *mother.* This cancer will *kill* her. *Soon.* Did they skip the definition of *hospice* in law school?"

"Don't talk to me like I'm a child," he

20

says, though he sounds like a child.

Rory slams her hand against the steering wheel of her still-parked car. "Damn it, Brian, THIS ISN'T ABOUT YOU. We're talking about forty-five minutes, once a week."

"That I don't have. I wish you'd stop treating me like a pile of shit for it."

"God. This is my fault, now?"

He clears his throat, which seems to strengthen his resolve. "We can't all be Rory Murray, Salt of the Fucking Earth."

"Fine," Rory says, defeated. "Focus on you. That's what you're good at."

This is my chance to get deeper into her thoughts. I zero in with willful concentration, intense to the point of exhaustion, and suddenly I feel it. A sensation. A flash. An *understanding.* Rory is alone and scared. She does not know what to do.

Brady and Eve can relate. And if I can read people's minds then certainly I can influence their actions. This woman is my chance to make things right. My family deserves more than I left behind.

EVE

Today is Mother's Day.

My first thought is stupid: my mom isn't here, so the holiday doesn't exist. But the

21

rest of the world doesn't celebrate *my* mom, they celebrate *their* moms, and their moms didn't recently jump off a building.

My father claims he'll be stuck in a hotel conference room negotiating a deal of "strategic importance" with a bunch of people I'll never know. I guess it's possible. He says when it gets to the end of a merger you work straight through till it's done, but the timing is suspect. Today is going to suck. A meeting that goes from freaking eight in the morning to eight at night on a Sunday is something even Mom would've considered a little too convenient.

I'm swirling cereal around the bowl when Dad walks in, suited up for his big meeting. If he's lying to get out of the tennis tournament he at least feels bad enough to wear a costume that matches his cover story. I wonder how he'll handle this moment. Baby me? Ignore the significance of the day altogether? Without Mom telling him what to do, he's a dud at parenting.

"Say you're sick," he offers. His eyes shift around the room, working hard not to land on me.

"Huh?"

"Skip the tournament. Everyone will understand."

He did *not* just say that. I give him an icy

glare. "Pretty sure Mom wouldn't tell me to bail on a commitment just because it was gonna be rough." He doesn't have a comeback, so he grabs a water bottle from the fridge and leaves for work.

I don't have time to be pissed that my father has the emotional maturity of a toddler, because my ride arrives. I wait for the horn to blare before getting up, delaying the start of this depressing day. It takes Kara all of thirty seconds to lose it. She's a spaz. On our eighth grade trip to D.C., she jumped in a fountain because she was hot, then freaked when they sent her home for it. She seriously has zero self-control. I ditch breakfast, grab my tennis bag, and head out.

Kara's ghostlike coloring gives away her hangover, which is strange since we never party before game days. I wonder where everyone met up, then remember I don't care. John is with his family opening their Cape house for the spring, so I'm not surprised no one thought to call. Mourning a parent is way too heavy for my crowd.

Kara drives while her mom rides shotgun, so at least I have the backseat to myself. Like my dad, they both avoid looking at me. Apparently, not having a mother on Mother's Day is something I should be embarrassed about. *Whatever.* Anything is better than the hysteria Kara brought to my mother's funeral, where she bawled as if she were the one left behind. I didn't get why she'd make such a scene until my father and I led the procession out and I saw her folded up in Jake's arm, a spot she'd been jonesing for all year. Always nice to see a tragic death exploited for a high-school hookup.

"Wind will be twenty miles an hour from the northwest," Kara reports. I nod, not that anyone's watching. "The end courts will be the worst, especially the side closest to the field."

Kara always talks up an excuse for getting her ass kicked. When her ball hits the net it's because of the wind, or a baby crying, or the sun's glare. It's never because she tilted her racket too far.

"Good point," Mrs. Anderson pipes in. "The court we get will matter."

Kara's mom considers her and her daughter a single unit, using words like *we* and *our* when referring to things Kara will experience on her own. She even puts her hair in a high pony and wears a tennis skirt to our matches, as though she might be called in to sub. My mom hated gossip, but I once heard her rag on Mrs. Anderson, "The coach needs to pull that lunatic aside and break the news she didn't make the team. Our turn ended three decades ago. Christie seriously needs to get over it." When Dad joked that my mom sounded jealous she said, "I'm not gonna lie, I'd take her body if it was completely detached from her heart and her brain." I find the memory particularly funny as Kara and Mrs. Anderson agree *their* court assignment will be critical.

"They still haven't fixed the crack on court three. Coach claims it isn't a tripping hazard, but I took a digger on it yesterday." Mrs. Anderson clucks like a chicken to show her disapproval. I swear she could be the billboard for what annoying looks like.

They're talking about this pointless shit because they don't know what the hell to say to me. It's the same at school. What no one understands is that it doesn't matter what's being said — everything makes me think about my dead mother because that's all I ever think about. Kara literally breaks out in a sweat when we're alone, as if suicidal mothers are contagious. I should tell her not to worry; her wannabe of a mom is way too vain to take her own life.

I've learned to completely block out my friends. I don't listen to their words, just the pattern of their speech. Each person is different. Kara doesn't take many breaths,

25

so her sentences come out in little sprints: *There's-a-sale-at-Nordstrom-today-and-I-need-a-new-strapless-bathing-suit-that's-not-plain-black-so-let's-go-right-after-school.* As long as you keep a smile on your face, she doesn't notice you're not listening. She doesn't give a rat's ass about anyone's opinion anyway. I haven't yet perfected zoning out Mrs. Anderson — though I'll be sure to get right on it after this car ride — so it's hard to ignore when she jumps in with more of a squeal to ask why I'm not wearing my team ribbon.

"Couldn't find it," I mumble.

"You should've called, dear. We have extras at the house."

Of course she does. I'm *not* her dear.

"I might have one in my bag," Kara says, "but it's in the trunk."

I stay silent while the two of them debate whether Kara does in fact have an extra bow in her bag and, if not, whatever will we do? There's a long list of possibilities here: ask the other girls, Mrs. Anderson running home, going to Jo-Ann Fabrics for a new one. . . . The topic isn't dropped until we arrive and Kara uncovers that — *praise Jesus* — she has an extra bow for me. Mother and daughter sigh with relief, proud of their impressive problem-solving.

I leave them in the parking lot congratulating each other only to discover that the make-believe-it's-not–Mother's-Day plan didn't stop with my dad and the Ribbon Police. I don't know who coordinated it, but there isn't a single cheesy WE LOVE OUR MOMS! sign, even from opposing teams. The buckets full of roses we usually hand out are nowhere to be seen. Mother's Day has *poof* disappeared, just like my mother.

As people spot me they look to their feet, pausing whatever pointless conversation they're having. Eventually the uncomfortable silence passes and heads pop back up like I'm a freaking zoo exhibit. They expect a dramatic breakdown, but I refuse to be the entertainment. I change my shoes without a word.

The match starts on time. Refusing to give the crowd even a frown, I take everything I've lost and put it in the force of my racket. Each time I connect with the ball I think, *Screw all of you.* My form suffers when I go all in with strength, causing a few stupid errors that catch the net or fall out-of-bounds, but I win all three matches. The losers will play it off as intentional. They'll go home to their intact families, proud of their sensitivity in pretending Mother's Day didn't exist. "I'm glad she won," they'll lie. "She needed it more than me."

Screw all of you.

No matter how people justify it, these cover-ups are not about comforting me. They're so people can skip the depressing conversation. Or not feel guilty they still have a mother. Or stall a private consideration that if it happened to me it could happen to them.

A week after the funeral I went back to school because Dad and I were such a mess together I was afraid we'd off ourselves too. It's hard to say which is worse. At school people are so desperate for me to talk that when I finally speak, even if it's just to say I have to use the restroom, they're all like, "Really, Eve? Wow. That's *soooooo* amazing." It drives me apeshit. Unlike the deep pain I experience with my dad, I feel nothing at all with my friends. In some ways it's creepier.

At lunch there's pressure to eat. Nothing is more loved at my school than a good eating disorder to diagnose, so I'm careful to finish what I pack. Anything is better than sitting through a food intervention with a bunch of teary-eyed girls and our clueless guidance counselor. We had one for Becky when she was making herself puke. I was all into it at the time. Lindsey told her mom, who told the guidance counselor, who helped us set Becky on the right course. All Becky took from it was the tip that everyone knows the sound of someone throwing up, so unless you're in a private stall, anorexia is a better option.

I'm at no risk for that particular societal trap. I despise puking and get wicked headaches when I go too long without eating. My problem is mental. Whole days pass where I don't remember physically walking from one class to the next. The dismissal bell rings and I can't remember where I parked or even driving to school. Teachers are divided on how to react. A few completely ignore what happened. They have no idea how to respond, so they treat me no differently than they did when I had a living, breathing mom at home. Most of the older ones are on a compassion mission. They ask how I'm doing before and after each class. No matter what I say, they flip their lips into their teeth and nod. The remaining teachers believe life is hard and, although it doesn't seem like it now, my mom's suicide will somehow serve me well later in life. They use the word *grit* a lot. Most of these assholes are now tougher when grading, as if to prove nothing is fair and life hasn't come to a stop.

But it has. This is a small town. I'll forever be branded the daughter of the stay-at-home mom who jumped off the Wellesley College library. My mom took my life with hers. I considered taking off in her BMW, but that only ever works out in movies. If I showed up in New York with no money I'd be spit right back out and my story would be even sorrier than it is now. This neighborhood already grieves my potential like a lost life. College is my ticket out, but I can't handle another year of this shit. I use Kara and her mom's silence over *their* devastating loss to finalize my plan.

When we pull into the driveway, I say good-bye and hop out. Kara doesn't say a word. No amount of pity could turn her into a good sport. When she didn't make varsity freshman year, she smashed her two-hundred-dollar Völkl racket into the court, probably causing that crack she's been bitching about all season. How was I ever friends with her?

Mrs. Anderson offers an insincere congratulations as I shut the car door. Her excessive mascara is smeared under one eye, so I know tears were shed over the loss. Real tears. From a grown woman. Over a tennis tournament. My mom was never that ridiculous. When I lost she'd sing that Sugarland chorus *"Let go laughing,"* then ask what I wanted for dinner. She could've picked sound tracks for movies — the woman had a song for every situation. Like when she belted out the Rolling Stones that time I sulked because she refused to buy me Tory Burch flats: *"You can't always get what you want, but if you try sometimes, you just might find, you get what you need."* I never admitted it, but the unique delivery did make her point stick. I wonder what she'd sing now? Would she encourage leaving Wellesley or want me to stick it out for senior year? As if in response, that Cat Stevens song she loved floats to my mind: *It's not time to make a change. . . .* I shiver, looking around the kitchen as if she could really be here, offering an opinion. The words echo through my head once more before I shake them free. *Screw that.* She's the one who ditched me; changing wasn't my call.

Dad isn't home yet, thank God. I leave the admissions folder I've been carrying around for a week on the kitchen counter with a sticky note that reads: *I want to be a boarder at Exeter next year. Need fresh start. Here's the info.* He'll worry what people will think — first Mom bails, then me — but in the end he'll agree. He has no energy to fight, and I know when he looks at me he

31

sees her.

She died on Good Friday. She wasn't religious but maybe it was symbolic, like her death was a sacrifice or something. Everyone at the funeral went on about how my mom was a giver, which means everyone at the funeral thought of Dad and me as takers. So that's it. We were both taking and taking and taking, and my mother, like a keg after only a few hours at a crowded party, was tapped. Her nod and smile meant the same thing as my middle finger. I just didn't know it. She certainly made her point. I imagine her looking down and shouting, "Do you see all I did for the two of you? Are you capable of being grateful yet?"

The struggle Dad and I have now is totally ironic. We're so used to her caring for us that we have no idea how to care for each other. We play a reverse game of hide-and-seek where the goal is to never be caught in the same room. Do we not know what to talk about or is there really nothing to say? We discuss only necessities, and even then he seems limited to specific words: *yes, no, maybe, when, where, why, who, okay.*

Every three or four days he attempts a deep talk, usually after he's had a few. Last night he asked if I knew "all about sex." I said it was a determination of whether you're male or female and laughed. His eyes watered. I felt bad, so I told him not to worry about it, that I was "all set in that department." When I realized how much I sounded like Mom, I started crying too. We both ditched the living room in opposite directions.

The truth is, I've been sleeping with John since my sixteenth birthday. I wish I'd told my mom while I had the chance, but I overheard her on the phone with Aunt Meg the night my cousin Lucy announced she was planning to do it with Keith: "It's so special she told you. I hope Eve trusts me when it's time." I knew instantly what she was talking about. "Make sure Lucy's smart about it, so you aren't a grandma at forty." There was a pause while my aunt spoke. "Well, I'll certainly keep you posted, but I don't think Eve is ready yet. Lucy has it right; seventeen is a respectable age to take the plunge. Not too old, not too young." I play the conversation over and over in my mind. I did trust and respect my mom, but I figured there was no harm waiting until I was the same respectable age as Lucy to tell her, which will be next month.

I was always deliberate like that. I got my first period when I was only eleven, not even in middle school yet. I calmly grabbed a quarter from the bottom of my backpack, snuck into the teachers' bathroom to buy a pad from the machine that we hid notes under between classes, and went on with my day. When I got home and told my mom she looked alarmed. "You could've called," she said. "I would've picked you up so we could talk about it."

"We already talked about it."

"I mean about the details of what to do."

"What details?" I asked, genuinely concerned I'd missed something. "Blood comes out and something needs to be there to catch it, right?"

"Huh, well, yes, but your independence does scare me sometimes. I hope you know I'm here if you need me."

"I do," I said. "That's why I can be independent."

She smiled. She had the best smile.

Technically I'm more independent than ever since there's literally no one looking after me, but independence isn't liberating when it's involuntary. I've been discarded like day-old milk. Even if I accept there's a lifetime ahead, I cannot picture how I'll live it without her. No Christmas cards will be sent, the vegetable garden will die, our sheets will have visible dirt before Dad or I think to change them, and we won't do anything to celebrate my birthday this year. Which is fine by me.

BRADY

My wife is dead. She jumped off a fucking building. I could watch the movie a thousand more times and still be shocked by the ending.

At the funeral her sister Meg kept throwing out possibilities like closet depression or a hidden trauma, but it's all bullshit. Maddy wasn't a secret-keeper. She couldn't tell a lie, even when it was the socially acceptable thing to do. A friend once hounded her for details on childbirth. She endeavored to avoid the question, advising that you don't think about the experience once that precious baby is in your arms, but the lady wouldn't relent. "You're *sure* you want the truth?" Maddy asked. The lady nodded. "Labor is like shitting a watermelon while getting felt up by your mailman. And when it's all over, you still look pregnant." The woman blanched. With Maddy, it was *ask and you shall receive.*

There's no room for a hidden life with a personality like that, so if Maddy jumped it was to abandon us. The total contradiction between who she was and what she did is

35

unfathomable. The last text I got from her read: *I have no idea how we're going to fit everyone @ the dining room table on Easter.* I have a hard time reconciling that this dilemma was enough to end it all. The psychologist at the police station claimed suicide is often an impulsive act, especially in cases with a "family history" like Maddy's, a history he pulled from me in pieces, then exaggerated to support his conclusion.

Maddy was nothing like Janine. She had one glass of wine a night. *One.* Maybe two. Sometimes three on Friday and Saturday. It was social. She considered her mother's suicide selfish, described it as a last *fuck you* to the few people who still cared. I remember the words exactly because it wasn't like Maddy to be so harsh. She walked in other people's shoes more than her own.

I'm avoiding the bedside drawer where her journal lives. Yes, I want answers, but only if they prove reality to be what I remember.

I made her laugh. I know I did.

Sometimes when she wanted to relax before bed, she'd ask me to tell her a story, any story. I reserved an arsenal for those moments. The key was to get her laughing straightaway. Laughter was Maddy's elixir. I'd jump right into a scene, as though she'd put a quarter in me. "Have I ever told you about the time I was six and got a tick on my dick?" Or, "Last night there was a guy at the airport so drunk he couldn't drive his luggage." The stories never had a point; they weren't supposed to. Current events or work updates revved her up, and the fact that I knew it pleased Maddy. When I was home, she was happy. But I often wasn't home.

I take another sip of bourbon. Is this my second glass? Third? I open the drawer and stare at the journal, curiosity fighting pride. When the glass is empty, I grab it with such force that my knuckles scrape against the bottom of the drawer. "Damn it," I mutter to the empty room. If Maddy were here she'd say something crafty like, "The drawer is winning, huh?" Of course, if Maddy were here I wouldn't be awake after midnight, drunk, pillaging her most personal thoughts.

I count the entries, an occupational hazard from my days as an accountant. There are just under three hundred spanning two years' time. If I read an entry a day, it'll last until after New Year's. It's unclear whether the ritual will be a source of torture or a gift. I pour another bourbon since no one is here to keep track. A small perk.

All I need is a unicorn on the cover and a heart-shaped key and I'll be seven all over again. As far as journals go, mine will be a bore. My life has been drama-free since my mom sucked back her last jug of wine with a handful of Klonopin. More on that later, I'm sure. Even dead she occasionally manages to be the center of attention.

Let me introduce the people I'll write about. My husband is Brady. He's short, 5'8", but I had a tall boyfriend once and spent a lot of time looking at nose hair. He's the CFO for HT (a company that makes software I don't fully understand). I refer to HT as Husband Thief, but I'm not allowed to be bitter about his working hours because we live a good life off his sweat.

Since my daughter landed her first serious boyfriend it's gotten a bit lonely — hence this pathetic journal. Eve turns fifteen next week. She's currently more a pain in my ass than the love of my life, but there is a bright light at the end of this teenage tunnel that keeps me warm. I can overlook that she says "like" every other word because she's bright and bold in a way that suggests her life will be fun to watch.

Today, she came home from school and declared, "I'm, like, so dropping out of confirmation class." She wanted me to be shocked, so I stayed silent. It's Brady's side that's invested in church. After I'd put away all the dishes without responding, she said, "You know what it is, Mom? They claim it's wrong to be on birth control, and then they teach everyone the rhythm method. But the rhythm method is birth control — it just, like, sucks. Why would I want to be part of an institution that totally sets people up?"

She's fifteen! I couldn't help but ask if she needs to be on birth control. Her face contorted with disgust. "You don't get me at all," she said. But she was wrong. I admired her point; I just had to be a mother for a second before continuing the conversation. But, being a mother for a second abruptly ended the conversation.

That's it. A book report. It's what I wanted — confirmation we were normal — but now I'm irritated. Blame doesn't stick well to the deceased; they can't fight back. I need Maddy to have a skeleton big enough to exonerate me, like a stash of cocaine in the laundry room, or a lover threatening to expose the affair. Something I played no part in, an offense larger than my offenses.

I'm haunted by her laugh. The first time I heard it was when the hospital receptionist requested my name and I blanked. I could describe Maddy's lemony smell. I could recall that her favorite color was yellow, her favorite movie was *Revenge of the Nerds,* and her favorite pair of socks were old and torn with little pigs jumping over the moon and jealous cows looking up from a field below, but I could not remember my goddamn name.

"Not trying to trip you up here," the receptionist said, giggling. Then Maddy joined, her laughter echoing in my mind. They hadn't yet discharged her body from the morgue but she was already with me. I cupped my hands over my ears to focus on the sound. This confirmed for the receptionist I was crazy. It was Eve who ultimately answered.

The second time I heard Maddy laugh was when Susan Dundel stopped over with a casserole after the funeral wearing a tight Red Sox tee that read BAT GIRL over the chest. Susan is a shameless flirt. At a neighborhood gathering when we first moved to Wellesley over a decade ago, Susan cornered Maddy and said, "You better take care of him. He'll have plenty of takers in this town, myself included." That same night Todd Anderson made a bizarre comment about how hot Maddy was — in front of his daughter Kara — then added he sometimes wished marriages had short time-outs. Maddy and I were shocked by their audacity, and she joked I should consider Susan a prime suspect if she ever mysteriously disappeared.

When Susan showed up at the door, it crossed my mind that she had something to do with Maddy's death. The thought triggered Maddy's casual laugh. It was exactly the sort of paranoid conspiracy theory she always teased me for. The sound of her laughter left me flustered, and I dropped Susan's dish onto the large Spanish tile Maddy redid a couple months ago. It shattered, spewing sticky chicken everywhere, the perfect excuse for Susan to come inside. She headed straight for the kitchen, grabbing a roll of paper towels and disappearing under the sink to collect cleaner and a trash bag. Susan looked so comfortable, like she'd staked out our kitchen with this exact scenario in mind. Soon she was splayed in

41

front of me, collecting the mess. She looked up and in an absurd attempt at a seductive voice said, "Brady, you and Eve need a woman around to help with your grief or you'll become overwhelmed by it." I couldn't muster a response, so I walked out the front door and kept going, a move I've resorted to a few times with Eve.

It's horrible, I know. But I have no choice. When the reality of my new life hits me, my response has to be physical — flee or fight. My instinct was to backhand Susan; it took great restraint to simply exit. It's Maddy's voice that calms me in those moments. *Leave,* her memory tells me, and so I do. I probably walked seven miles that night, mostly wondering why my wife went through the headache of changing the foyer tile when she planned to kill herself.

Things aren't as bad when I hear her laugh. It's far worse when people invade my grief and Maddy doesn't come to the rescue. That's when my anger clots and detonates. It started a week after the funeral when Eve hightailed it to school. Maddy's best friend Paige offered to work with the guidance counselor and homeschool Eve the last two months of the year, but Eve rejected the idea outright. She glared at us — chin jutted out like Maddy's — and said,

"So you think it's a stellar idea to isolate me even more?" Paige and I cowered.

The next day Eve left for school, so I went to work. What else could I do? Paula greeted me outside my office door with a rehearsed look of sympathy. Maddy loved that my assistant was old enough to be her mother. "How are you holding up?" she asked, patting my back.

Each time her hand connected with my shirt my jaw clenched tighter. "Fine," I replied, realizing I'd be answering that question all day. "Is everything rescheduled? Can Jack catch up this afternoon?"

"Oh, I don't think that's such a good idea," Paula said with the curt smile of a flight attendant. "I was talking to Sally this morning . . . we agreed you probably aren't ready just yet. Maybe spend a little more time with Eve? Work some half days?"

Sally is the CEO's assistant and evening companion when he's not with his wife, an interesting person to dole out family advice.

I clenched my fists, willing them firmly by my sides, and enunciated every word as if English was Paula's second language. "Something tells me the auditors won't care about my wife's death, and I still have a daughter to support with a career of some sort. Reschedule. My. Goddamn. Calendar."

Paula stood there, stunned, expecting an immediate apology. I'd never been terse with her or anyone else at the office. But given the giant pile of shit that recently became my life, I enjoyed the power of it. I shut my office door and got back to work.

There is nothing Maddy in my office. Not even a family picture on my desk. There never was. I treated the two separate: there was my career and there was my family. Now, there's work and there's my daughter. Buying and selling companies is infinitely easier than communicating with a pissed off sixteen-year-old. And being wronged is easier to accept than being made a fool.

CHAPTER TWO

MADELINE

It's hard to keep track of time here. I suppose I'm negative one month. The stunted scale reminds me of when Eve was a newborn and people asked how old she was. (Or *he* if they were unable to piece together basic gender clues from the color of her clothes and bow in her hair.) At first I kept track daily. "Two weeks tomorrow," I'd say with pride. When Eve was a month I acquiesced slightly, moving to fifteen-day increments. "One and a half months," I'd report, marveling at the speed of time. After her second birthday it jumped to years and from there it's a haze — Eve went from three to five to sixteen in what felt like one season. Wherever the hell I am now, time holds me accountable for every minute. It's slow going when there's no laundry and all you can do is watch.

"Look at me please, Toby," Rory prompts.

"Okay, but don't freak."

A pudgy boy with impressive bedhead turns to face her. Rory covers her mouth to stifle a laugh at the raisin lodged in his nose. "*Oh my . . .* how did that get there?"

"I wanted to know what raisins smelled like."

Rory gives a doubting look. "You don't need to put something in your nose to smell it."

"Yeah huh. I did! I couldn't smell a thing until it got up there, but now I can."

Rory smiles. "Before you head to the nurse, I have to ask: What do raisins smell like?"

"Like raisins," he says, exasperated.

I'm addicted to watching Rory in action. Earlier a little girl tugged on her skirt to say she lost a pencil. "Okay, ready?" Rory replied. The girl nodded. Rory swooshed her hands in a circle, then flung them toward her desk shouting, "Abracadabra!" The girl looked, wide-eyed. "Did it work?" She shook her head no. "Then I guess you'll have to handle this the old-fashioned way and go look for it."

As the kids line up for music, Rory reflects on the simplicity of Toby's answer. *He's right,* she thinks. *Life is not as complicated as adults make it.* I remain singularly focused

46

so I can intercept her thoughts, which flow from one to the next like notes in a symphony. Rory's musings leave me certain she's the answer to my mess. I just need to get her to step in it.

I relish my newfound ability to mind-read. I now know Brady *can* hear my laughter and exit prompts — abandonment is better than battery — and the song lyrics do reach Eve. With practice, I'll be able to influence their actions.

Though I'd rather keep Rory's light-hearted company, there's work to be done. I turn my attention to Eve as she moves my things to her closet. I find myself oddly flattered. When my mother died, nothing tempted me. Her color palette was extensive, the woman never met a hue she didn't like. Meg and I packed her entire wardrobe into moving boxes and dropped them off at Salvation Army. The chore was completed in an efficient, no-nonsense manner, which my mother no doubt applauded from the grave. Even wasted, she pooh-poohed sentimentality. Her intoxicated breath smothered any hint of it by reminding everyone the moment would not be remembered. Eve and I had more in common. We wore a similar preppy style, though I splurged on nicer brands. My wardrobe will be an upgrade for her.

She transports the clothes with a luggage set I bought after my Christmas wish list was ignored in place of cashmere sweaters I didn't need. It was a routine I didn't mind. My friend Paige and I got what we really wanted during postseason sales, so what did it matter that our families were the world's crappiest present pickers? It became a running inside joke. I looked forward to seeing what Eve and Brady came up with, knowing Paige and I would howl about it later over a glass of wine: fancy moisturizers for oily skin I didn't have, holiday-themed clothing I'd never wear in public, IOUs scribbled on note cards we all knew would never be cashed in. I found their disregard for detail amusing, but as Eve comes across the forgotten gifts of celebrations past she rues her carelessness.

Her remorse is constant. She wears guilt like a jacket on a cold day, clutching it. She's unable to eat a meal without lamenting that she never said thank you after I cooked. She can't watch TV without chastising how frequently she cut me off mid-sentence when a commercial break ended. Eve was central to everything in my life, so from her limited view, she's inherently culpable for my decision to leave. If only she knew what I really went through. I can't stand the emptiness of her expression. I need to make her smile. It will be fuel for us both.

I focus on the old duffle bag tucked behind my long dresses. It was my go-to hiding place for gifts, and my baby girl needs a pick-me-up. I struggle to call her attention to it. If only there was a hit song with the chorus *open the bag at the back of your mom's closet.*

Nothing I do draws her in, but once the clothes are gone, Eve notices it in the corner. The rectangular outline inside sparks her curiosity. Her train of thought makes me laugh: *Oh my God . . . it's like in the movies when old people have secrets stashed in a forgotten shoe box.* Eve thinks she's going to unzip the duffle and uncover my dirty laundry. Instead, she finds the Tory Burch flats she's been pining for since November. I'd planned to give them as a Christmas gift, but she threw a teenage fit over waiting a month. *One month.* For two-hundred-dollar shoes a sixteen-year-old has no business owning. Her display of entitlement made me uneasy, so I decided it'd be a good lesson to hold out until her birthday.

Eve squeals the way she did a decade ago when Cinderella strolled by during our first trip to Disney. For a tenth of a second she indulges the self-absorbed teenager she has every right to be. The sight of it leaves me giddy. Yes, I need to solve the escalating tension between Eve and Brady by putting a buffer between them, but I also need to bring moments of peace.

It takes four trips to get my things upstairs and several hours to unpack. When the work is done, Eve puts on my favorite springtime pink polo and pulls her hair back with one of my old silver clips. She looks in the mirror. Tears gather. She watches them fill her eyelids and overflow, imagining it's me she's looking at. Our resemblance will be a curse for her now, an inescapable reminder.

Wearing my outfit comes with an urge to play house. She heads for the kitchen and, donning my yellow rubber gloves, starts in on the dishes. There aren't many, but she's acting a part, so she takes time scrubbing each one, ignoring the efficiency of the dishwasher. I'm horrified to realize this is how Eve pictures my days. No urgency, no goals, just a series of tasks to scroll through on autopilot like an indentured servant. There's no room in Eve's version of my life for personal pride, which explains why she hasn't questioned my intent that night.

Brady enters the kitchen as Eve absently

swirls a sponge around a stubborn ring at the bottom of a coffee mug, her back to the doorway. He gasps. It isn't only my clothes; it's the way Eve stands with her weight to the right, her left foot barely touching the tile. He blinks twice before processing it isn't me. They're kryptonite to each other right now; what helps one hurts the other. Remembering me at my best is cathartic for Eve and hell for Brady.

Eve senses a person behind her and drops the mug in the sink, startled. "S-sorry," Brady stutters, still shaken by the mirage. He continues his course to the fridge.

"Did you see?" Eve asks. "I emptied Mom's closet."

He stops mid-step. Brady worked most of the day, as he does most Saturdays, and hadn't yet noticed. Eve senses his irritation. "I mean, I figured, what do you need with a bunch of women's clothes? And we're the same size. Well, not in dress pants, but when do I ever wear dress pants? So, I moved it all upstairs. That's okay, right?"

"It's fine," Brady manages, wishing he meant it.

There's nothing more to say. *Subject change,* I encourage.

"Did you see the info on Exeter?" Eve asks.

Did she receive my suggestion or change subjects on her own? I can't tell.

"Yeah." He flipped through the folder at work to check how much it cost. I tried to sway his decision, but got nowhere. Brady was too busy assigning an honorable justification for why boarding school makes sense — *it's what she wants; she'll have more supervision; I travel all the time.* The menacing truth is that, for Brady, Eve leaving would be a relief. Without even asking the distance of the school from our house, he gives his answer. "If that's what you want, go ahead and apply."

Wonderful: my life's work compromised after fifteen seconds of deliberation.

Boarding school is for the von Trapp family pre-Maria. Eve needs unconditional love staring at her twenty-four hours a day, massaging her stubbornness. Without attention, her sarcasm will turn to cynicism, her independence to isolation, her grief to depression. She's too young to process the complexities and nuances of the world, but she's astute enough to think about them and puerile enough to assume she understands — a dangerous combination. Everyone expects Eve to mourn dramatically like the teenager she is, but Eve mourns intellectually, trying to understand why it happened

52

and what it means and how to move on. She needs to stop picking a fight with the future when there's plenty to mend in the present. Who will help her with that in the middle-of-nowhere New Hampshire?

Eve smiles at Brady, holding back tears. It's the answer she wanted, but she didn't want him to make it that easy. She craved a fight, even for show, so it wouldn't be obvious he'd rather her gone.

My husband has never been one to catch the subtleties of a situation. He called every Valentine's Day to ask if I wanted him to stop on the way home to get a card. Every year I said no, don't bother, and he'd say something like, "Okay, but I want to go on record I asked, so you can't say I'm not romantic." I never did point out that any chance the gesture had of being romantic was lost when he asked whether he had to do it.

EVE

"Massage is a documented remedy for sadness," Mrs. Simpson says, handing me a gift certificate and patting my shoulder like I'm a household pet. Lindsey beams with pride over the incredible generosity of her family. How freaking annoying. I look at a crack in the ceiling until I can open my mouth without informing them a back rub won't cure shit.

Getting out of this town can't come soon enough. The only person I'll miss is my mom's friend Paige. She at least has the balls to admit this whole thing sucks and leave it at that. Everyone else is either a moron or offensive. Usually it's adults who piss me off and my friends I find stupid. Lindsey and her mom just managed to accomplish both with one sentence. I know they mean well, but I'm starting to see that the high-school social scene is a math formula. What you look like + athleticism + the clothes you wear = who you hang out with. I'm pretty enough, MVP of the tennis team, and wear mostly J.Crew, so I date the cocaptain of the soccer team who wears mostly Abercrombie and we hang out with the other athletes as long as they don't buy clothes from Target. Lindsey and I are about equal in where we fall on this plastic equation, so we're besties. It's lame.

I shove the gift certificate in my backpack and beeline to the parking lot. It was another miserable day in my new miserable life and I just want to go home and sleep through the rest of the school year. But John is at my car.

"Hey, beautiful," he says, certain I'm

happy to see him. Before Good Friday I would've blushed and given him a peck on the cheek, but you can't fake blush and I don't have the energy to get on my tippy-toes.

"I paid for our share of the limo today. What time do you wanna meet at Lindsey's for the preparty?"

"Preparty?"

His eyes bug out. "Prom? Next Saturday?"

Now my eyes bug out. How does he expect me to go from dead mom to the prom? Or dead mom to kissing? Or dead mom to anything at all? If I go with John, we'll probably win Junior Court and I'll have to pretend I actually care. It'll be impossible to look grateful for the honor of wearing a fake tiara, sitting on the back of a Jag convertible on loan from Kara's dad's dealership, and waving to a crowd of people who are all wondering what horrible, unmentionable things happened during my childhood. If I don't go, the guidance counselor will consider it a "red flag" and pull me from class for another progress report on where I am at "dealing with my grief." I decide to play both sides. I'll buy a stupid dress so people assume I'm going and then claim pinkeye like my mom did the night she bailed on her twentieth high-school reunion. She claimed it was the perfect excuse because it's highly contagious but only lasts a day.

"Right. Prom," I say. "I'll check on the preparty and let you know."

"Great."

He stands there waiting for more — an invite to hang out at my house, a promise to call later tonight, a hug, something. A small wave is all I have to give.

When Dad gets home from work, I approach him about prom-dress shopping. It's ten past seven; the stores close at nine. "Why didn't you go this afternoon?" he asks, as if I created the prom to bug him.

"Mom liked to approve what I picked out. You should see some of the choices."

He loosens his tie and shakes his head as though that's the dumbest thing he's heard all day. "Well, I trust you."

I bite my tongue hard with my molars because I can't stand his expression when I cry. "Pretty sure Mom trusted me too."

He sighs. I exhaust him. He disappoints me. "That's not what I meant, Bean. You know that's not what I meant. I just can't fathom anything I want to do less than go to a mall right now."

Oh. My. God. How did I miss what an ass he is when Mom was alive? No wonder she bailed. "Don't call me Bean. I am not, like, five." I turn to the stairs.

"Come on, Eve," he says to my back. "Don't be dramatic. It's a damn dress. Take the credit card and get one tomorrow. Or ask Paige to take you. She only has boys. She'd love —"

I slam my door.

Last year, Mom and I made a whole day of dress shopping for homecoming. We went to Newbury Street, got our nails done in a matching hot-pink color, and had lunch at a fancy Italian café. She even let me sip her chardonnay. I pretended to be surprised by the taste. She laughed and said, "I'm not as clueless as you wish I were." Then she asked whether I trust her.

"Of course I do," I said.

"Good. Tell me a secret." I thought about it. We were sitting in a window booth. Every woman who walked by looked so put together, so confident. I remember wishing I were older. I pictured Mom as a coworker or a college roommate or the wife of one of my husband's colleagues. When I snapped back to reality, she was still waiting for a reply. Mom wasn't afraid of silence. She claimed when you gave people time to think you got a better answer. I had loads of little secrets I could disclose to make her happy, but I wanted to be clever, so instead I said, "I'll tell you a secret, if you tell me one."

"Deal," she replied, rubbing her hands together. "You go first."

I smiled. "I've heard you and Dad before, like, at night."

Mom gasped, but then smirked. "Fine," she said. "Two can play at this game. My secret is that Christie Anderson called last month to say she saw you and John under their deck, and you had your hand down his pants." She took a bite of her caprese salad, satisfied.

I stared at her in complete shock. "Shut up! *What?* Why didn't you tell me?"

She raised her eyebrows. "I should ask the same question."

"Mom, seriously, why?"

She smiled to let me know it was all in good fun. "For a lot of reasons. Christie is a ruthless gossip. I didn't want her to be the basis for one of our talks."

"And?"

"*And* . . . and . . . so what? We've talked about all that stuff. I trust that if you need anything, advice or anything at all, you'll come to me."

It was confusing. She never dodged hot topics. I have friends whose mothers get all cray-cray over hand-holding. Not my mom.

She figured that stuff was natural. Last year I confronted her, disgusted, with a tube of K-Y I found in her nightstand. "I don't get why you're upset," she said, not bothering to ask what business I had in her room. "You're mad I have vaginal dryness?" When she worded it like that I felt silly.

"So why tell me now?" I asked.

"You embarrassed me, so I wanted to embarrass you."

That was how she was: ask a question, get an answer. We laughed nervously for a couple minutes before moving on to safer topics. It was a great day.

I obviously didn't expect my father to re-create that Newbury Street scene on a Tuesday night with one hour to shop, but I had hopes for something. It's laughable since I don't plan to wear it either way, but I pictured coming out of the fitting room after trying on a few dresses and him saying, "That's the one, Eve. You look wonderful."

Instead, he offered his credit card. Typical.

BRADY

"Thank you, it looks delicious," I say without looking. The door is almost shut when she thrusts her arm out as if to hold an elevator.

What's with the divorcées in this neighborhood? They scare the shit out of me.

"Wait! Please wait," Mary begs, doing a maneuver that somehow replaces the wedged arm with her full body.

"I actually just walked in, so I really need to check on Eve." Mary doesn't change her expression or stance; she's on a mission. They all are. Random women "drop in" with offerings from soup to wine to homemade cheesecake. Maybe I'm paranoid and they're only being charitable, but it's a statistical aberration that none of these philanthropists are still married. I know Maddy would be calling me a cynic, but the most plausible explanation for Mary's benevolence is discontent with her spousal maintenance package.

Mary bites her lip. I think it's supposed to be sexy, but it looks like it hurts. "That's so sweet," she says. "I hear you're a great dad. Eve's a great kid. I see her drive by sometimes. Really, *really* great. Just great." Her limited vocabulary makes the conversation more irritating. Whenever Eve talked like that, Maddy took out a thesaurus and had her look up replacement words. I consider leveraging the tactic now.

"Did you know I don't have children of

my own?"

Jesus Christ. Did she seriously just bat her eyelashes? And how would I possibly know that? Until two minutes ago, I didn't know her name was Mary. "Nope."

"Yeah, no, I never took the plunge. So I have time to help out if you ever need a hand."

Great. A crazy lady with a strategy. Launching a defense against divorcées with kids wipes out everyone except her. "Okay, well, thanks again." I step forward so Mary has no choice but to step back or be trampled. As soon as she's over the frame I swing the door shut.

How am I considered a good catch? You'd think these women would be at least marginally concerned by Maddy's proactive exit. How do you overlook that my first wife opted to eat pavement over one more day with me? I head to the kitchen for a cocktail. Eve is at the table with a giant grin on her face. *Fucking perfect.* She overheard that entire discourse. I decide to preempt her jab. "We should put a sign on the door that says, 'Food won't make us feel better. Go away.' "

"I don't know, Dad," she teases, "those were some impressive legs. I think Mary is a hiker."

What the hell do I say to that? It's not like I reach out to these vultures. I get a tumbler from the cabinet. Eve huffs. I'm growing accustomed to her sounds: a huff preludes criticism. I put ice in the glass, waiting.

"Good to see you can find time for a stiff drink given your busy schedule."

And there it is.

I assume she's referring to the fact that I didn't go gallivanting around the mall last night. My shoulders and neck tense, but I manage to walk away, drink in hand. *Fuck that.* I got up at five this morning, ran five miles, and worked a fourteen-hour day; I can have a goddamn bourbon. Or four. As long as I get up at five again tomorrow, what the hell does it matter?

If only Maddy and I had discussed her day-to-day communication with Eve. How did she know when to remain silent? Laugh instead of yell? Pick a serious talk over a punishment? And what compelled Eve to heed what Maddy said after she'd decided what the hell to say? It's such a goddamn cluster. I observed Eve growing up without much thought as to how she was raised. That was all Maddy.

We met at a coffee shop in Boston. Maddy was head down in a book. Later I learned that was the rule, not the exception — if

Maddy wasn't working she was reading. There was a fly buzzing around her head that sounded like it was attached to a bullhorn. I could hear it from the line ten feet away. There was no indication Maddy had a plan or even that the noise bothered her, but when the fly dared to land on her book she slammed the pages together, victorious. There was quiet applause from surrounding tables. She looked up, startled to realize people had been watching. "I hate that sound," she mumbled to no one, flicking the fly off the page with a napkin.

After paying for my coffee, I approached the table. "I don't want to disturb your reading, but do you mind if I sit here?"

"You can," she answered, immediately turning her eyes back to her book, "but there are plenty of open tables, so I don't know why you would."

I am not a pathetic puppy-dog guy, but I was intrigued enough to sit unwelcomed and slowly drink my coffee. Maddy was beautiful in a classic Hollywood sort of way: pale but not ghostly, thin but not skinny. Her blonde hair was organized, not hard with hair spray as was common at that time, but instead pulled up softly on the sides. Her lips were defined and shining in solid red.

She paid absolutely no attention to me. A half hour had passed when I got up to leave. "I'm not usually so rude," she said, her eyes still dedicated to the book.

"Just my lucky day then?"

Maddy snorted, a real pig snort, then covered her nose with her hand and snorted again. "I don't believe in luck," she said playfully. "Well, I believe in bad luck, but I don't believe in waiting around for good luck." It was like having a conversation with an inspirational poster.

"Does that mean I shouldn't leave?"

She shook her head. "No, you probably should. I can't put this damn book down. It's that good." She thought a second before adding, "Plus, the last guy I dated was a complete disappointment." I ignored her advice and sat back down. I was hooked.

We had a tumultuous courtship. One of us always cared more than the other. Sometimes she returned my messages, other times not, then it'd flip and she'd call every day. That was when I pulled back, canceling plans or not answering the phone. I was afraid of marriage. My parents never seemed at all pleased by the arrangement. The hitched guys at my office tried to talk me into proposing, but their arguments weren't persuasive. One guy likened getting married to going from a lawn mower to a landscaper. I still lived in an apartment, so the analogy eluded me. Looking back, I think he was getting at how women execute an entire life plan whereas men mostly consider their next meal.

Eventually we got to the point where it was time to get married or move on, and I couldn't imagine moving on. With Maddy, I was at peace. When she fell asleep first, which she usually did, I'd stay awake to sync our breaths. Sometimes it was easy, a steady pace in and out, but sometimes she went from short to long to nothing for seconds at a time and I'd have to focus to follow her cue. It was my way of handing over control without letting her know. I'm textbook Type A; it was the best I could do.

I packed a small picnic we never ate and took her to a rocky beach on the South Shore. She loved the sound of water hitting rocks. *Simple music,* she called it. I think she must've known what was about to happen because she acted uncharacteristically aloof and spoke in tired clichés. "Well, what a perfect day for this. There's barely a cloud in the sky. I'm surprised more people aren't —"

I interrupted with the question that changed our lives. "Madeline, will you please marry me?"

She tucked her hair neatly behind her ears, nodded, and said, "This won't change anything really, right? Except I get to wear a beautiful diamond ring?"

The only distinction between her words and a joke is that we didn't realize it was funny. We were naïve enough to believe that marriage wouldn't change things that much. But it changed everything. We loved harder, and in the beginning, we fought harder. We both contrived every concession into a lifetime concession. You couldn't simply share your dessert without inadvertently agreeing to only eat half until death. Now I look back and think, would that be so bad? I'd gladly eat half of every dessert and make a million more sacrifices for one more day with my wife. What I can't get over is this: she didn't feel the same way.

So our marriage wasn't perfect. Whose marriage is perfect?

I pull out her journal and flip to the next page, dated June 16, 2013. The day Eve turned fifteen. I'm thankful for the reminder of her impending birthday until the words sink in.

How DARE he miss it. How can someone so bright not be capable of prioritizing something so obvious? "I know it's shitty, Maddy," he said. That's it — shitty. No, you incredibly shortsighted ass, shitty is when you go on vacation and get the runs. It's something bad that happens that you have no control over.

My heart dropped when the phone rang at six-thirty. Eve rushed to pick it up and, with a smile on her face, asked how far out he was. The limo was already out front.

He didn't have the guts to tell her. The phone was passed to me.

Eve wanted to cancel. I recited my speech about practicing love, compassion, and forgiveness, inwardly thinking how great it'd be if I didn't have to practice quite so often on my husband. We went and made the best of it. I assume Lindsey will look back on the night as awkward and Eve will look back on it as miserable or, to use her teenage terminology, a fail.

What could possibly be happening in the software world that trumps your daughter's birthday, you number-crunching, tunnel-vision, selfish, selfish man?

That's it. Each word was penned with such ferocity that it dented several subsequent pages. Maddy never said a word about it after the fact. Or had she and I disregarded it? It's disconcerting how little I recall from our daily conversations. I search my laptop to see what meeting I chose over this extra memory. All I had on the evening of June 16, 2013, is a chunk of time reserved to catch up on Q2 numbers for an eight a.m. board meeting, with a note from Paula that I might be asked to present. That's it. That's what I did instead. The possibility of speaking at a board meeting felt bigger than my daughter's actual birthday dinner. I was a new CFO. Work felt so important. *I* felt so important. And now look at me. I'm the guy whose wife offed herself.

I should have gone shopping with Eve for a prom dress yesterday. I'm still a number-crunching, tunnel-vision, selfish, selfish man.

CHAPTER THREE

MADELINE

Seems silly to pray given the mounting evidence I'm stuck here for eternity, but please God, if I haven't been forgotten already, let today be the day I do more than just comfort them. Let today be the day I sway their future.

Brady's boss, Jack, is an active Exeter alum who pulled strings to get Eve accepted even though they don't usually take senior applicants. Jack knows all the right people. Looking for a good price on a luxury car? Want to rent an oceanfront house in Nantucket during the height of the season or get your hands on a rare black truffle? Jack is the man who can make it happen. He could arrange to have a word added to the dictionary while it was his turn at Scrabble.

I was disappointed at first — Exeter's rejection would keep Eve home — but then reality checked in. Brady and Eve are at war.

Distance will at least make it harder for the damage to be permanent. Exeter's acceptance came with the condition that Eve complete precalculus this summer, and, lucky me, Rory's name showed up on the list of eleven local math tutors. A first grade teacher helping with calculus might not be in Eve's best academic interest, but her emotional well-being is more important. If Eve picks Rory, the two of them will be together on a weekly basis for the entire summer.

In past attempts, I've padded my guidance with reasoning and related emotions. My intent was to be compelling, but perhaps it's too much to transmit. Catchy songs and laughter get through; simple equals successful. I knead Eve's subconscious, repeating Rory's last name. *Murray. Murray. Murray.* There's no evidence it's working. She moves through her day like a puppet, every action forced. At lunch, John, Kara, and Lindsey surround Eve at the table farthest from the smelly lunch line, a coveted spot. Kara doesn't acknowledge Eve, her remorse won't allow it, but John and Lindsey study my daughter as if she's a research project. Their hovering drives Eve batty.

Murray. Murray. Murray.

My daughter never struggled to fit in the

way I did. High school didn't interest me. I spent all four years buried in novels. Sal Paradise, Holden Caulfield, Jay Gatsby — these were my people. My mom never understood. "You're gorgeous," she'd say, not as a compliment. "Why don't you have friends?" Once, when I was a junior and she was on a bender, she asked if I was a lesbian. "Nope," I said to the relief of the Catholic still in her. "I want to kiss boys; I just don't want to kiss any of *these* boys." What I wanted was hot sex with Jack Kerouac, but Mom didn't fish for details. I was prepared to support Eve through the isolation I associate with that time in life, but there was no need. Even now, in her grief-stricken funk, people seek her out like a front-row seat.

Despite Eve's popularity, I remained detached from the other mothers. Paige was the only one who *got* me, and she was a decade older. We met at a PTA meeting nine years ago when the then president, Evelyn something, shot down my request to set aside a small field-trip fund for the few kids in Wellesley who qualified for lunch assistance. When I pointed out that teachers often paid their fees personally, Evelyn said, "If no one steps in, the families will step up. We're talking about twenty dollars a year

71

for a couple dozen students. Wellesley doesn't have a low-income issue."

The meeting proceeded. What I should've said was, "You mean the people *in this room* don't have a low-income issue, which makes it all the more insane that *teachers* are the ones jumping in." But I was paralyzed under the fluorescent cafeteria lighting. I hadn't yet hit the fuck-you forties where you say and do whatever you damn well please. I was about to grab my purse and leave when Paige pulled a chair next to mine and whispered, "Have you met Evelyn's high horse? She rides it quite a bit." I failed to suppress my unexpected laughter. From then on, Paige and I sprung for the field-trip funding and replaced PTA meetings with a glass of wine in town. God, I could use her practicality right now. We think so much alike; she'd be easy to influence. The thought inspires me: Paige can be my courier for Eve. Meg can't. She's too bogged down with her own guilt-laden grief and she isn't local. *But Paige . . .* Paige I can prod on my behalf. I need to get creative.

I drone on: *Murray. Murray. Murray.*

A girl I don't recognize leans toward Eve, unaware her personal space is protected. "Are you gonna eat your turkey?"

"No," Eve says in a trance, handing over

the protein.

"Are you *serious,* Katy?" Lindsey snaps, swatting the turkey from her hand. "Leave. Eve. Alone. She needs to eat." Katy reddens. She likely just lost her spot with the cool kids tomorrow. Eve doesn't seem to notice. Someone could tie her down on train tracks and she wouldn't scream.

I continue the boring chant, *Murray. Murray. Murray.* Over and over. During tennis practice I make a game of it to break up the monotony, timing my delivery to the exact moment the ball connects with her racket.

By the time Brady hands Eve the list of twelve names, she doesn't hesitate. "I heard Ms. Murray is nice."

"Ms. Murray it is," Brady agrees, circling the name and shoving the list back in his briefcase.

I want to celebrate my first real success, but Eve's mood darkens, snapping me back to attention. "Are *you* gonna schedule it?"

Her open-eyed expression tells me this is a test. Eve set me up like this all the time, reeling me in with a seemingly casual question that had only one correct answer in her stubborn mind. If — no, *when* — I responded incorrectly, she pounced all over the perceived mistake. I try to send Brady a warning, but it unravels too fast.

"Sure. I'll have Paula do it tomorrow." He continues scanning the mail, oblivious to the missile en route.

"Does Paula wipe your ass too?"

Brady's brown eyes squint until his stare is a laser on Eve's head. The Fireman has arrived. The veins above his eyebrows pulsate under his skin. He looks like a man about to throw a punch. *Walk away,* I instruct them both, but Brady is too incensed to be persuaded and Eve is frozen with fear.

Brady moves so physically close that they suddenly share the same kitchen tile. "I have tolerated enough of your bullshit," he shouts at her. Eve does not retreat. She can't. Her firm stance enrages Brady more. "You can-*not* talk to me like that. What happened to your mother is NOT MY GODDAMN FAULT." He slams an open palm on the counter, knocking over a water glass. The sound of it shattering whips Brady out of his fury, returning his eyes and face to normal. Eve backs out of the kitchen, startled by the stranger before her.

Brady stares at his hand as if it's a foreign object. With Eve safe, I stop watching. I don't want to fall any more out of love with my husband than I already have.

■ ■ ■ ■

I find Rory on a blind date with a man who looks like Herman Munster. He has the height, flat forehead, baritone voice, and unfortunate luck of sitting in a spot where the green backlight of the Mexican restaurant hits his face, leaving a Kermit afterglow. The only thing he's missing is a bolt lodged in his neck.

"Rory is such a beautiful name," he says, leaning in as she simultaneously sits back. "I love the whole New Age, hippy look you have going."

Rory slaps an artificial grin on her face. "Thanks."

He clears his throat to buy time while he figures out what to say next. When he considers a line I know will horrify Rory, I encourage him to go for it. I wouldn't sabotage the date if there were any chance it'd end in true love, but these two aren't kismet, so why not make it an entertaining disaster?

"I had a newt named Rory once," he says, "only it was a boy."

"Really, a boy newt," she repeats, not bothering to feign a smile. "What a coincidence." Her thoughts are crazy with chatter: *Did he seriously just compare me to an amphibian? What was Danielle thinking? How desperate do people think I am?*

"I mean, what are the chances of that? Rory is not a common name, you know? And yet, five years ago, I *happened* to name my newt Rory. And then we both *happened* to get a divorce. And now you *happen* to work with my second cousin's wife. That's all pretty unbelievable, even if the newt was a boy."

It certainly is unbelievable, Rory thinks. *Who in their right mind married you?*

He waits for a response to that random statement of facts with a creepy grin on his face. "Ahhh, yeah, no, it is. So, David, Danielle mentioned you own your own business in Dedham?"

It's a successful shift in the conversation until he replies, "Yes, a funeral home. I'm a mortician."

I didn't have to do anything to make that funny. Rory coughs to cover the laugh that escapes and considers the possibility she's on *Punk'd.* She looks at the pepper shaker for a lens of some sort, then around the bar for anyone who could be in on it. She truly expects an explosion of applause and laughter at her expense. Instead, the mortician continues, "You know, the industry is misunderstood. They paint it out to be full of people taking advantage of families at a vulnerable time. But that's not it at all. I think of myself as someone who gives families one last favorable look at their loved one. I had this guy last week who got hit by an eighteen-wheeler. I'm not exaggerating when I say he was *messed up.* I mean eyes popped, arm detached —"

Rory's last sip of wine threatens to come back up. "Jesus, please," she says, using a hand as a stop sign.

He wears a sympathetic expression I imagine is universally loathed by his clients. "I'm sorry." He reaches across the table and gives her hand a pat. "Have you lost a loved one in an auto accident? I should have asked before I told that story."

"*No, no,* well . . . yes, actually," Rory stammers, "but regardless, it doesn't feel right to be so flippant about someone's death."

He laughs. "Okay, you're sensitive. I get that. Frankly, I like it. Because I gotta tell ya, some women your age are bitter." Rory frowns. "What I mean is, it's refreshing you're so easily upset." She remains visibly displeased. "Okay, I declare a subject change." He claps his hands to make the declaration official, drawing attention to their table. Rory shrinks in her chair. "Let's share divorce horror stories. That's a safe zone since our exes are unfortunately still alive — ha ha ha — am I right?"

"I'd rather not," Rory replies with a hint of teacher authority behind her voice.

"I'll go first. It's a total cliché. My wife left me for the UPS driver." Rory and I have the same thought: there's nothing cliché about that. Hollywood maybe, but not cliché. UPS drivers don't carry the same sex appeal as, say, personal trainers. "He went the extra mile carrying our new Bowflex into the living room and, next thing I knew, he lived there and I didn't." Rory looks longingly through the window to her car in the parking lot, then back at her date. "Your turn," he says.

"My husband and I weren't a match anymore."

"Come on," he pushes. "Was he an alcoholic? That's pretty common. I have three aunts and a cousin who hit the bottle *hard.* I'm talking drunk before church. Not Danielle, of course. Don't be a bad girl and spread rumors now — ha ha ha."

"He wasn't an alcoholic."

"Abuse?"

"No."

"Oh God, did he cheat on you?"

"No."

"Please tell me you didn't cheat on him. Did you? Because I have to say, after my last experience, that's the only thing that could stand in the way of me taking this date to the next level."

Having no intention of taking the date to any additional level, Rory retrieves her purse. "Listen, David, thanks so much for the glass of wine. It was nice to meet you."

She sticks her arm out for a handshake. He stands too, awkwardly rubbing the condensation from his glass onto his pressed khakis. "Oh, okay," he says. "You're heading out? Can I walk you to your car?"

Rory graciously explains it'd be best if he stayed at the table so the bartender doesn't think they're skipping out on the tab. The mortician does not appear fazed; this is not the first time drinks didn't turn into dinner.

Brady hasn't been on a date in twenty-three years, but he'd never describe a mangled body over cocktails. Rory's disaster of a night is, selfishly, perfect. Even with a temper, if this is the competition, Brady will do fine.

EVE

Thank God Lindsey's aunt is a flight attendant who thinks her stash of in-flight cocktails is well hidden in the corner of the guesthouse closet. While the parents in attendance have the luxury of openly enjoying their wine and beer, we take turns ducking out to the privacy of the back deck. It's clutch to keep your buzz going till you get in the limo or the dance will be cheesy, but for me it's more than that. I have to keep my buzz going so I can pretend I'm somewhere else. Anywhere else.

Unfortunately, it's not my turn to be drinking when the Andersons stumble over. They make a perfect couple because they're both totally clueless no one in the room likes them. Mrs. Anderson has on a blue sequin tank with a way-too-short white skirt that I can see Lindsey's mother dissing in the kitchen. Between her slutty outfit and the hangover she's working on, you'd think it was Mrs. Anderson's prom night. Her husband plays the part of a horny date well. His hand creeps closer and closer to Mrs. Anderson's ass as they make their unwelcome rounds. It's fine that parents still do it and all, but they should be considerate of the fact that it grosses everyone else out.

"Did you pick your dress beforehand?" Mrs. Anderson asks while her husband scopes the room for someone less depressing to talk to. I can't believe so many fools buy cars from a man who obviously goes to a tanning salon.

I assume Mrs. Anderson is referring to before my mom voluntarily plunged to her death. A classy question. Thankfully she blabbers on without waiting for an answer. "Kara and I found hers in February in the middle-of-nowhere Springfield, and you know Kara, she somehow convinced me it wasn't too early to buy it. I'm just relieved she still likes it. I mean, it's not as though we could return something we bought four months ago. And Springfield is a million miles from here. That would've been my worst nightmare."

I want Mrs. Anderson to suffer a real nightmare. I'd like to see how nice her Botox looks after finding out something whacked, like her *GQ* husband has a hidden family in the city. That'd teach her to be more careful with her words.

I consider informing the Andersons that their daughter is puking her brains out in the woods right now, probably getting backsplash on that gorgeous Springfield catch, but instead I walk away. I'm beginning to understand why my dad likes that move — it's badass to peace out in the middle of a conversation.

I should've stuck to my original plan and pretended to have pink-eye, but then it would've been Dad and me, alone. At least here I can be drunk. Before I left, he asked if he should come to take pictures. *As if.* I laughed in his face, but stopped when he looked like he might smack me. Maybe I shouldn't have backed off; a black eye would go perfect with this night.

Paige offered to come as my bodyguard, but I passed, knowing she meant it literally. Mrs. Anderson would have been escorted out by now. That's why my mom loved Paige. Tonight she showed up just before I left with a boutonniere for John, which I flaked on getting, and two condoms. I have no plans to put out tonight, but it was the first time I've laughed since Good Friday. It was something my mom would do. No awkward conversation necessary, a simple gesture that said it all.

I scan the room. Preprom is nothing more than a parade of mothers showing off how close they are with their daughters. The fussing, the makeup, the pictures, it's all a performance, and tonight gossiping about my dysfunctional family is the main act. I hear them, the way I do at school: *It's so sad. . . . I heard Madeline was a big drinker. . . . I always thought she seemed so happy. . . . Look at poor Eve. . . . My God, how selfish do you have to be to kill yourself when you have a child?* I want to scream between camera flashes that losing my mother did not make me deaf.

Someone snaps the back of my strapless bra. I spin around to find Katy, who social-climbed all year to get invited to this stupid party, giving me air-kisses like she's some sort of movie star. "I'm so glad you came tonight," she gushes. "There's no good excuse to miss prom."

"Hmm," I reply, pretending to think about it. "I think my excuse would've been pretty fucking good." She wipes the fake smile off her face and leaves me alone. It's the first hint she's taken all year.

I can't face another conversation like that, so I wait until no one is looking and truck upstairs to lock myself in the master bathroom. It reeks of hair spray and perfume, but I'd hole up in a Porta Potty right now if that's what it took to be alone.

I sit on the toilet lid and stare at the ceiling. Sounds from the party mush together and become easy to ignore. *Why didn't she leave a note?* After the funeral I checked the mail every day, certain she sent a letter explaining it wasn't my fault and offering loving advice on how to move on. Suicide really is the ultimate fuck-you.

On the morning of the day she jumped,

she told me to prepare myself because it was going to be a crazy Easter weekend. I assumed she meant no one would get much sleep since Aunt Meg, Uncle Dan, and Lucy were staying at the house. Now I see it was a big joke. She must have felt powerful knowing she'd be dead before bedtime and we'd be left to realize how much she really mattered.

There's a knock at the door. "Eve, open up. It's John."

I turn the lock. He lets himself in and sits on the vanity, taking a swig of the mini vodka I left on the counter. For a second I remember what it's like to be normal. Sneaking away for a quick drink with your cool boyfriend is ordinary. But I'm not here for a flirt-filled drink, I'm here to chug as much as I can without puking because my tragic life is being advertised like a Super Bowl commercial downstairs.

"I guess you're not into the whole prom thing this year," he says. I nod. "Makes sense."

"Yeah." I run a finger under each eye to catch the tears before my eyeliner does. If John weren't here, I'd let them slide into my mouth. I've come to enjoy their salty taste.

"It's good to see you cry," he says. "You're

supposed to be sad."

Hopefully he isn't saying that to be nice, because his words unlock a full sob. I am so completely alone. I run through all the life moments that are ruined. The prom is nothing. What about graduation? My wedding day? When I have children of my own?

John hops down for a hug but I push back. I find no comfort in physical touch. Everything feels fake.

"I'm so pissed." I want to yell it, but I don't want anyone to hear, so it comes out as an angry whisper. "I can't take this *shit.* Seeing everyone here, joking, getting dressed up like it matters."

"I know —"

I stumble backwards. "No. *No.* No one knows. That's the whole thing. Freaking Lindsey asked if I thought she and Noel had a chance at winning Junior Court. I looked at her, like, does she honestly think I give a rat's ass? She can be the damn princess or whatever you even call it."

I'm wicked drunk. We both are. John sensed I'd be a bummer date and tucked a flask into the back suspenders of his rented tuxedo. It's already empty. "Let's get through this and we'll bail on the dance," he suggests.

I look in the mirror at my swollen eyes,

puffy cheeks, and running makeup. There's no way I can go back out there. "I want —" I pause to think what it is I want. "— to go home." It's a lie, but I can't stay here, clearly, and I can't think of anyplace else.

"Let's leave together," John says. "We can go to my house. My parents are at a wedding tonight." He reaches for my hand. I stare at it. I once heard my dad describe this guy he worked with as airspace. When I asked what he meant he said, "He's nothing to me. He's not good. He's not bad. He's just there." That's how I feel about John now. Before Mom died, dating him was everything. We claimed we loved each other. Now he's airspace. But he can get me out of this hellhole, so I take his hand. We walk out of the bathroom, across the foyer, and out the front door without anyone noticing.

A prison break.

BRADY

"Brady Starling?"

I know the voice on the other end of the line. My breath catches. "This is."

"I am calling from Newton-Wellesley Hospital regarding your daughter, Eve."

I drop to the floor as though someone took a baseball bat to my legs. This can't be happening.

86

"She's here at the hospital," the voice continues, unaware of my frantic state. "There was a car accident. She'll be fine, but you need to bring her insurance information and pick her up, if you have a safe means to get here."

I replay the call about Maddy. *Your wife is in critical condition,* the same voice said. *Please find someone to drive you to the hospital immediately.* "You're lying," I shout now. "You fed me this bullshit before, but my wife was *dead.* Dead. She had died instantly."

My right hand claws at my chest, drawing blood. I feel no pain. The woman falters for a second but then insists, "Sir, calm down and listen. There are times we say that to protect people in extreme circumstances, but I promise you your daughter is *fine.* She needs a few stitches. That's all."

I hang up, get off my hands and knees, still begging, bawling, and sprint to the car.

When I got the call on Good Friday, I was at work. Meg was already at the house for Easter weekend, so she brought Eve to the hospital and I used the drive to set perimeters around what happened. Maddy and I had been lucky in life. Too lucky. Everyone pays dues at some point. I settled on the fact that Maddy had been permanently

87

disabled. It was the maximum sentence I could conceive, and my giant ego actually believed I had the power to contain the situation. It was my turn to serve Maddy, and by the time I parked the car I was prepared to take on my new duties. I hadn't realized how high the stakes were then, or how little say we mortals have on these matters, but I damn well know now. You only confuse hope with power once in life.

I can't remember the drive — did I speed? stop at streetlights? — but suddenly I'm at the ER. A double-wide door opens for an exiting patient and I walk through, ready to shout Eve's name. I stop short when I notice clumps of her hair on the floor of the first exam room. It's the same sandy blonde as Maddy's.

I throw the curtain aside and there she is. My daughter. Alive and looking rather bored. The front part of her hairline is shaved and covered with a bandage about an inch long. My instinct is to collect her hair off the floor, to keep every part of her together.

"What happened to you?" she asks.

I follow her stare to the bloodstain on my shirt, but don't answer. Hearing her talk is such a relief to my senses that for the second time my legs buckle, only this time in gratitude.

"Dad, seriously, are you all right?"

I kneel by her side and grab her hand, crying into the sheets. This is the scene I was robbed of having with Maddy. I'd been directed straight to a conference room, where a doctor came in, looked at his feet, and apologized. I replied that we'd find a way to work it out, still certain the tragedy consisted of installing wheelchair ramps and accommodating physical limitations. "You don't understand," he said, shaking his head. "Your wife didn't survive."

Maddy is dead. Eve is not. For some reason that feels like breaking news.

"There's blood on your shirt," Eve says, trying to lift my head with her other hand. I stay furrowed, my forehead pressed into her arm. I picture her veins beneath me. Working. Pumping life through her.

I play through our history. Eve and I have memories without Maddy. They pop to mind as if someone's spoon-feeding them to my brain. *Tennis.* We played together. When Eve was younger, I let her win, but at some point her lessons paid off and we routinely and legitimately split the victories. I'm stronger, but she's more strategic, and a trash-talker like her mother. "You're getting too old for this," she jabbed on our last trip to Florida. "Maybe we should play bingo instead."

I go back further. *Bean.* When she was an infant, skinny and long, I was the only one who could calm her down from a fit. The trick was to hop from foot to foot at an even pace. The faster I jumped, the more she relaxed in my arms. I'd press the right side of her face against my heart to keep her head steady and whisper, "It's okay, my little jumping bean." That's where the nickname came from. We had a connection, she and I. Maddy actually called me home from work one day when Eve wouldn't let up. I think she was only four or five months at the time. "If Daddy's little girl doesn't stop crying Mommy is going to have a nervous breakdown," Maddy said. I knew she was serious from her use of the third person. Maddy wasn't one to disassociate from her thoughts.

There's more. When we were en route to her first day of kindergarten, Eve announced that she and I were getting married. Maddy laughed and asked what she'd do without us, alerting me this was not cause for alarm. "Don't worry, Mommy," Eve said, "you can live in the guest room."

Yes, there was a time when Eve preferred

me. I know I'm now forever relegated to a pinch hitter, but I have to step up. I am all our child has left. And it suddenly seems so obvious, this detail I've been overlooking: she's all I have too.

Eve gives up competing with my internal trip down memory lane and instead gently rests her hand on my head. It's soothing. I wonder how Eve thought to do it. How do women just know?

The doctor appears, forcing me to stand. He looks a little put out by my lack of composure, but then softens in a way that suggests he knows about Maddy. It's a small town. Our neighbor is the chief of surgery here. With a series of nods he directs me to a little room off the registration area. I'm confused why our discussion requires such privacy until he speaks.

"She's a tough young lady. No one else got hurt, but there was heavy drinking involved. The boy who was driving — Jim? John? — will definitely be charged. Your daughter might too, for underage consumption, although with your family's recent struggles, I wouldn't be surprised if they let it go. That's what I intend to recommend."

If he expects a thoughtful response, mine will come up short. "Okay. Can we go?"

He seems ready to repeat his speech, assuming a miscommunication of some sort, but instead yawns. "I'll send a nurse to give care instructions. The staples in her head are going to hurt once all the medicine and booze wears off."

I linger in the room. I haven't prayed in years. As a kid my knees were permanently scuffed from all the kneeling we did as a family, but Maddy and Eve weren't into it, and my hectic schedule left me content to drop the extra obligation. I have no right to ask for anything, but I make a pledge. I intertwine my hands, still standing, and say, "Thank you, God, for keeping my baby girl alive. I'll do better."

When I return to Eve, she's asking the nurse about John. "He'll be fine," she assures. Eve asks if she can see him, but the nurse says, "I'm sorry. I really am. He asked the same thing and his parents forbid it."

Eve's expression is unmistakably grateful. We've become loners. Maddy was our spark. When we get in the car our words are short and to the point.

"I'm sorry, Dad."

"Me too, Eve."

Sorry for her. Sorry for me. Sorry for Maddy.

CHAPTER FOUR

MADELINE

The worst part of watching the cars collide was Eve's eerie calm. Her eyes were wide, not with panic, but acceptance. She's become comfortable with tragedy having a seat at her table. The lesson she's pulling from all this is that misfortune is commonplace; chaos lurks everywhere; no one can be trusted. It pains me — those were the realities of my childhood. I worked tirelessly to give Eve a different start, and yet here she is, arriving at the same conclusions.

I was helpless in that moment, desperate to transcend the invisible boundary that separates us. Eve isn't done yet. She still needs to find her true voice and chase down a passion and get married and have children who will no doubt expand her perspective like she did mine. She needs time. Decades more time. As metal crunched into what sounded like a cacophony of death, I pleaded, *Oh God, please, please, no, please don't take her.* An unexpected calm warmed me like a slow-burning fire that carried with it the knowledge Eve would live. More than live. Eve would prosper. And then a peculiar thing happened: my position in the universe, which hadn't budged since death, shifted higher. A slight but discernable rise. After the noise ended and Eve was still in one piece, I questioned what transpired. My plea was more a wish than a prayer — I didn't realize I had an audience — but the response was authentic, spiritual. *Thank you,* I said. *Thank you, God.* My gratitude pushed me up higher still, and Eve's promising future stayed rooted as a fact in my soul, not something crafted for comfort, but the truth, offered as a gift.

So maybe I haven't been abandoned after all. I didn't acknowledge my unease until hope presented itself, but I've had a nagging fear about what will become of my spirit after Eve is grown and Brady remarries. Today I'm a ghost with a purpose, but if I'm successful, at some point I'll be reduced to a plain old ghost. Bored and frightening. The possibility that I'm still on some cosmic radar is a tremendous relief.

Eve's apathy at death's door also made me realize that Brady should show her my journal. Not all of it, but pieces. Enough to prove that in many ways I am who she remembers me to be. She needs reassurance that my happiness was real to affirm that happiness is possible. I distill my request to two simple sentences. *Show Eve the journal. It documents Maddy's love.* I match Brady's communication style because, secretly, everyone is their own biggest fan. I wouldn't use the word *document* and *love* in the same sentence, but Brady would. He once wrote in an attempted love letter that he was "nearly certain" I was the love of his life. He was confused by my disappointment. "It's the most anyone can hope for," he said in earnest, "since nothing in life is an absolute guarantee." Clearly I married a pragmatic man.

I start during his commute, but even at seven in the morning Brady's subconscious offers fierce competition. I chant, *Show Eve the journal. It documents Maddy's love,* while he sings a song to the tune of "Swing Low, Sweet Chariot" that goes *Maddy's dead. . . . She killed herself. . . . And now I'm stuck all alone.* It's rather hilarious. His thumbs tap the steering wheel to the beat for the entire thirty-minute ride.

When Brady gets to the office, the song is pushed aside and work takes over. He poses questions to himself formally, then answers as though he's presenting to an audience. His process is methodical enough to border on disturbing. *What are the risks of outsourcing development to India? Well, quality for one, management for another. You don't save money if you spend as much time fixing code as you would to develop it in the first place.* On and on he goes. Paige is easy to infiltrate. I said, *Grab a condom for Eve* one time; she smiled and stopped at the pharmacy on the way to our house. Brady isn't as malleable, but I stick with my plan. *Show Eve the journal. It documents Maddy's love. Show Eve the journal. It documents Maddy's love.*

Standing at the urinal appears to be the only place his mind rests. For a short moment, I have the stage. *Show Eve the journal.* Brady tilts his head to one side, straining to hear. I say it again: *Show Eve the journal.* His voice comes back, talking over mine. He asks it to himself as a question because, of course, it has to be his idea. *Should I show Eve Maddy's journal?*

I shoot right back. *It documents Maddy's love.* He receives it, but still as a question. *Will it help?* I have one more chance as he washes his hands. I repeat the full sequence. It works. Brady adds my request to his mental checklist, which is more reliable than death and taxes.

I wish I'd discovered this rational, simple approach while I was alive. Brady and I would've avoided so many confrontations. Every couple has one never-ending fight, one conflict that rears its head again and again. Each time it ends, you assume you've found resolution moving forward, but the same battle reinvents itself under a different pretense and *bam!* you're right back where you started. For Brady and me, it was about vacation. I wanted to go; he didn't. By our second night away, tanned and relaxed enough to wear a Tommy Bahama shirt, he'd offer a toast as an apology: *To my beautiful wife who realizes that taking a wonderful vacation is worth a fight. I promise I'll remember this moment next time.*

And yet, when vacation rolled around again, getting Brady to agree to time off was like getting dried Parmesan off a dinner plate. Somehow his previous epiphany of appreciation was overshadowed by everything he was juggling at that moment. The fight always commenced the same way. I'd say, "Eve has a week off coming up and I thought we could go somewhere as a family." Brady would agree to check his schedule. Tension steadily mounted over the next two weeks as I sought confirmation on our pending plans, until we hit the true beginning of the fight, when Brady said something like, "You know, honey, with work it's just not in the cards for me right now, but you and Eve should go anyway." Some variation of this sentence started about two fights a year throughout our entire marriage. That's forty fights, fierce and long, on the same subject.

I went ballistic twice a year, calling him everything from a martyr to a cheater. I cried and questioned why he didn't like spending time with his family. I stormed out of rooms. I cursed. One time, after a few glasses of wine and to my sincere embarrassment, I broke a plate on the floor. That night he accused me of acting like my mother. He's lucky he survived the insult.

Listening to his systematic thought process, I now see that the fight for him was no longer about taking off work, it was that not taking off work didn't make a person a masochist or adulterer. Logic owns my husband — being a hard worker does not equate to screwing someone else. That's a fact; that's what he was arguing.

"Maddy," he'd say, "listen to yourself. You're not making sense."

His analytical response burned me. "You

don't care how upset I am."

"I care, but come on, you're being theatrical. I can't take time off right now, that's all. I don't have a secret life, or any of the other crazy shit you've rattled off."

I should've stated my case more simply. Brady is a numbers guy. Things add up to be correct or incorrect, not because of hype but in spite of it. I wonder how he'd have responded if I'd said something like, "We need to vacation as a family. It's important for our marriage and your relationship with Eve. You can bring your iPad and check email, but I'm asking you to make this a priority." I bet with a concentrated message like that, he wouldn't have fought so hard. He would've respected my reasoning and agreed to go, perhaps with the caveat that we shorten the trip from seven days to five.

I could have lived with that.

EVE

Another lecture about drinking and driving is on its way. I'll apologize and my predictable father will say, "That's not good enough this time," and announce the punishment he's been "mulling over" all week. Whatever it is, I won't give a shit because there's nothing he can take from me that matters. This entire conversation is a waste.

"Help me understand what happened," he says instead.

Oh, I get it. He's attempting to approach it how my mother would have. I slouch, not knowing how to answer now that we're off-script. I decide to make him uncomfortable so he'll drop the act.

"I'm not a respected executive that people are afraid to offend, Dad. I hear people whispering about us. Not just Saturday. All. The. Time. It blows."

"Not having to hear it doesn't mean I don't know what people are saying."

He's talking to me. For real. Maybe I should've gotten in a car accident sooner. "Well, it's humiliating."

He twitches. Humiliation is new to us both. I used to be proud of our family, not that I appreciated it at the time. Dad was successful and Mom wasn't like the other moms who spent like three hours a day at the gym and kissed everyone's ass. When I was twelve, she overheard this girl Lauren (whose dad owned practically every gas station in Boston) call this other girl fat. Mom barely knew either of them, but she paused her conversation with Paige, looked Lauren right in the eye, and calmly said, "That was mean. You should consider saying you're sorry."

"You're not a teacher," Lauren said.

"And that girl's not fat. You saying otherwise was unkind."

"But, I —"

Mom was never a fan of the word *but*. She turned back to Paige, leaving Lauren looking foolish at the sideline. Something changed that day for those of us who saw it — we stopped giving Lauren the power to stomp on us. She switched to private school the following year, and I always thought we had my mom to thank for it. I wanted to be exactly like her.

So what do you do when you find out the person you most admire hated her life?

In the ambulance after the accident I ignored the EMT moving around the stretcher with air masks and tubes and his personal judgment showing in huffs, and thought about how unfair life is. My mother was wrong; there's not a reason for anything. I don't even know what to want anymore. I don't want to die, but I'm no longer excited to live. Not that I can say that to my dad. He'd freak and ship me off to some high-end loony bin for suicide watch.

"I still don't understand how you ended up in a car with John on Route 9."

Why can't he drop it? The case is closed. With John's family connections, the city got everything settled in four days — John lost his license for two years and I got thirty hours of community service — yet here we are a week later still on it.

"It just . . . happened. Everyone was talking about Mom and then Mrs. Anderson was wasted and asked if I picked out the dress with her beforehand and I lost it. I had to get out of there."

"Christie Anderson is a douche bag. Your mother and I used to call her Cruella de Vil."

Finally something he and I agree on: Mrs. Anderson is a douche bag. The channeling has stopped; Mom never would've admitted that.

"The thing is, Eve, you should've called. I would have picked you up, no questions asked."

That's crap. He would've picked me up, but he would've been a pain in the ass about it. And he probably would've been as drunk as I was. I debate calling him out but decide it's not worth it. "Well, you don't have to worry. That was my last school dance."

"Still, you're grounded."

"Fine, I'm grounded."

I don't even ask how long. There's nowhere I want to go with a runway of missing hair where my wispy bangs used to

102

hang, and there's no one to hang out with anyway. John's father is on the Massachusetts Supreme Court and viewed our actions as a call for help. He added thirty days in rehab with no communication from me to John's sentence. John's friends are mad at me and my friends are tired of begging me to care. I have officially become what I've felt like for months, an outsider.

Dad gives me a weird look, then jumps to his feet as if he forgot something. He returns with a book tucked under his arm. "It's your mom's journal," he explains, rubbing the cover. I reach for it, but he pulls it close to his chest. "I've been reading an entry a day. You have to respect that these are her personal thoughts and there's only certain pieces you'll benefit from at this point." He flips through a few pages and hands it to me opened on June 23, 2013, my last day as a freshman. "I thought you'd appreciate this one."

Well, Eve is officially a sophomore. The cliché "Where have the years gone?" doesn't seem so trite when it's your child. I'd never hear the end of it if she read this, but sometimes I stop and smell her laundry before putting it in the wash. She's my favorite smell.

As anticipated, the status of our relationship swings wildly based on her needs, fears, and struggle for independence, but I continue to find evidence there's more going on in her head than she lets on. Today I told her I was proud to be her mother. I expected an eye roll but instead she said, "Thanks for not judging me." Just like that, a compliment.

She's wrong, though, I do judge. She's perfect.

Mom had a journal? She loved my smell? She thought I was perfect?

I was wronged, cheated out of a gift that was right in front of me at a time when I was too selfish to open it.

I ask Dad if I can read more, but he gently tugs the journal from my hands. "Someday," he says. "Some of it will serve you better later. As I read ones like this, about you, I'll pass them along."

" 'Kay." There's no point fighting about it. The man is never home. What's he gonna do, lock it in a safe?

Out of nowhere he asks if I want a party for my birthday in two weeks. I don't point out that he just grounded me. It's a short conversation.

"No."

"Why?"

"Because."

If he pushes the list is long: because most likely no one would come, because I'm not excited enough about life to celebrate, because it would be a total sham if I got presents after driving my mom off a rooftop. Luckily for both of us he just says, "All right."

It's not really, but I'll keep pretending.

BRADY

If Paige hadn't printed a wiki page on why it's disgusting not to, I would've left the bedding from when Dan and Meg stayed for the funeral. But here I am, home from work an hour early, in a three-way wrestling match with sheets and a mattress.

Paige has morphed into a representative of Maddy's previous interests, operating a step ahead of my next mistake. How she knew I planned to throw a guest into a dust-mite haven I'll never know.

Goddamnit it . . . No matter how high I lift the mattress to shove the hanging sheet underneath, a section still falls lower than the comforter. And no matter how many times I circle around tugging each side, the top border isn't parallel to the headboard. I can't believe Maddy did this every week, on every bed in the house, without complaining. Or, at a minimum, bragging. I'm adding it to the cleaning lady's list, which used to take four hours a week and now requires two full days. I hope she doesn't quit, because I'd have no idea how to recruit a replacement. Every week I leave more money on the counter next to a note outlining additional requests, praying it's still worth her time.

I'm redoing a particularly sloppy corner when Eve walks in. "Why are you grunting?"

"I'm not grunting," I snap. "I'm making the bed for Bobby." Her expression is blank. Now I grunt. "I've told you a hundred times." Still nothing. "My friend from high school? He's coming for the weekend."

She ticktocks her index finger in sarcastic recollection. "Ohhhh, that's right. I think it's hard to remember because I didn't know you had any friends."

I remind myself that a normal person would laugh, then force myself to act like a normal person. It's amazing how quickly in life your standards can change. At Christmas, a good moment was eating Maddy's homemade tortellini, listening to Michael Bublé, and hanging out with my family. Now, a good moment is getting made fun of by my daughter and not losing my temper.

Eve turns to go so I can complete this impossible domestic task, but I stop her. "Did you see my note? The Y called to confirm your lifeguard schedule for the summer." She nods. "I told her you were volunteering at a special-needs camp every morning, so afternoons were probably best. I left out that it's mandatory community service."

Eve flaps her wrist. "Whatevs. I'm not working anyway. I'll call to let them know."

I put the last pillow in place — it looks like the work of a monkey — and sit on the bed, trying to hide my disappointment. "Why not? You love that job."

"I don't feel like saving lives right now."

I've noticed showing I care about an outcome tends to work against me, so I stick with questions. "What will you do all afternoon?"

Eve purses her lips, annoyed. "Mom found plenty to keep busy around here."

"But how will you earn spending money?"

She shrugs. "You only need money if you're going places."

Apparently, that's the end of the conversation, because she walks away. Of all my behaviors, it serves me right that this is the one she emulates.

Clearly Eve needs therapy, but even thinking about that conversation makes me wince. Her moodiness gives her an upper hand. I'm the lion in *The Wizard of Oz,* searching for my courage. Maddy once shared this whole working theory about professional men who spend the day building an empire and ego at work, then come home assuming they deserve the same status, despite the fact that it's a different audience. I'm such a moron; I missed the obvious connection that she was referring to me. Maddy made the façade succeed in our house. She was the liaison between Eve and me, negotiating my sense of entitlement down while playing up my role as provider with Eve. Without my wife's intercession, Eve doesn't see me as successful at work, at least not as much as she sees the failure I am at home.

I am trying. I put a moratorium on travel until Eve leaves for school, and I get home from work by seven with dinner in hand, cognizant that forgetting to secure food for my daughter over the past several months is a substantial parenting offense. But these are easy, tactical changes. My temper still wins more than it loses, and I end each day housing reprehensible thoughts, like, *What if we never had Eve?* Appalling, I know. But when night hits and loneliness takes over, I imagine our life as it was in our late twenties, when all Maddy and I had was work and each other. Without a child, we wouldn't have gotten rid of the cappuccino machine we sold when Eve turned one and it consumed prime bottle-cleaning, baby-food-making real estate. And if we still had the cappuccino machine, I would've had coffee with Maddy every morning instead of alone at Starbucks. And if we had that extra time together, I would've known she was unhappy. It's at this point in my nightly spiral that I start to gulp the bourbon I'm plowing through, drowning my despicable-ness until Maker's Mark tucks me in for the night.

Perhaps my daughter isn't the only one in need of therapy.

The doorbell rings. Hearing Eve greet Bobby brings me back to the now. My daughter won't be impressed. I should've had Paige host a sleepover. Bobby is an entertainer who never found a career that sponsored his talent with a paycheck. Twenty-seven years after highschool graduation and he's an insurance adjuster for auto claims, the same job he held when I left for college. It seems a cruel waste of a great personality, but the job does feed him good material. When I get to the kitchen, he's already started on a story.

"She didn't want her husband to know she'd hit the boat trailer, but she had a huge dent that needed to be fixed, so the genius decided to hit her mailbox too."

"How do you know it was intentional?" Eve asks, I assume to be polite versus actual interest.

"When the mailbox didn't tip on the first try, she backed up and hit it again. A neighbor called nine-one-one thinking she was having a stroke or something."

"For real?" Eve questions, skeptical.

Bobby holds up a hand. "Take everything I say, divide it by three, and it's exactly what happened."

They laugh until they see me standing there. "Wow," I say. "I really know how to bring down a room."

I expect Eve to disappear to her bedroom straightaway, but somehow the three of us end up parked in the living room listening to Bobby's tales. They all end with an observation like, "Look at any couple where both people have a visor on and one person will also have a fanny pack." Or, "Women tell their estheticians everything. Eve, you should know there's no client confidential-

ity just because some lady did your Brazil-
ian." I don't appreciate his uncouth delivery,
but Eve seems to be enjoying herself.

Bobby and I are a six-pack in when he
gets going on a guy who totaled a classic
Corvette by self-installing a six-hundred-
pound chandelier in his garage. "The wir-
ing was old, and apparently the installation
was shoddy too, because when he flipped
the switch it pulverized the car."

"Why would someone put a chandelier in
a garage?" Eve asks.

Bobby's lighthearted air evaporates. He
shifts his weight on the couch and takes a
sip of beer. "His wife liked them."

"I bet his wife died." I meant to think it,
but I can tell by their faces I said it out loud.

Bobby takes another sip, bigger this time.
"Yeah," he says. "Sorry, man, I forgot that
part."

"I bet they fought over it," I continue, not
wanting to put myself out there, but unable
to shut up. "Now the guy understands what
a waste that was, and he wants to make it
up to her, but he can't."

I'm greeted with silence. I can read Eve's
mind; she's wondering about my failures
with Maddy, about the regret behind the
tears in my eyes.

I am too. Until this moment, I've allowed

anger to grant me absolution. *Who jumps off a building?* Now the chandeliers of our marriage present themselves. *Who refuses to go on vacation? Who routinely comes home an hour late without calling, knowing two people are waiting to eat dinner?* The epiphany would be meaningful if Maddy were here and I could do something about it, but she's not, so I get up and head to bed. There's no off switch once my mood sours. I need to sleep it off.

Not wanting to be left sole hostess, Eve also stands and exits without a word. I hear Bobby finish his beer in the living room before calling it a night. I'm sure he spends the time lamenting his decision to visit.

I apologize the next morning on the way to golf, but the awkwardness can't be undone. Bobby waits until we've finished a Bloody Mary to attempt a serious discussion about loss, but some people aren't wired for topics like that. Neither of us knows how to pull it off. I'm trying now with Eve, but it's not smooth. I say things like, "I missed Mom a lot today," or, "You sounded like your mother when you said that." She just nods. Now, with Bobby, I take Eve's approach and stay silent, hoping he'll shut the hell up. But, like me, he doesn't. On the sixth hole he says, "It must suck."

I don't stop walking until I get to my ball. "It does."

"If you want to talk about it, I'm here."

"Nah," I reply, swinging hard. The ball goes far, but not straight. Story of my life.

"Remember the time I brought that girl from Rhode Island to your house?" Bobby asks as we head to the seventh. I nod. "When she was in the bathroom, I asked Maddy what she thought. 'Well,' Maddy said, all sweet-like, 'she wears a shirt that covers her entire abdomen, so she's better than the last girlfriend I met.' She was a pistol, your Maddy. Funny and brutally honest. I always wish I found someone like that, you know? That I had a chance to have what you guys had."

"I said I don't want to talk about her, Bobby."

He scratches his cheek. "Yeah, you did. Sorry."

It's a relief when Sunday comes and he leaves. I guess Eve's comment that I had no friends was more a prophecy than a joke.

CHAPTER FIVE

MADELINE

Eve was an accident. It's hard to admit that my greatest accomplishment was thrust upon me, but it's the truth. I was convinced women lacking strong maternal mentors had no business procreating. Friends accused me of being careless; I was not. I took that small blue pill every day at noon sharp, but Eve wanted in.

We'd been married almost three years. Our advertised stance on not having children was very sophisticated. (Or maybe *self-righteous* is more accurate.) We circled around topics like population growth, questioning the responsibility of adding life when we were educated enough to understand the long-term consequence on humankind. We poetically feared raising a child in a world where the most violent show on TV was the evening news. We regurgitated statistics about the pathetic state of public education, giving ourselves a pat on the back for having the foresight to not have a child who'd fall victim to it. But this hyperbole was a cover. I didn't know the first thing about being a good mom and I was at a selfish point in life, loving the attention corporate America doled out to hardworking women in the nineties. That the pay wasn't commensurate to the work didn't bother me as much as it should have. It was the era of DINKs — Dual Income, No Kids. Brady and I took last-minute weekend trips, went out for nice dinners on a whim, and procured whole outfits worn by shop mannequins. We'd recently returned from Jamaica when that powerful little stick made a plus sign.

My immediate reaction was terror. Not regarding our carbon footprint or in fear for our future child's safety in this ever-violent world, but because of my overabundance of vacation indulgence. Jamaica was a blur of rum punch and mai tais. I didn't need to worry about how terrible public schools were because I'd probably done enough brain damage to the baby on my own.

When our first sonogram showed a healthy heartbeat and viable fetus, Brady and I made a silent agreement to ditch the political rhetoric and be grateful. And I was, at least publically. Privately — and by that I mean without even whispering the words in an empty room — I dreaded the impact a baby would have on my career and marriage. Who the hell was I to be someone's mother?

I was a kick-ass saleswoman. I found it intoxicating to use femininity and charm to seduce stores into buying more from me than my male competitors. And — this was the heart of it — my career stomped out an innate fear of turning out like my mother, a homemaker who didn't take care of her home. How much of my persona would be stripped away with a hungry, crying human to tend to? Were Meg and I the reason my mother became what she became?

In a way my fear was justified; Eve changed my life. But it wasn't the sacrifice I imagined. When she arrived I felt this tremendous call to action, like a soldier going to war, and I was honored to serve. Without acknowledging it, I'd never cared about anyone more than myself, not even Brady. Motherhood enlarged my heart. I found a reserve capacity to love that trumped my initial supply tenfold. I had more to give everyone because I had more to tap into. When I quit, my boss warned that it was the biggest mistake of my life. I told him I certainly hoped he was right. That'd be a damn good life.

Eve arrived at midnight on her due date. When she was young, I kicked off the celebration of her birthday with a gentle kiss as the clock struck twelve. Later, when she reached double digits, I awakened her to tell the story of our labor. I'd sit at the edge of the bed, careful not to disrupt the covers since Eve sleeps naked with sheets tangled around her like a full-body bandage. From the moment she was born, Eve preferred to be nude. When a bottle and diaper change failed, stripping Eve naked to rest in front of an open window saved my sanity. She loved it so much that we pushed the envelope on how old was too old to swim with no bathing suit and walk around the house in only underpants. Brady joked she'd better grow out of the preference before puberty. At six, I finally called it, and we slowly adapted her to society's expectation of clothing, but she never succumbed to pajamas overnight. She'd wear something right up until bedtime, then strip before jumping under the covers. Don't get me wrong; she was shy about this penchant and as she grew older she got mad when we teased her about it. An oddity. Brady's mother suggested I send Eve to a therapist.

"Nip it in the bud before she's old enough to be sleazy," she cautioned. I replied that there are worse things in life than being comfortable with yourself.

I consider the beginning of Eve's life the true beginning of mine. Motherhood put to rest a slew of unhealthy anxieties and obsessions. People's opinion of me became wholly insignificant, while my opinion of me was considered for the first time. No more social climbing. No more following seasonal fashion trends. It was time to find a cause and give back. To become a role model. Eve was the catalyst for everything I'm most proud of. I will not break our birthday tradition; I've disappointed her enough already. So here I am, at midnight, telling the familiar story.

It was ten when my water broke. Your father's plane was supposed to land at eleven-thirty, so I assumed he'd be able to take me to the hospital, but an hour later it was clear you had no intention of accommodating Dad's travel schedule. We were new to the neighborhood, so I settled for a cab. Your father had gotten his first cell phone two weeks before for this exact occasion. I left a message that he'd probably be a dad by the time he listened to it.

The taxi was stuffy. The driver went faster

and faster as my contractions got closer and closer. I tried to space my breathing how they taught at Lamaze, but it felt better to scream, so that's mostly what I did. Through the pain I pictured you making your way, on your first true adventure.

When we arrived, I thought the driver would stay with me, like they do in the movies, but he took the cash from my shaking hand and sped away. For a brief moment I felt alone, but then you reminded me of your presence. I walked in the waiting room, convinced by the pressure that I'd give birth right there on the gray vinyl couch. I howled deliriously at the thought of it.

You were the world's fastest delivery. I only pushed for twenty minutes. Your father ran in right as you came out, fists clenched, arms raised, and one eye open. You looked intense but ardent, ready for anything to come. When I saw you I knew I was looking at my life's purpose.

Eve, you're still intense, ardent, and ready for anything to come. Happy birthday.

When I finish, Eve has her knees tucked to her chest. We're embracing; I feel it. I send a burst of energy. As the sensation flushes through her, she's aware it's unworldly. I'll remember that trick, a way to send love without competing with her thoughts.

The next morning Eve wonders whether it was all in her head. On a whim I belt out the words I sang whenever she questioned my love: *Ain't no mountain high enough . . . ain't no valley low enough . . . ain't no river wide enough . . . to keep me from getting to you.* When the chorus ends, her concentrated face breaks into a smile. She squeezes her knees to her chest one last time, saying good-bye.

Brady wrote *Happy Birthday!* on the bathroom mirror with lipstick, the way I always had. Eve giggles at the effort, and also, I think, at seeing the display in a man's handwriting. It does look funny. Yesterday I repeated the words *lipstick mirror* about three thousand times so he'd remember the tradition. His Come-to-Jesus-Moment after Eve's accident hasn't been the miracle transformation I'd imagined. He's still too raw, too angry, and — since there's no reason to sugarcoat anymore — too innately selfish. He wants to put Eve first, but not as much as he wants whatever the hell it is he wants. His inner dialogue is a wheel of excuses: *next time . . . she won't care . . . if I'd been sober I'd have handled it better.*

Eve brushes her teeth, stupefied by the idea that I'll miss her seventeenth birthday.

And eighteenth. And nineteenth. As the number ticks up, she presses the brush harder and harder against her gums, lost by the enormity of how much time she has on earth without me. Minutes pass where Eve mentally disassociates from her physical action. *Stop,* I command. *Stop. You're hurting yourself.* She receives my plea and returns to the present, spitting toothpaste into the sink. It's bright red, her gums exposed. Eve swishes fresh water in her stinging mouth, then heads downstairs.

Brady has chocolate-chip pancakes going. That hasn't been Eve's favorite since she was nine and ate too many despite my warning, but she keeps that to herself. I'm nervous for them. I watch the scene play out as I imagine a writer finishes a chapter, hopeful the conclusion complements the rising action, but unsure it will.

"Happy birthday," Brady says, as apprehensive as I am.

"I don't know about that, but thanks." She smirks. "I got your note. Was that color Kissalicious pink or Heart Stopper red?"

"It was called The One on Sale at CVS."

Rory was at the pharmacy when Brady bought it. I didn't want them to meet in that moment — Rory was frenzied, picking up nausea medication for her poor mother, and Brady wanted to get in and out without anyone noticing the lipstick he was embarrassed to be buying — but I was overruled by fate. Brady grabbed a basket on his way in, planning to hide the lipstick under a bag of chips. When he got to the cosmetics section, he realized he was being foolish and, rudely, abandoned the basket in the middle of the aisle. Along came Rory, rushing toward the exit, prescription in hand. When she tripped on his booby trap, Brady rushed to help. "I can't believe someone left that there," he said boldly.

Rory waved off the hand he offered. "Oh, I'm fine. But I am beginning to wonder at what age I'll learn to watch where I'm going." She picked up her purse before meeting Brady's eyes.

Smile, I instructed Brady. He did, so she did. "You're all right?"

"I am."

"Too bad," he said with a grin. "No grounds for a lawsuit."

Rory laughed. "Which is a shame since my brother's an attorney and I could use the money."

As she turned to leave, Rory registered the lipstick in his hand. "Have a nice night," she said, walking away.

"It's for my daughter," he called to her back.

She turned to wink. "Whatever you say."

I couldn't have orchestrated it better. They have a natural chemistry. With Eve's tutoring starting next week, the timing is perfect.

"Hungry?" Brady asks, bringing me back to the moment.

"I'll eat if you will," Eve says.

"Is that a critique?"

"No," she replies carefully, "but it's a birthday wish."

I help Brady take in the meaning of her words — *your daughter is worried about you.* He wonders when their roles reversed. "I've been eating, you know," he says. "Just not at dinner."

"Yeah, I figured, since you're still here and all, but I'd like to see it firsthand."

I've been encouraging Brady to show Eve his sense of humor, trying to lighten their interactions (as much for me as them), and I can tell he's about to go for it. "You know what I absolutely love?"

He says it in a childish voice that piques Eve's interest. "What?"

"Those cracked honey-mustard pretzels. They cut my mouth like shards of glass and give me cold sores, but even in my grief I can't help myself. I'd have disappeared if it weren't for those damn things."

It's such a genuine exchange, which is all Eve wants. She rewards him with a smile. "Whatever works, right?"

"Right."

There's a knock at the door. "It's probably one of your adoring fans," Eve says. "I'll get it."

"If you're right, I'm not here."

I find it hilarious how royally they've both misinterpreted the neighbors' intentions. Susan Dundel aside, the women who stop by are doing so out of concern, for Eve more than Brady. They aren't stalking him. It's an organized schedule of twice-weekly check-ins. And they're not all divorced; Brady's innate cynicism has combined with his huge ego to determine that they have an ulterior motive and it must be him. Mary is a happily married therapist who was aggressive because she wanted to see Eve in her home environment to ensure everything was kosher. She wasn't batting her eyelashes at Brady — she was scanning the foyer. The conversations are awkward because no one knows what the hell to say. It's not like I died in a car accident.

Eve opens the door to Paige holding a laundry basket filled with gifts. I teed up the delivery, but the timing is off. Brady will be irritated.

"Oh good, you're not crying yet," Paige says.

Eve looks at the size of the offering and whistles. "Think you got a little carried away there?"

Paige flaps her hand. "Yes. Usually I'm desperately scouring Pinterest for a suggestion, but for some reason ideas kept surfacing. What can I say? I became a woman possessed. And why not? You've been through hell; this stuff won't make anything worse."

"Way to aim low."

"I find I'm rarely disappointed." She follows Eve to the kitchen.

Brady tenses. He plotted out the morning, and Paige isn't in the script. She's the ultimate reminder of what he lost.

"Is your better half at church?" he asks. That's how the guys refer to their standing Sunday golf game.

Paige nods. "He said to tell you they're holding your place in the foursome until you officially tell them to screw off."

"You should go sometime, Dad," Eve urges.

"Nah," Brady says.

He's been branded and he knows it. Men aren't as obvious with their judgment, but it's there. Inwardly the guys at the club use my death to puff up what great family men they are. Their wives spend their money all-smiles — they can't figure out how Brady botched such an easy equation. Even Paige, who was my trusted advisor and had a front-row seat to my life, doubts Brady's innocence. We shared every marital grievance, but Paige now assumes I held back. She wouldn't be here now if it weren't for Eve.

"Should I open them?" Eve asks, looking at the gifts.

"No," Paige says in a serious tone. "They're for your *eighteenth* birthday." They both giggle. Brady puts tinfoil over the pancakes, sensing this will take a while.

The first few gifts are to get Eve into yoga — videos, a mat, Athleta clothes. My primary intention is to offer an outlet for her anger, but I also want to establish a commonality between Eve and Rory.

Eve thanks Paige without enthusiasm. "Try it," Paige presses under divine inspiration. "It's not like your schedule is booked solid."

"Thanks for pointing that out."

Paige's eyebrows rise. "Well . . . am I wrong? Do you have time to give it a try?"

"No, you're right, I do. But I can't promise I'll like it."

"Fair enough," Paige agrees. "Next present."

Their exchange leaves Brady jealous. If he called Eve out like that there'd be backlash. *What gives Paige the right?* he wonders. *Is it just maternal confidence?*

Eve unwraps a paperback copy of *The Celestine Prophecy* by James Redfield. I'm convinced it's the right book to further open Eve's mind to the possibility that the energy she senses, the vibrations I send, are real. The more she believes, the easier it will be to get through.

The final present was not at my behest. Paige bought Eve four-hundred-dollar Frye boots. Eve does a double take at the branded box. "This is a pity present."

"Completely," Paige admits. "I love ya, kiddo. Since your mom isn't here to spoil you, I figured I'd step in."

Eve tears up while they embrace. Brady shuffles behind the counter to remind them of his existence, but Paige shoots him a look that screams, *Back off.* Brady shrinks, admonished. After his friend Bobby left, Brady did a masterful job pushing back the nagging possibility that he'd played a role in my unhappiness, but Paige's contempt resurfaces his doubt.

It's time for her to go. I poke Eve. "I'll

127

walk you out," she says.

When Eve returns to Brady, they stare at each other, looking for a way back to their earlier momentum. Eve starts to say something, but abandons the thought mid-sentence. "Spit it out," he says lightly.

"Mom shared the story of her labor last night."

Respond carefully, I coach. "I hear her laugh sometimes," he divulges. "It's in my head, obviously, but still." He wipes away a tear, but not before Eve sees it.

"You never told me that."

"I thought it sounded crazy."

"It does."

Brady snorts, "Yeah. Yours too."

Eve pours two glasses of orange juice while Brady puts the pancakes in the microwave. "Do you think it's 'cause we want to hear her so badly? I mean, it's not real, I know that, but then, what is it?" She places a hand on her collarbone. It's a gesture of hers I know well — she's scared of the answer.

"I don't know," Brady admits, "but hearing her makes me happy, which so little does right now, so I'm trying not to overthink it."

"*You?* Overthink something? Never."

Laugh at yourself, I instruct Brady. And, with mammoth effort, he does.

EVE

My hands are still sticky with syrup when he hands me a blank version of my mother's journal. I thought he'd have Paula buy a bunch of random shit and try to pretend this birthday is normal, but he gives the one gift, unwrapped, as if to prove he had no help. I don't know how he tracked down something Mom bought over two years ago, or how he thought to get it in the first place, but it's the perfect present. He wrote a note on the inside cover.

Eve,
I know this birthday will be unforget-table in the most negative sense. It's unfair that grief doesn't take time off. I'm a poor substitute, but I promise we'll make it — you and me. Our grief will mature. Although in despair, I cherish your life today, as I do every day.
There was a saying your mom used to quote by Adrienne Rich: "If we could learn to learn from pain even as it grasps us . . ." I hope this journal helps you do that.

Happy birthday,
Dad

The note is proof that out of freaking

nowhere, it's no longer *me* versus *him;* it's *us* versus *them,* where them is everyone who didn't lose Her. We're a team. A totally dysfunctional team, but still.

"Remember the Clean Plate Club?" I ask.

"Remember it? I invented it." He looks down and sees my food is gone. "Nice work."

I eye the three-quarters of a pancake still on his plate. "I think we should reinstate the Clean Plate Club."

He folds his arms. "I disagree."

"Why?"

"Because I don't like playing games I won't win. Any other questions, Chatty McGee?"

He's right. I'm not usually this talkative, but I don't want breakfast to end. The second it does, his laptop will come out, his office door will close, and I'll be left alone with my ghost of a mother. "Yeah, actually . . ." I draw out the words while I think of a question. "Why did you guys name me Eve?"

He wiggles his jaw to find the memory. "Umm, your mother picked it. It means 'life giving' and she loved the idea of that. But Eve had been a favorite of hers even before we looked through those crazy name books. A friend of Gram's was named Eve. Mom

130

talked about her quite a lot when we were first dating."

"Who was she?"

"She was the one who turned your mom into such a bookworm. Highly intelligent. Men proposed right and left, but Eve balked at the whole idea of it. If memory serves, she was one of the first women to get a law degree from Boston College."

"Did I meet her?"

"No," he says, "and neither did I. She died while Mom was in college, before we met. Lung cancer, I think. She was a big smoker."

I grin. "I was named after a dead woman you never met who smoked a lot?"

He frowns. "It's all in the details you pick. Mom would say you were named after the most inspiring, independent woman she knew. That's what she wanted for you, you know? She believed everyone had the right to create their own life, so she was inherently wary of people who told her how to live."

"What if I choose to be a belly dancer?"

I mean it as a joke, but Dad keeps it serious. "Whenever we were around parents who had black-and-white goals for their children, your mother felt sorry for the whole family — the parents because they'd be perpetually disappointed, and the kids because they'd always feel nothing was good enough. She believed there was nothing worse a parent could pass on to a child than guilt."

I have to ask the obvious question, even if it ruins the moment. "If that's true, why'd she do it?"

He takes a long sip of coffee and looks out at the garden. "She must not have considered it that way."

I give him a moment, then ask why she never told me I had a namesake. I'm surprised when he has an answer. "She was saving it, I think. For when you needed to hear it."

"And that's today?"

"I don't know, Eve. I'm sure I'm hosing the timing, but you asked, and let's be honest, it's not like I'll remember it at the perfect moment anyway."

I double-check I'm talking to my dad. He never admits things like that. Maybe he's on antidepressants.

"What about Mom and Gram? Did they get along?" I only saw Gram once a year. She used to slip me Rolaids as candy.

Dad chuckles. "Not so much. Gram subscribed to the guilt-ridden formula of motherhood. That's probably why Mom was so conscious of it."

"Like how?"

He takes a huge bite of his pancake and holds up an index finger. I watch the bite travel down his throat. He's the world's slowest eater. It drove Mom batshit.

"Gram struggled," he finally says. "She wasn't comfortable in her own skin, you know?"

I stick out my tongue. "That's weak. I want examples."

"Really taking advantage of your birthday clout, huh?"

"Oh, come *on*," I push. "What could you possibly have to be hush-hush about now? I'm seventeen and they're both dead." He grimaces. "Sorry," I whisper. "I didn't mean to say it like that."

His head hangs. I assume I've lost him, that he's about to get up and leave me with the plates to bring in, but after a minute he says, "Secrets clearly aren't the way to go. We need to learn to learn from pain, right?" I nod. "Gram was a drunk."

My face contorts. "What?"

"She sobered up once a year so Mom would let her see you."

This conversation is as interesting as her journal. Why didn't I think to ask these questions sooner? "So what, like, she passed out every night?"

"Eh. It was more substantial than that. Things soured between her and your grand-father, and Gram just sort of holed up with a bottle. She wasn't abusive or anything, but there was a lot of chaos in the house. Neglect. I think that's why Mom needed everything perfect all the time."

This info gets me thinking. Mom's child-hood could be the source of her depression. She told Dad she wasn't abused, but who knows? Clearly her goal was to put up a front, a beautiful family portrait that never really existed.

"Is that what Gram died of?" I ask. "Alco-holism?"

My father coughs — a strange, forced cough designed to distract. Something about it clues me in. Before he can string together some bullshit story I say, "Oh. My. *God*. She killed herself, didn't she?"

He puts up a hand to slow me down. "Hold on," he says calmly. "We don't know that. She had early-stage Alzheimer's, so she wasn't of right mind."

"Holy shit."

His eyebrows rise. "Language."

I ignore him. "How'd she do it?"

"A nurse left anxiety medication in her room by accident and Gram overdosed. They found an empty jug of wine, which didn't surprise anyone, and no note. I still think there's a chance she got drunk and forgot she'd taken her meds."

I roll my eyes. "She just kept forgetting? Over and over?"

"You sound like your mother." He looks exasperated, as if it's nine years ago and I really am her and this is still up for debate. "It wouldn't take much. She was in poor health. Dialysis and all that."

I don't buy it. I don't remember anyone ever saying Gram had Alzheimer's. If she got drunk and housed pills it was on purpose, which means we have a family history of suicide. Maybe there are more hands on Mom's corpse than I thought.

Dad takes a big sip of his orange juice and points his glass toward me. "So now you know."

"Any other skeletons you can pull out for my big day?"

"Cool it," he says. "It wasn't my story to tell."

Halfway through the day I shut off my cell, but people just call the house phone instead. Everyone has the number since I was the *last* of my friends to get a phone. "You're not getting one until *I* need you to have it," Mom said every time I asked. That turned out to be freshman year when I started getting rides from older kids on the tennis team and Mom worried I'd need to get in touch with her. She called me all the time. I never called her once.

Today, I only answer for Aunt Meg. It's not worth ignoring her call. It's a once-a-week thing, and if I don't pick up she hounds me until I do. Before Mom died our relationship was weak: I saw her on holidays and birthdays where I spent most the time hanging out with my cousin Lucy. But she and Mom were obsessed with the whole sisterhood thing. They talked every morning during Aunt Meg's hour-long commute. Mom must've blabbed her face off about me, and that's why Aunt Meg thinks we're so much closer than we actually are.

I dread our talks. She knew Mom better than anyone. I'm a little jealous of that, but mostly I'm pissed she missed whatever walked my mom off that building. She's also a mother, with a daughter my age, and both of them are alive. That obviously shouldn't bug me, but it does anyway.

Aunt Meg knows I'm not into our little chats, but instead of taking the freaking hint it's made her superaggressive. She's full of stupid suggestions, as if she's going to replace my mother with a ten-minute weekly pep talk, as if I don't need a mother at all. Giving advice to someone in mourning is like offering pretzels to someone dehydrated. It doesn't help.

"Happy birthday, beautiful," she sings when I answer, chipper as a former teen model turned successful business executive because that's exactly what she is. "What are you doing to celebrate?"

"Not much," I say, flipping through channels on TV.

"I know it must be hard, honey, but your mom would want you to celebrate. It'd kill her to think of you moping around on your birthday."

"She already took care of that." I do not feel bad for being bitchy. Aunt Meg set herself up by saying something so stupid.

"I'm not suggesting I know what you should do, but —"

I half-listen, deciding whether to hang up or call her out. I don't know which I'll pick until the words come out: "Yes, you are, Aunt Meg. I-I don't mean to be rude, but . . . you totally are. You want to fix this for me, but you *can't.*"

"Oh, Eve, sweetie, I know," she coos in a baby-talk voice.

"*Shut up!* Please. You have no idea —"

"She was my *sister,* Eve. I lost her too."

"*Yes.* You lost your *sister.* I don't know how that feels. I lost my *mother,* the person who did everything for me. You don't know how that feels."

I must be speaking louder than I realize because my father appears in the family room to see what's going on. He stands at the door, motioning me to surrender. "Look, *whatever,*" I say. "I shouldn't have even answered. Thanks for the gift card. I'll call later or something."

I assume I'm in for a lecture, but Dad just walks away. There might have even been a smile on his face. I think my fight with Aunt Meg signaled that he handled the day well. He's so freaking competitive. I guess you never grow out of wanting approval.

BRADY

I'm on my way to pick up take-out Chinese at Eve's request, which the two of us will eat alone. The day Eve turned sixteen she was on the phone with her friends every second she wasn't physically with them. I delivered my birthday wish while she put one hand over the receiver, telling whoever was on the other end to hold on a sec.

This year I was promoted to birthday coordinator. My only goal going in was to not walk out of the room when grief punched and — even with the bar that low — I've been craving a drink since breakfast. The energy it takes to focus on Eve's needs drains me. How Maddy made a life out of it is baffling.

I hadn't registered how rarely Eve is on the phone these days until birthday calls rolled in and she ignored them. Most of the messages broadcast from the answering machine were painful to overhear. Lindsey sounded timid, like she was leaving a message for someone terminally ill who may or may not have survived the night. It struck me that Eve mourns the loss of her mother while Lindsey mourns the loss of her best friend.

Some guy called to say John asked him to wish her a happy birthday since he couldn't from rehab, then added how lucky Eve is that John still cares. *Prick.*

Kara Anderson's message was bizarre. "Happy birthday, Eve," she mumbled in a way that sounded so involuntary I envisioned someone with a gun to her head. The phone shuffled around as if she tried to hang up but the line never disconnected. In the background there was a weird whimpering that continued until I got to the machine and cut the recording.

Kara has always been a troubled kid. Last

139

year she and Lindsey spent the night after
the homecoming dance. Maddy and I had
tied one on while the girls were gone, so I
woke up at two in the morning needing a
glass of water. I dragged myself to the
kitchen in gym shorts and there was Kara,
sitting on a bar stool in a see-through white
tank top and underpants, eating ice cream
out of the container. The second I processed
what I was looking at I turned to leave, and
she said, "I don't bite, Mr. Starling," then
laughed as I trotted back to my room. I
should've told Maddy, but I was out of sorts
enough to question my recollection the following morning.

I'd call Todd and Christie to make sure
everything was okay over there, but as the
guy with a wife who committed suicide and
a daughter who just got in a drunk-driving
accident, I'm not in a solid position to offer
up familial guidance.

Eve erased every message. When I asked
why she didn't want to talk to her friends
she said, "Trust me. They'd be forced
conversations. Everyone's glad I didn't pick
up."

I'd like to say my daughter's perceptive-
ness is a new part of her, something she
found in her grief, but Maddy's journal
documents otherwise. The entry last night

recounted a time after Eve got her driving permit when she said to Maddy, "It must be funny to be driven around by the person you usually chauffeur." They fought over the comment. Maddy was upset at being labeled a chauffeur; Eve claimed she was only joking and Maddy needed to "chill." When they were less than a mile from the house, Maddy made Eve pull over and walk home. Eve got back ten minutes later, and said, "I get why you're mad and I'm sorry. You weren't being a chauffeur all those years, you were being my mother."

Damn right, I thought as I read it. But now I'm struck by how often I took Maddy for granted. It frustrated me when she claimed to be too busy to get something done. One time I questioned what she was so busy doing. "Mostly putting together the pieces you leave behind," she replied. I thought it was a snarky retort until the pieces were left to me. It's not a dust pile but a landfill, and I'm not accounting for her volunteer work in that assessment. On a regular basis, I came home an hour later than expected, usually without the courtesy of a phone call, anticipating Maddy would be in a good mood with dinner ready. She was; it was. Often the school or library would call at night after someone had bailed, asking

141

Maddy to commit time or resources the next day. I preached she needed to set boundaries and say no. Once I even suggested the reason she got summoned was because she'd been identified as a sucker. "Not a sucker," Maddy corrected, chin up. "A giver." In the end she always agreed to help, which I inanely took to mean she had spare time. God, I was a jackass.

I return with takeout and a troubled conscience, determined to get through dinner without ticking Eve off or losing my cool, but anxious to retreat to my bedroom with a generous bourbon and brood.

Eve senses my mood has soured, so we eat in silence. She got the gift of intuitiveness from her mother — Maddy could always tell when there was more to a story. I once went on a business trip to Las Vegas when Eve was three. There was a guy, Jason Donahue, who I'd been working for since graduation. He was my boss, but he was also my friend; Maddy and I knew him and his wife, Stacy, well.

"How was Vegas?" Maddy asked casually at dinner. I must've changed my posture, or something out of the ordinary, because after responding it was business as usual, Maddy went radio silent. When dinner was done she marched Eve to bed, without offering a kiss good night from me. I listened as she gave Eve a longer bath than usual and let her pick five books instead of the customary three, dragging out her time away. When she finally returned, I asked why she was mad.

"What the hell happened in Vegas?" she responded, hands on hips, certain. Maddy was not a paranoid wife, and I was not a careless husband. How had she sensed there was a story at all?

"Nothing," I answered. "Jesus. What's wrong with you?"

"You're lying. Your poker face isn't any better than Eve's."

"I didn't do anything wrong."

"Then it won't be difficult to tell me the damn story."

She pulled it out of me like a splinter. Jason and I went out for drinks one night and Jason left the bar with a hooker. Maddy was horrified. First, she confirmed under intense scrutiny and implied threat of divorce that I had nothing to do with it, had never done anything like it, and would never consider doing anything like it in the future. With that contained, she turned her emotions to Jason's wife.

"What if he got a disease or something? Stacy needs to know."

"Are you out of your damned mind? It's none of our business, Maddy. Besides the fact that it could cost me my job."

"Your *job*? That's what you're worried about?"

"Yes . . . my job that supports this family."

Her eyes cut into me. "I support this family too."

She wished she didn't know more than I wished I hadn't told her. At least once a day we fought about what to do.

"It couldn't have been a one-time thing," she'd blurt randomly, when I thought the topic was dead. "You don't just say, 'Hey, it's Tuesday and I'm on the road, I'm going to try out this whole hooker thing.' " Then the next day, "What if Jason has another child somewhere?"

"I'm sure he was smart about it," I'd reply, trying to end the conversation but never succeeding.

"*Smart about it?* Smart about getting a hooker? There's an oxymoron for you."

I'd sigh and offer the same line I'd been touting for years without success. "You need to learn how to let other people tend to their own problems. It's not your job to fix everything." I blamed that propensity on her mother. Janine never addressed anything, so Meg and Maddy never let anything go. It was a rebellion of sorts.

She was uneasy every time I had a business trip with Jason after that. She couldn't shake the story; it hit too close to home. Eventually, I was promoted above him and our friendship dissolved, but I often think about that night. I never had Maddy's intuitive talent. She always held an element of mystery for me, and I liked it that way. I never felt bored. With the suicide everyone wants to know what was happening behind closed doors. I think they'd be surprised to discover I'm wondering the same thing. I was so rarely here.

When I got home from the hospital the day she died, there was a to-do list on the counter. I showed it to the police as undeniable proof her death was accidental. The officer read the list and said, "You can take this as whatever you want, sir, but there's no evidence to suggest anyone was with her, certainly no signs of a struggle, and no reason for her to go out on the roof in the first place. The investigation is over." He handed it back to me. "Maybe the list was for you."

In case he was right, I did everything on it — buying ingredients I had no idea how to use, refilling every bathroom with toilet paper, replacing the kitchen sponge. When I was done, I decided she left it so I'd appreciate the effort that went into making our lives run smoothly. She left it so I would walk in her shoes, even once. But getting a grocery list didn't scratch the surface. It's days like today, Eve's birthday, when I can't even make it through dinner without my own selfish distractions ruining the moment, that I finally appreciate the life she breathed into this house. She carried the weight of me and Eve's happiness.

"Shit," I say, breaking up the silence. "I forgot a cake."

Eve doesn't look up from her plate. "A cake wouldn't help."

"No, I guess not." I get the bag off the counter and scour for fortune cookies. Even though I ordered for three out of habit, there's only one in the bag.

"Let's share the fate of whatever it says," Eve suggests. I throw it to her. When she cracks it open, the message catches us both by surprise: *The only way forward is through.*

I clear my throat. "You know, Eve, they say that the time we're going through right now, after the funeral is over and everyone else has moved on, is the toughest part of grieving."

"Yeah, well, I think that's complete

bullshit." I half-laugh, which she finds encouraging enough to continue. "Every day sucks in some new way. It'll never end."

I don't know if it's the right thing to do, but I nod in agreement. How can I pretend there's a bright side here? Acknowledging that everything sucks is technically progress, at least we're agreeing.

We part for bed with a simple hug. I swallow hard, realizing that Eve and I haven't made physical contact since the day of the funeral. I could compete on a reality show for the world's shittiest dad. Eve has faced this disaster in total isolation. I have a daughter who is bold and smart and I cannot take any of the credit.

CHAPTER SIX

MADELINE

The downstairs of Rory's town house has been converted into hospice care for her mother, Linda. Yesterday, as they sat on the couch watching TV, Linda looked up to the ceiling, hands in the air, and said, "Come and get it." Rory slapped her mother's arm and said it wasn't funny, but they both knew she did it for Rory's sake, to prepare her. Death leaves Linda thinking of nothing but her daughter's future. Her thoughts often parallel my own.

I worry about Linda's sorrow when she's welcomed by no one, greeted only by air, but question whether Linda's death will be the same as mine. Even now, as she sleeps, her breath releases with an indecipherable whisper, like she's already conversing with people on the other side. If I focus my energy, I sense their presence, and though I fail to interpret the dialogue, the effort draws me farther from the ground below, the way it did during Eve's accident. However slowly, I'm ascending.

The curtains stay drawn while Linda sleeps, which is now most of the day. To respect her failing appetite and growing sensitivity to smells, Rory and the day nurse, Greta, consume only benign food. Linda wakes to them murmuring about dinner. "Eat something plentiful, you two," Linda begs.

Rory grins. "No way. My new waistline and miniscule grocery bills are the high points of your cancer." The ladies all giggle. If Rory can entertain her mother on death's door, certainly she can get a smile from Brady and Eve.

They need it.

Eve is in the kitchen studying for finals, waiting for Brady to come out of his room for dinner. She's come to look forward to their evening routine. During the workweek, Brady rushes in with a bag of takeout like they have a standing seven o'clock meeting. (It's on his calendar, so from his standpoint they do.) On Saturday and Sunday they mostly eat leftovers from the week, but they do it together. This is the first night since the accident Brady has bailed. He's holed up in our room. His room, now. The idea that he played a role in my misery gnawed at him all week; tonight he has nothing left to give.

Sundays, in particular, are hard. It was our day. Saturday Brady worked and Eve usually had a tournament of some sort, but Sundays everything clicked into place. Nothing sensational, errands and togetherness mixed with a little daydreaming, but that was all we needed to wind up for another week.

The Sunday before I died I woke up to the smell of bacon. Eve and I wandered into the kitchen at the same time. Brady had already set out plates. "Breakfast for me ladies," he said, taking a medieval bow.

There was a reason he felt compelled to put on a show. He'd been traveling most of the week, but only bothered to call home once. I'm not high maintenance, but I expect an evening check-in.

I played along, anxious for him to earn my forgiveness. "Thank you, my lord."

"Yuck. Get a room," Eve snapped. Brady and I lost it in laughter, giving each other a kiss while she turned away in disgust.

The day got better. I needed to go to an antique store to pick up a lamp that finally arrived. Brady surprised me by wanting to tag along, and again when he asked for a tour of the Wellesley campus on our way home. I'd volunteered at the library for two years, but he and Eve rarely acknowledged my time there. He was surprised how many passing students and professors knew me by name.

"Whatever you do, you go all in," he remarked. Brady wasn't one to throw around compliments, so I relished them when he did.

We returned home to a note from Eve saying she was having pizza at the Andersons'. Normally I'd have been irked she didn't get permission — especially since it was at Kara's and Eve knows I'm not a fan of that family — but that night I let it slide. I made lemon-broiled salmon over risotto while Brady set the table and opened a bottle of pinot grigio. We laughed, flirted, and made love. Our last time, it turned out. Afterward we danced to our wedding song and he whispered the lyrics in my ear: *You came along and everything started to hum. Still it's a real good bet the best is yet to come.*

Untrue, of course, but Brady didn't know that at the time.

Now he lies in bed, replaying the day, unaware Eve sits a room away, worried. I should motivate him to head to the kitchen, but I'm as swept up by the memory as he

151

is. I don't want to be remembered by how I died, I want to be remembered by who I was that Sunday, when I wasn't competing with Brady's and Eve's many distractions.

Our thoughts crisscross. Am I leading him or is he leading me? I can't tell. He lets out a keening sob that startles me. Most of his time grieving is filled with anger, but this moment is pure loss. He looks like a toddler, tucked into the fetal position, grasping his knees for strength. His mind stays fixed on that wonderful day, remembering details I forgot.

"I don't tell you often that I know how lucky I am," he said during our walk.

"No, you don't, but I don't need to hear it that often."

Why did I always acquiesce like that? Perhaps if I didn't enable his inattention he would've learned how to nurture. I allowed him to be distant, to disappoint, and it worked because I was there to make up for it. Now Eve is stuck with those qualities in her only parent.

Brady struggles through his tears to remember how we picked our wedding song all those years ago. *New York City,* I whisper. It slips to his consciousness. The weekend after our engagement Brady took me there to celebrate. We stayed at the Park Plaza, even though we could barely afford to park the car. All our money still went to student loans. I asked over and over how we'd pay for the weekend. "I'll take care of it," Brady assured. "I'm going to take such good care of you." It turned out I'd be the one taking care of everyone, but we didn't know it at the time. That night we went to a bar called The Rat Pack and danced to "The Best Is Yet to Come." I'd never felt more certain.

Before retiring to her room, Eve checks on Brady. His audible sobs stop her from knocking. Picturing him broken down, only yards away, hits her hard. Eve is not enough for Brady, which of course she knew, but resents confronting so plainly. She listens over a half hour, wondering whether to knock. *Let him be,* I pass down to her softly, and she does.

This can't be undone.

EVE

Today is my grand finale at Wellesley High School. I didn't think of it as a big deal until Paige stopped in on her run this morning to see how I was feeling. She seemed surprised to find me unfazed. I want to feel sentimental — I do — but my emotions peaced out with my mother. Now I'm just water and bones.

The hall is packed with kids emptying out lockers. Lindsey and I shared since mine was in a clutch spot by the stairs and vending machines, but she cleared her stuff out days ago, probably to avoid us doing it at the same time. This won't take long. I rip down the pictures we hung like wallpaper on the back wall and shove the spare makeup bag in my backpack, embarrassed I used to refer to an unexpected pimple as a 911. Everything else goes from my locker to the trash.

The inside of the metal door is covered with penciled graffiti where Lindsey and I passed gossip between classes. I'm supposed to erase it so I don't start next year with detention, but they can't exactly track me down in New Hampshire. *I heard Jake say you have a fine ass,* I wrote, starting the exchange in September. *OMG — he's such a drooler,* Lindsey replied. And on it goes, until the day before Good Friday. No hot gossip after that unless I was the butt of it. I notice a new message across the bottom of the door: *I so hope you find a way to be okay.* That's it. A simple wish from my old best friend. It doesn't bring a single tear. I've become a freaking zombie.

I consider how different this day would be if my mother were alive. Everyone's headed to Noel's because his parents totally don't give a shit what happens there. I'd be passing twenty bucks to Katy whose big brother is hooking everyone up with beer for a small profit, and John would be working on cover stories so we could both spend the night. Instead, I'll walk out alone and go home to an empty house. My father won't realize today was the last day of school until I don't go back tomorrow.

I turned in a poem for my creative-writing final. Picking it up stands between me and the end of junior year. The assignment was to write a short story, but Mrs. Ludwick gave me an *A* for these four lines.

SILENCE SAID

I have no idea where to start
How to repair a broken heart?
Where a laugh means more than the mere
    amused
It means a tear has been refused.

The grade was probably because she felt sorry for me, but still. At the top of the page, she included a handwritten note: *You seem to have something to say. You should try writing without the constraint of rhyming.* I hold the paper up, pretending the message

155

is longer than it is to avoid eye contact with everyone. The cover-up is probably unnecessary; there isn't exactly a line of people looking to chat it up. Everyone's sympathy ran out when my mourning came at the cost of the soccer team's starting lineup next fall: John's DUI got him benched the first five games.

The seniors are all hugging, shaking their heads at how fast it went. The juniors, my classmates, are running around in a tizzy announcing that the Class of 2016 has officially taken over. "Get ready to be hazed," Jake taunts, knocking the baseball cap off a kid I don't know. Kara shrieks the words *as if* over and over about some freshman who made a pass at her. She's clearly started drinking already, which is bold even for Kara. They all sound like assholes. When the big metal door shuts behind me, I'm numb.

I once saw an *Ellen DeGeneres* where kids cut themselves with knives. There were pictures and video clips, but I still didn't buy it. I figured if they were really cutting themselves it was to get on *Ellen* and not, as they claimed, for the pleasure of feeling something, anything. Now I'm not as sure. I walk to the car, letting my backpack dangle from my elbow and smash uncomfortably into my legs with each step. It hurts, but it's better than nothing. Mom sometimes carried pots off the stove with her bare hands. She claimed her skin was callused from years of cooking, but maybe the burn made her feel alive. I can practically hear her denying it, begging me to take better care of myself. It's a new low: I'm so desperate for affection I'm inventing conversations with a dead person. I pinch my arm to distract me. Indifference is scarier than pain. It makes you think there's no point being here.

I stupidly left my writing final on the kitchen counter and when I come down for dinner, Dad has it in his hand. "Wow, Eve. This is poignant."

I refuse to turn it into a whole big talk, so I say nothing.

He squints his eyes like he's afraid of the words that want to come out of his mouth. "I've been thinking you . . . well, you and I, should go to therapy." I stare at him. "Not together or anything. On our own."

I laugh. He doesn't. "Does the poem worry you?"

"Not at all. The poem is fine. Beautiful. It's the note from your teacher. She's right. You probably have a lot to say. I know I do.

But who am I going to say it to? You're the only one who can relate, and I don't want to be a burden." He shakes his head to show that's not what he meant. "Not that you'd be a burden to me. You can talk to me anytime. I-I hope you know that." He's flustered. "God, my sales pitch stinks, but will you go? To counseling?" He extends his arms in a *whaddayasay* gesture.

"Whatever."

"*Whatever* as in you'll go?" he confirms, unable to hide his shock.

"Sure."

I play it cool, but the truth is, it sounds like a damn good idea. I'm not completely losing it, but my masochist moment this afternoon was pretty close. And a couple nights ago I woke up obsessing over an old picture of my mom and Gram cooking. I needed to find it. Right then. It felt enormously important. I got up and emptied an entire bin of prints from the guest-room closet, flipping through each one, as if this random photo held the secret to their deaths, as if this random photo would bring them both back to life. Eventually sunlight filtered through the window, snapping me out of it. Hours had passed. I was ankle deep in photos, sweaty and tired, but mostly confused. I couldn't remember why I wanted to see the stupid thing in the first place. When I calmed down, I remembered the picture was in a frame at Aunt Meg's. I don't know how I'd forgotten (or how I suddenly remembered). The whole thing was flat-out psycho.

Dad was expecting a fight. He stands there, holding the counter as if he might need it for protection. When he processes that he won, that I'll go to counseling, he pulls out a copy of an email from his briefcase.

"Here's a list of all the local therapists covered by our insurance."

This went from casual idea to concrete plan mighty fast. "God, Dad. How long have you been, like, scheming for this?" He confesses it's been a few weeks. I arch my eyebrows. "And . . . you never said anything . . . *why?*"

"I booked my appointment already, but I've been waiting for the right time to ask you." He stops there but then pushes on. "Admit it, Eve, you're temperamental. I never know how you'll react to stuff."

It's true, and he called me out the way my mother would have, so I pick up my cell and book an appointment with the first female shrink on the list. I love shocking my dad. It's one of my few remaining kicks.

That night, to prepare for therapy, I write in my new journal for the first time. I only get out fifteen words:

June 15, 2015
There are so many things I dare not say I have quietly stopped being me.

I stare at the sentence for a long time, questioning what it is I want to say. Who was I, really, before my mom died? I was a self-absorbed, materialistic, conceited, naïve child. So maybe what I want to say is simply that I'm sorry. Only the person I want to say it to is gone.

BRADY

I fired Paula. It's not what I put on the paperwork, but she knew too much and dug too deep. She had come to think of us as confidants. We talked casually before Maddy died, but asking how my weekend went is a little different from asking if I'm eating enough. Then today she started in on Eve. When I said she was hanging in there, Paula had the nerve to reply, "I lost my mother too. I'd be happy to talk to her if you think it'd help."

Eve would destroy her. "How old were you when your mother died?" I baited.

160

"Thirty-nine."

"What did she die of?"

"Cancer."

I scratched my chin. "I'm no professional, Paula, but I'm going to take a swing here and say that losing your mother to disease when you're a grown adult with children of your own is, just maybe, a little different from losing your mother a month before you turn seventeen to suicide." It was the first time I'd said the word out loud and I despised Paula for putting me in the position. We can't work together anymore. I'm the asshole, but it's easier to change my assistant than my personality.

I tell Eve at dinner, sans all details.

"Is it hard to fire someone?" she asks. A thoughtful question.

"Yes," especially when they don't deserve it. I take a sip of wine to ease my guilt. "She has a family too, you know?"

Eve smirks. "Can I make a joke that you promise to take as a joke?"

"Shoot," I say, nervous I won't be able to deliver.

"Who's going to wipe your ass now?"

I don't miss a beat. "I'll probably get a temporary ass-wiper until I can find someone to take over full-time." We laugh, but the sound is so foreign it prompts a moment of silence. Eve spins a fork around in her pasta, but doesn't take a bite.

"Can I read some more of Mom's journal?" she asks. I expected this request, and earmarked one a couple days ago that I thought could serve as a foundation for Eve and me to have, as Maddy would say, a serious talk. I bring it back to the table, already open to the page.

June 25, 2013

Eve got sent home from her boyfriend Aaron's house because they were caught kissing. Aaron's mom escorted Eve to the door like a common criminal, reporting the aforementioned kissing like it was a close second to murder. Poor Eve's face was red as a fire truck. I'd never met the woman before, so I thanked her for giving Eve a ride home and reached to close the door.

She put her hand out to stop me and said, "If you don't mind, I want to know how you plan to handle this. I think it'd be best if she and Aaron had the same punishment, so we can send a consistent message."

I nudged Eve inside and took a deep breath, trying to decide how to respond to this lunatic. I first confirmed they were only kissing.

"Yes, but I wouldn't say 'only' kissing," she replied. "That does lead places, you know."

I laughed. "I think as mothers we can certainly agree there." She didn't find that funny, so I said, "Look, Eve isn't getting in trouble for kissing your son. I'm sorry if she broke one of your house rules, but she hasn't broken one of ours."

The woman stormed off, leaving the distinct impression she'd be praying for my soul this evening. I sat on the floor in the foyer and laughed until Eve found the courage to come in. It seemed like a good time for installment two of "the talk." Brady is away, so I took her out for Japanese. During our last talk, when she was eleven, we covered the scientific stuff. This time, at fifteen, I gave her details, including the dreaded birth-control lecture. She asked questions like, "How do you know when you're in love?" and I asked questions like, "Are any of your friends having sex?" We probably should've ordered in — we got odd looks from the table next to us — but it was a great night. She let me peek into her world, giving me confidence in her ability to control her own destiny. Eve is not a girl who's going to sleep with someone out of pressure. Curiosity maybe, but not pressure. As we drove home she said, "You really are good at the whole mother thing." A kudo of the highest order . . .

I wait until Eve reads the entire thing before speaking. When she looks up I say, "I know I'm not her, but if stuff comes up, questions or whatever, I hope you know I'm prepared to be here for you. I'll leave all judgments at the door. And if you can't talk to me, you can always talk to Aunt Meghan or Paige. The most important thing is that you get answers when you need them." It was my most eloquent speech yet.

"I heard you crying Sunday night," Eve replies, so that I'm the vulnerable one. She refuses to let me parent.

"Sorry," I mumble. "It was a tough one."

"No," she says. "Don't be sorry. I'm trying to say that the same goes for you. If you ever want to talk, or whatever, I'm here. I didn't want to, like, interrupt you. Your door was closed, so I figured you wanted to be alone. But if you ever want company, I'm up for a good cry anytime."

Huh. "Thanks." I force a smile, wanting to keep the goodwill flowing. "So, are you and John still dating?"

She pouts. "Do we seriously have to get

into this right now?"

My gut commands me to stand my ground. It's been instructing me a lot lately, and it's usually right. "It's a simple question."

"We never technically broke up, if that's what you mean," she says, "but once he's back from rehab I'm sure he'll get right on that."

I begged to have this conversation and now I don't have a fucking clue where to take it. "You don't know that," I offer.

"Ah, yeah Dad, I do. We hadn't been speaking much before prom and his dad like banished me after the accident."

I look at Eve. Her expression is firmly that of someone who doesn't give a shit. I know the look from firing people who are excited to collect unemployment. Eve used to explode when we made her get off the phone with John late at night, now they haven't spoken in three weeks and she couldn't care less. Maddy would find that disconcerting, but what would she do about it?

"Well, maybe that's best with you going to Exeter. No shortage of boys there." What's wrong with me? Why am I advising my daughter to stake out another boyfriend when I won't be there to vet him?

Eve snorts. "You're a geek, Dad."

I decide that's an apropos ending to this disastrous bonding moment. Before she leaves I move in for a hug, determined to break our physical barrier, but she steps out of reach and says good night.

I stay up late thinking about all the things I told Maddy, and all the things I held back. Where was my opinionated gut back then? I offered lots of *I love you*s and *thank you*s, but those words are overused. Lying in the bed we shared, lights out, I say it aloud, as though she's here with me, as though it isn't too late.

"If you can hear me now, and I swear you can, I loved how you quoted your favorite writers to describe how you felt about something. I loved your thick, loud laugh, and how over time you wore less and less makeup instead of more. I loved how you treated everyone like they were equally important. I loved how you occasionally cursed like a truck driver, and I loved that you never apologized for it. I loved how you made me feel like I was the smartest, funniest, most generous man in the world, even though I'm learning I wasn't."

It's my second speech of the night, only this time I get the response I was hoping for. Echoing through my head I hear Maddy whisper, *I love you too.* Present tense. And I allow myself to pretend that's true, as though she's here with me and it isn't too late.

CHAPTER SEVEN

MADELINE

You'd think dead people, with the ultimate consequence exhausted, would be free from traditional worry, but Rory is on her way to the house and I'm a wreck. If Rory and Eve don't hit it off there will be no point adding Brady to the mix.

At my request, Brady called last night to confirm the tutoring session. Expecting it to be a simple back-and-forth, he worked on an outbound email while the phone rang.

"Hello?"

"Hi. Is this" — he paused to look at the list with her name circled — "Ms. Rory Murray?"

"I'm sorry to be rude," she said in a near-whisper, "but would you please take me off your list? My mother is unwell . . . I can't risk disturbing her."

Brady almost took the easy out and disconnected, but I reminded his subconscious he's a grown damn man with a reason for calling. "I'll be brief. I just want to —"

Rory was aghast at his audacity, still under the assumption he was selling vacuums or life insurance. "Look, I have no money to buy whatever it is —"

"*Oh.* No. *No.* Tomorrow you tutor my daughter, Eve Starling, in calculus? I'm calling to confirm and get an address to remit payment."

Rory laughed. *"Remit payment?"*

Realizing he was the butt of the joke, Brady stopped multi-tasking. "Sorry. Long day. I just want to make sure we're square."

She giggled. *"Square?"*

He laughed so she'd know he's more normal than initially presented. "Geez, tough crowd. I apologize for wanting to pay you."

"I don't mean to give you a hard time," Rory said, the smile showing in her voice. "I'll take any excuse for humor these days."

Brady thought back to the comment about her mother, which he'd chalked up to a genius *stop calling* tactic, and kicked himself for not hanging up. The idea that he woke an infirm old lady was too much for his already overworked conscience.

Me too, I suggested he respond, keeping him in the moment.

"Me too," he said to my delight. "And I did sound a lot like a man about to offer zero-transfer fees."

"Well, *clearly* I appreciate your concern with payment as I just inadvertently confessed I have no money. Are you okay leaving a check with Eve?"

"No worries," he said, switching from telemarketer to surfer dude in a multiple personality disorder sort of way.

She arrives fifteen minutes early. Eve is upstairs finishing a thirty-minute beginners yoga DVD when the doorbell rings. By the time she gets downstairs, Rory is at the garden, humming the tune to "Everybody Plays the Fool," which I stuck in her head on the ride over. Eve freezes, remembering how I sang that chorus every time she came home devastated or embarrassed by one social travesty or another. Whenever I did, Eve demanded to hear about a time *I* played the fool. There was no shortage of material; the challenge was keeping the story age-appropriate. Eve got to picture me as a freshman tripping in front of the entire football team — or whatever other humiliation I opted to reveal — and I got to ease my daughter's there's-no-way-I-can-go-back-to-school-tomorrow anxiety. It was a healing song for us.

I couldn't have directed the scene better; Eve's association draws her to Rory.

"Ms. Murray?" she says, sad to interrupt her own memory. I watch like a gambler with money on the game as Rory flashes her hypnotic smile. I send energy to complement it. Eve relaxes and so do I.

"It's summer. Call me Rory." She steps into the foyer and slides off her Birkenstocks, clearly a learned, long-standing habit. Eve has never seen a guest do this, but she's a hostess like her mother and follows suit. Rory notices and it endears her to Eve.

"Thanks for agreeing to come to the house," Eve says, leading her to the kitchen. "I really didn't want to spend all summer at the library." She leaves out the detail that her mother recently died at one.

"It doesn't matter to me, as long as you're able to focus. Covering precalculus in one summer is a tall order. I had to brush up before coming here."

"Yeah, I know, but Exeter doesn't usually accept people for only senior year, so I was at their mercy."

"Oh, you won't be here in the fall?"

"No, I've, umm, always wanted to go to boarding school, and . . . well, my dad, he finally agreed."

The word *dad* catches Rory's attention. Or rather, lack of the word *mom.* Our story clicks into place. *Starling. Spring. Suicide.* The elementary teachers who had had Eve in class all those years ago were in absolute shock. "Madeline Starling was the nicest, most normal mother I ever worked with," her friend Sarah attested. "I truly can't wrap my head around it."

Rory hides her discovery well. "My brother Brian went to Exeter. He graduated about eight years ago now, but I remember the campus. It's beautiful."

Small talk complete, they sit at the kitchen table and get to work. I struggled to focus on calculus when my GPA was on the line, and it's immediately clear nothing has changed in the stimulating world of mathematics. When the hour is up, their good-bye is lamentably efficient:

"Same time Wednesday?"

"Works for me."

The challenge is clear: calculus is too dry a topic to foster a meaningful bond between Rory and Eve, and they meet while Brady is still at work. Nurturing their relationship will take prompting.

Eve is still in the kitchen doing practice problems when Brady gets home and announces they're having gyros for dinner. "What the heck is that?"

"You've never had a gyro? Where've you been?"

Eve crosses her arms. "Ah, living here with you."

"Touché." He unwraps one to showcase it. "As you can see in Exhibit A, a gyro is shaved lamb with red onions and this cucumber-y, yogurt-y sauce on a pita."

Eve pretends to throw up in the sink. "That sounds heinous. I'll stick with ramen noodles." I repeat Rory's name to Eve, trying to break through their banter so she'll mention the tutoring session.

"That's too bad," Brady entices. "I had a proposal for you, but it requires someone with a taste for adventure."

This mysterious comment commands Eve's full attention; she pushes my message to the side. "I'm listening."

"Try a small bite of the gyro."

Eve gives in, but only on her terms, munching off a quarter of the pita in one bite. With a full mouth she grins and says, "It's good," her words barely discernable.

"*See*. Next time, don't share an opinion until you have one." Brady opens the second wrapper and they sit at the table.

"What's up?" Eve asks.

He claps his hands together. "All right, what are you doing after your required community service is done, but before school starts?"

"Can you stop calling it 'required community service,' please?"

Brady taps his foot, anxious to get to his announcement. "Sure. What should I call it?"

"Camp."

"Fine. How about we go on vacation when camp ends?"

"Ha-ha-ha, very funny. You never want to go on vacation."

Brady looks wounded. He didn't need to be reminded of our fights. "I'm serious," he says. "You can bring a friend."

Eve waves off the offer. "I'm in for vacation, but pass on the friend."

Brady wipes his mouth with a napkin. "It might be nice to spend time with Lindsey or someone before you leave for school. Just don't pick Kara. She's too much, and I'd go nuts figuring out logistics with Todd and Christie." In truth he doesn't want a repeat of homecoming night.

Eve pretends to gag again. "We don't even speak. It's like she's mad at me that my mom died." Eve looks down at her half-eaten gyro. "I've sort of figured out that I

174

don't really, like, have any friends." She holds her hand up in a preemptive defense. "I don't want to talk about it. I'm not upset or anything. It's just so totally obvious that no one gets me right now."

Let it be, I suggest. To Eve's relief, Brady does. "Okay . . . so vacation for you and me?"

" 'Kay. Where?"

"Anywhere we've never been."

Eve snorts. "So that rules out . . . Florida."

Brady concedes the point. His mind's eye scours the globe. "How about Paris?"

Eve slaps the table. "*Paris?* For real?"

He inhales her eagerness like the drug it is. "Paris for real."

"Oh my God. Seriously?" She's out of her chair now.

"Seriously," he repeats in his best teenage-girl imitation.

I urged him to suggest vacation; he's been thinking about it since a journal entry documenting our semiannual fights, but I was not expecting Paris. I'd have relished an opportunity to vacation in Europe. If Brady had ever given the slightest inclination he'd go for it, I'd have planned the perfect trip. "Touring cities isn't relaxing," he always said. *"Trust me."* And with that weak reasoning I was relegated to Naples.

I'm jealous. Not a cute, envious-from-afar jealous, but a raging this-is-total-bullshit jealous. How ironic: I'm dead and we're still having the same damn fight, only this time arguing opposite sides.

While Eve leaves the table to look at places online, and Brady tosses the wrappers from dinner, I vent. *Paris, now? I've had to beg you to take even a couple days off to go to Florida for the past twenty years, and suddenly you're game to gallivant across Europe?* I'm ranting, not even thinking I can get through his noise with my thoughts, when suddenly he fights back.

Yes, Paris, he thinks. *And you don't get to be upset, Maddy. There were other ways to get me to change besides taking your life. You wanted to send a message? You wanted to demonstrate that I wasn't engaged? Grateful? That work isn't everything? Well, message fucking received. And the prize for sending it so dramatically is that you're not here to enjoy it.*

It's the first fight Brady's won in a long time.

EVE

Reading Mom's journal is total crack. I can't stop. The selections Dad deems Eve-appropriate are the lame ones where she's all Mary Poppins. The ones I read while Dad is at work are *her,* the real her, uncut. She was tired of serving our every whim without any recognition. It's all right there:

December 14, 2014
Even my wrists are tired from this day. Eve's school had winter festival, and I got roped into baking ten dozen cookies, which would've been fine if I didn't also agree to individually wrap each one in a red cellophane baggie with a ribbon. When will I take Brady's advice and learn to say no? I was up until two a.m. tying the damn things.

I awoke with a cold coming on. In between sneezes, Brady casually mentioned his boss Jack leaves tomorrow for the holidays, so he needed a gift today. I went from the festival to the liquor store, which was completely insane, and bought a bottle of Dom. The stupid carrying case alone was thirty bucks, but whatever, it got the job done. I dropped it off at Brady's office and made it back to school in time to watch Eve's talent show, which took forever because some kid on an oboe thought it'd be a riot to see how long he could play before someone made him get off the stage.

Brady and Eve came fluttering in tonight, starving as usual, and after dinner, as I cleaned the kitchen alone, I realized that my mother never did anything for anybody and Meg and I turned out fine. So who's the crazy one — the lady who spent her life doing whatever the hell she damn well pleased or the one running errands full-time for two people who don't even appreciate it?

I remember the day because I was annoyed Mom didn't videotape the lame lip sync I did with Lindsey and Kara. "I reminded you this morning to bring the camera," I scolded. She mumbled something about the only predictable thing in life being human imperfection. Reading the day from her point of view I see she was a punching bag and my dad and I gave her a daily workout. I'm starting to wonder why she didn't jump sooner. I'm never getting married or having kids. We suck.

I return the journal to the nightstand, depressed, and head to my first therapy appointment. The conversation is totally pointless.

"Keep in mind, Eve," the counselor says, uncrossing and recrossing her legs for the hundreth time, "time heals all wounds."

I can't believe anyone considers this lady a real doctor. She should have a distinct title like Talking Doctor so people know not to trust her with a scalpel. I've spent the last thirty minutes explaining that time doesn't heal jack shit, but she doesn't get it. Whether it's my birthday or Mother's Day or prom or random, lonely Tuesdays, time is my worst enemy. It slaps me over and over by reminding me how permanent a mess I'm in.

Someone needs to publish a list of things not to say to people in mourning and start it with *Time heals all wounds.* Runners-up include: *Everything happens for a reason; God only dishes what you can handle; I know how you feel, I lost my* — whatever —; *It's good to have an angel on your side;* and, my personal favorite, *How are you feeling?* To that brilliant question, I want to yell back that I don't have the goddamn flu. My suggested response to someone grieving is no response at all; just shut the hell up.

I call Dad on my way home to explain that therapy isn't for me. His temporary asswiper puts me right through. "I'm not going back," I reply to his overly animated hello. Every time we talk he's either trying too hard or not even listening. The man doesn't know how to act normal.

"Why not?"

"It was cheesy. She was all, 'You know it's not your fault, Eve.' So I'd be like, 'Yeah, I know, but I wish I knew why she did it.' Then she'd say something asinine like, 'It's normal to ask yourself questions like that,' and I'd say, 'Yeah, I know.' The whole thing was a waste of time."

"Who did you see?"

"Dr. Cliché."

He laughs, which makes me feel weirdly proud. "Well, how about trying your next session with someone else on the list?"

"How about not going again?"

He makes a *tsk* sound. "I'd like you to try one more time. You might find someone you relate to."

I agree to that. I don't want to give him an excuse to skip out. He needs a shrink more than me.

"Listen," he says, "if we've reached a verdict, I need to hop back into this meeting."

I love the idea that there's a group of people my dad left hanging to take my call. "Sure, but one quick thing. Don't bring food tonight. I'm cooking."

"You don't —"

"Love you," I say. "Bye."

I'm glad I'm not working at the Y, but he

was right about needing more to do. I think it's possible daytime TV kills brain cells. I'm only a week into *The Young and the Restless* and most of the cast have already slept together. The only entertaining part is imagining my mom's take. *I have yet to see anyone pause to put on a condom. All of these people must have gonorrhea by now.* Or *It takes an awful lot of Botox to always look that surprised.* Or *He's a second-rate personal trainer. He doesn't drive a BMW.* Fun as it is to crack up with a ghost, I'm getting dumber sitting on that couch.

It was Paige who suggested I cook. I don't know how she knew I was lounging around all day in pajamas, but she showed up yesterday obsessed with the idea. It's a logical thing to take on. I've been my mother's sous chef forever. Before I was tall enough to reach the counter, Uncle Dan built an adjustable shelf for the island so I could be in the action. I don't know how he thought of it. Aunt Meg doesn't cook, so there has never been anything for Lucy to watch.

I unpack the groceries and wash my hands. Mom preached that the best cooks keep it simple. Spinach with a little garlic and salt, rice simmered in chicken broth with pepper. Fish with lemon. Easy peasy.

With the warming drawer full and the table set, I head outside to light the grill. I've watched Mom do it a million times. It hasn't been touched in months, so the gas clicks several times. When it finally catches, flames shoot straight up, scaring the crap out of me. I jump back, touching my eyebrows to make sure they're still there. *Holy shit.* I exhale, looking at the grill as if it were a living thing that just tried to kill me, then I laugh — a loud, creepy laugh that doesn't sound like mine. *What a rush!* That's what my mother's death took from me — I'm now only truly present during extremes. Anything ordinary is dull.

I go back in the house to grab a smoke from my purse, hoping to keep the surge going. I'm not hooked or anything; it's just something to do. I usually wait until Dad is in bed, but it's windy enough he won't smell it on me. I flick the butt when I hear his car coming down our long driveway. The fish is done. I shut the grill and bring it inside.

He can't hide his surprise at the set table. I follow his eyes as he takes in the new seating arrangement. Dad used to sit at the head of the table closest to the door, with Mom and I on either side. We've been preserving her spot, even though it makes no sense to have two people sitting kitty-corner. Tonight I busted out, putting both plates on the far end of the table across from each other.

He looks tense but manages to sit down and say, "Dinner smells great. What are we having?" His point is clear — he can make the change, but he can't handle a whole conversation about it. It's better than having him walk out the front door.

The whole scene is awkward, like I'm on a date with my dad. I take a scoop of each dish as I run through the menu, then pass it to him for a helping. Our exchanges are clumsy; it's supposed to be a circle. Tomorrow I'll set the plates with food already on them.

"Do you smell something burning?" Dad asks. I sniff. We both look to the patio at the same time — the grill is engulfed in flames. "Call 911," he says, running to the laundry room for a fire extinguisher. By the time he gets outside the flames have spread to the plants, so the dinky red can doesn't help much. It's been a dry summer. It's definitely a job for professionals.

While we wait, Dad stares at the fire as if they're in a conversation. I stand there, praying the cigarette butt disintegrates with the flowers and everything else, assuming it won't. Luck and I haven't been getting along.

The firefighters arrive and put it out quickly. They then start in with questions. When they realize I was the grill operator, they eye my dad. "But you were home, sir?" the cutest fireman clarifies.

"Yes," he answers. "Well, no, not when she cooked."

"Have you ever operated a grill before?" they ask me.

"No."

They look back at my dad with disgust, which he puts right back on me. "You've never used it? How did you know how to turn it on?"

"I'm not an idiot. Mom used to do it herself."

"Goddamn it, Eve, you are *not* your mother."

The words sit in the air between us, stinging more than the smoke. I look at the charred patio and ashy garden and start to cry. The three firemen stand there, attempting to piece together our backstory.

"At least I'm trying, okay, Dad?" I shout through my tears. "I cooked so you'd maybe eat more. And it worked. You were. I mean, who the hell gets takeout every night? We're turning into freaks." I move to go inside but one of the firemen reaches for my arm.

"Don't touch her," my father says firmly.

Everyone freezes.

"Sir, we need to file a report on this fire, and I don't have the information I need. Now, I can call the police if you want, for assistance, or the two of you can answer my questions so we can leave you alone to work out whatever" — he waves a hand between us — "is going on here."

"What questions? It was clearly an accident."

"I need to know if she turned off the propane tank."

He nods at me to answer. "No," I say, biting my lip. "I only turned off the switch. And it's a really old grill." I'm taking a dig at my dad with that. Mom wanted a new one. She was always cutting out magazine pictures of custom outdoor kitchens. She claimed the only reason Dad wouldn't go for it is because he never did the cooking.

"There's probably a leak in the line somewhere. On a hot day like today, that's a dangerous mistake."

"Yeah, got that," I snap.

"Lose the attitude, Eve," my dad warns, playing both sides.

The firemen look at the grill for another twenty minutes wearing full protective gear while my father and I watch in silence. Finally, the cute one declares the fire "accidental misuse," citing that "something combustible must have hit the leak in the gas line." They don't mention what the flying combustible might've been, and my dad doesn't ask. I can't tell if they're doing me a solid or suck at their job.

After they leave, we stand in the soot, looking at the mess. I ruined our patio. I could've burned down our house. Mostly I feel stupid, but there's a small part of me that finds it funny. Mom would've laughed at this scene the way she laughed the day the washing machine hose detached and flooded our entire mudroom. She called it a this-situation-is-so-horrendous-it-is-absolutely-hilarious moment.

My dad looks beyond pissed, so I remove my smile. I guess you have to be my mom to pull that off. And as he so sweetly pointed out, I'm not.

BRADY

My shrink looks like a cross between Albert Einstein and Abraham Lincoln. From Albert he inherited thick glasses and electrocuted hair; from Abe he acquired a lanky physique, hanging nose, and the stark impression that he's usually right.

186

"Before we dig into a more natural dialogue, I'd like to run through a series of questions relative to your social history and spousal loss that will help me create a picture of your current state."

I'm glad he takes immediate control. Now that I'm here I have no idea what to say. "Shoot."

"Have you been sleeping well?"

"Yes," I say, omitting bourbon's role.

"Do you wear a seat belt each time you get in a car?"

"Yes."

He carries on at a steady pace, reviewing my concentration level, work schedule, and eating habits. It runs like a legal deposition. Eve's right. This is a waste of time. It's not as if I'm going to tell this random man truths I'm not yet ready to confront myself.

"Has your interest level in other people changed during that time?"

"Yes."

"How?"

"I no longer care about anyone except me and my daughter." Dr. White stops firing off questions and makes a note. I'm pretty sure he writes it down as an exact quotation.

"Can you elaborate on that?"

"I used to joke around with colleagues, play squash, go to an occasional Patriots game. Maddy took care of everything at home, so work was my only real responsibility. The rest of our life was hers."

He tilts his head to indicate he's about to state something insightful. "Financial stability is a substantial thing to take on."

"I thought so at the time," I reply. He writes that down too.

"Do you work out?"

"Yes, daily."

"Do you view yourself as a worthwhile person?"

"Yes, but I guess I probably shouldn't."

"Explain that."

"My wife killed herself."

"And that changes your value how?"

I consider what I'm willing to put out there. It might feel like a legal deposition, but it's not. I can edit as I see fit. "Well . . . it'd be arrogant not to question what I did to contribute. Mostly I'm mad at her. I think, *She did this to me.* She left us. She had no right to do something that radical without informing me something was wrong in the first place." The truth of it fills me with rage. No matter how much I neglected our home life, the salient point is that Maddy never said anything was wrong.

"What would you have done if she'd alerted you she was unhappy?"

"I would've fixed it." Of that I'm certain.

Dr. White shrugs. "Okay, but she didn't point it out, so you couldn't."

I can't accept his easy out. Jesus Christ, I'm in a fight with myself. "I missed *something*. A hint. A clue. I didn't pay enough attention."

"Okay, we'll circle back to that. What do you do for fun?"

"I don't do fun."

The click of his tongue suggests Dr. White doesn't find my answer entertaining. "Be serious now, have you made any attempt to get out there since your wife died?"

"One time. Last Sunday. I went to dinner and a movie alone for the first time in my life. I won't be doing it again anytime soon."

"What happened?"

I don't want to get into it. There was a time when I looked at people unaccompanied at restaurants like it was their fault. They were the type to sue their parents or sleep with their best friend's spouse. Why else would someone my age still be alone? Now I know what it's like to be on the receiving end of those stares. I sat there waiting for my food, looking at people until they caught me, and I realized something: going out to dinner has nothing to do with eating. It's about the conversation, or the celebration, or the hope that something will happen after dinner. That's why the person alone is so disturbing — if all you want to do is eat, you can go to a drive-thru or get takeout. But I'm not going to say all that.

"What's the point in putting your solitude on display? I can eat and watch movies in the comfort of my own home."

Dr. White doesn't disagree. "Give me a little more color, if you don't mind. Share one specific detail about the night."

"I don't know. I thought the movies would be better than dinner. Who cares if you're alone or paired up in a dark room where everyone expects silence. I took an aisle seat, only to get a glare from a couple that apparently left one chair free to be closer to the center of the screen, assuming no one would sit there. The woman got up to use the restroom as soon as I sat down, then switched seats with her husband when she returned, like I was a high risk for a cheap feel."

This he does find funny. "Hmmm," he says, when he's done chuckling. "I don't think you are clinically depressed." I frown. I definitely want to be clinically depressed. "You look disappointed."

I shift uncomfortably in my seat at how perceptive he is. "Well, like I said on the phone, I feel depressed."

"You're appropriately sad, and justifiably angry. You're in mourning. But you're doing it with a clear head." I have an overwhelming urge to cry. "That's good news, Brady. It means we can talk through the changes you're experiencing, the hurdles you're facing, and get somewhere without medication."

I voluntarily confess my recent temper in the hopes he'll up the ante. I want a big fat fix-it-all pill that I can chase down with ten milligrams of Ambien every night. "Your volatility makes sense," he replies, unimpressed. "You said it yourself, you only have the capacity to worry about you and your daughter. That means your patience is on a short string. Your brain now deems everything else unimportant."

"But it's not just work. I lose my temper with Eve too."

"Of course you do. You're in survival mode. Seventeen-year-olds are terrible at dealing with adults in survival mode. It goes against every desire your daughter has right now. She's grappling for independence and you're looking to keep her safe; you have opposing goals. When anything questions the stability you seek, it sets you off."

"Okay, so how do I fix it?"

He combs a hand through his wild hair and sighs. "You don't."

"Then why the hell am I here?"

"Easy, Brady. It fixes itself. You'll see. You'll become aware, you'll ease up on yourself, forgive yourself a bit, and in so doing, you'll be more forgiving of others."

Forgive myself.

Tears fall. However implicitly, I let this happen to my family.

CHAPTER EIGHT

MADELINE

Rory is lonely, I repeat to Eve as they tackle "Chapter Three: Evaluating Limits." Eve's expression softens, but I can't decipher what she'll do with the information.

"Do you see how we got here?" Rory asks, showing a long workflow.

Eve purses her eyebrows. "Why can't you test the limit by plugging in a value?"

"It's a good thought. This is a hard concept, and that question proves you understand what we're trying to calculate here."

Rory knows the material. I shouldn't have doubted her. Linda raised a daughter with flawless ethical boundaries; if Rory didn't feel comfortable teaching calculus she wouldn't have accepted the offer. *My mom?* Not so much. If I was taught anything it was that a good lie could ride you to the next argument.

The doorbell rings. "I'll be quick," Eve

says, getting up from the table. It's Paige.

"Whose car is that?" she asks, peering inside to investigate.

"My drug dealer's — oh, errr — I mean, my math tutor's."

Paige smiles. "Feisty, are we? This is just a drop-off." She hands Eve a bag of organic vegetables and a roasted chicken from the farmer's market. "Just chop up all the veggies and sauté it for a nice succotash. The chicken will be fine in the warming drawer until dinner." Eve gave up cooking after the fire, and I'm desperate to get her back into it.

"Thanks," Eve says. "Hopefully I don't burn the house down."

"That grill was ancient. Don't beat yourself up." My message exactly.

"Oh, and here." She hands Eve a Butterfinger from her purse. "I don't know what possessed me to buy it, so don't ask. But take it before I eat it."

Eve's heart pounds. Butterfingers were our secret obsession. We laughed about it all the time: of the candy bars on the market, Butterfingers seemed the most embarrassing one to love. It isn't just the neon wrapper announcing from fifty feet away that you're not indulging in, say, a protein bar; it's the name. Butterfinger. Like butter fingers. Like you're eating a finger-sized chunk of butter. We bought them every time we bought tampons, which we found doubly amusing.

Eve stares at the wrapper. She's reading into it, exactly as I hoped she would. Our Butterfinger passion was truly an inside joke. If Paige felt compelled to buy one, I had something to do with it, which means my spiritual presence is real. "My mom and I loved these," Eve whispers, more to herself than Paige.

"*Really?* I never saw her eat one."

"No, you wouldn't have," Eve says.

Paige senses a shift in Eve's mood, but doesn't know what to make of it, so she gives her a hug and leaves. Eve returns to Rory, lighter with the perspective that I haven't completely abandoned her.

Orchestrating mini moments of comfort is great, but Eve leaves in two months and I continue to ascend in little surges, so my timeframe to help is shrinking in both directions. So far, elevating hasn't weakened my clout, but I'm nervous it soon will. I need to establish Rory as a permanent replacement while I can. I continue my initial incant. *Rory is lonely. Rory is lonely.*

Back and forth they go, evaluating wind speed, the efficiency of different containers, heat's exponential decay. . . . Rory lost me during the introduction on the first day, but Eve leverages Brady's gene pool to follow along. It's amazing to witness Eve learning from her mind's eye. She's brighter than I appreciated. Eve always delivered good grades, but I assumed she had to work for it. She doesn't, not really, not the way I did. Her brain operates in the fast lane, absorbing most concepts without much concentration, and once it's there — *zap* — so it remains without notes or flash cards or zany mnemonic devices. If I hadn't worked hard I'd have been a *C* student. I was motivated solely by the ambition to not end up like my mother (and, yes, I appreciate the irony of that). My father, who publically lamented having no sons, said he'd only pay for his girls to go to college if we earned straight *A*s, no exceptions. Meg and I both knew he was the kind of man who'd look at a *B+* in wood shop and say, "Damn. You were so close," completely ignoring that the rule was arbitrary. So we both got 4.0s. For Meg, it was a breeze. For me, English was the only freebie.

When I quit work to stay home my mom didn't consider their college investment a waste. "She landed a great husband because of that degree," she claimed, unaware people stopped valuing her opinion decades ago. "Brady wasn't going to end up with some nitwit."

My father wasn't convinced. He pulled me aside and said, "You do realize what your mom has — the crazies and the drinking — is genetic. You squirrel away in a house all day long enough, you'll end up a drunk. Don't screw with your potential." But there was no genius in me. I memorized information whereas Eve consumes it. It's an important nuance. I could only recite what Eve understands.

Rory collects her papers to leave. I pick up the pace. *Rory is lonely, Rory is lonely, Rory is lonely.* "If you tackle the practice problems before Monday we can start in on chapter four." Eve stares at Rory's left hand, not responding. Typical of our society, she associates loneliness with lacking a man. "Earth to Eve," Rory says, waving. "What are you looking at?"

Eve blinks, embarrassed to have been busted. "Sorry. I'm out of it today. I-I noticed, I mean, I was surprised that . . . well, not surprised but, are you married?"

"Divorced, actually."

"Oh, sorry."

Rory slings a blue tote over her shoulder. "Don't be. I'm confident you had nothing to do with it."

"Do you have children?" Rory stops mid-step. Her expression sags. "I don't mean to be nosy," Eve backpedals. "You don't have to answer that."

Rory regains momentum toward the door. "No, no worries. I don't have any. Call if you struggle on those problems."

Rory walks to her car with the same distant expression I observed that first day in the grocery store, only this time I intuit what happened. Her daughter is dead. Rory blames herself. She has more in common with Eve and Brady than I realized.

The usual lyrical flow of Rory's thoughts crumbles into a litany of random observations as Rory tries to fend off her emotions on the ride home: what's for sale, what needs to be repaved, what's closed during normal business hours. She pauses in her driveway before going in, knowing she can't afford a slump with her mother sick. "People need you," she says aloud, willing herself motivated. The pep talk is well rehearsed but unsuccessful.

Greta is surprised Rory doesn't ask for details about Linda's day, but graciously takes the hint and leaves. After giving her sleeping mom a kiss on the forehead, Rory pours a tall glass of Chianti, and plops on the couch in the dark room. If you substitute the Chianti with chardonnay, the sight is similar to my early evenings after Eve got older and didn't require as much doting.

Enveloped in a silence disturbed only by the steady click of Linda's IV machine, Rory stares at a picture of her daughter smiling, revealing a first tooth popping through swollen gums. She has the same chocolate-brown hair as her mother. I cannot fathom the heartache and desperation of such a loss. Losing Eve would've taken me to that ledge without bait.

Rory looks older sad. Her mood deflates me. I've learned *how* to get through, but not *what* to get through. I wanted Eve to invite Rory to stay for dinner, not tip her into depression. I want — oh hell, I don't know what I want. I guess to be better at death. It should at least be easier than life.

I turn my attention to Brady as he interviews new assistants, quick to notice that none of the candidates are over thirty or at all hard on the eyes. I'm horrified by the prospect of Brady turning into a gawking old man. I prepare to haunt some sense into him until I listen to his reasoning. His hypothesis is that, human nature what it is, The Fireman might be less likely to lash out at a younger, more vulnerable woman.

The idea of it repulses him — he wants to be wrong. I find his analytical approach fascinating. It's scientific self-awareness.

"What were the working hours of your last position?" Brady asks.

The stunning applicant looks rather peeved. "I already told the HR lady that."

Brady is equally annoyed. "Her name is Meredith. Do you mind terribly sharing the answer with me too?" His tone makes it far from a cordial request.

"It depended on what quarter we were in, and also Mr. Breack's travel schedule." She wiggles in her chair like it's tickling her.

Brady twitches at the immature display, happy to be irritated despite her good looks. "So your schedule is flexible?"

She folds her arms. "Not really. That's why I quit."

Brady pauses the interview to scan the rest of her resume. She's been out of college five years and held four jobs. She never should've made it through the screening process. He makes a mental note to discuss the infraction with Meredith, then glances at his iPhone, pretending to read an important email. "I'm going to have to cut this short. Something's come up." He shoos the lady with the tight ass out of the room, relieved. He's an asshole, but he's an equal-opportunity asshole.

Watching the scene play out unnerves me. I recount all the times when, in the middle of a conversation and without any prompting, Brady looked at his phone, then dismissed me because "something popped up at work." This lady was a rude, job-hopping idiot. What was my offense?

EVE

Rory looked so whacked when I ask about children there has to be more to the story. As soon as her car is out of sight I get on my laptop. It's what everyone did when my mom died. They switched to a whisper as I passed, but teenagers don't whisper well. They want to be heard so badly. *Did you read* The Townsman? *She didn't leave a note.* Or, Go Boston *said she might have been on meth.* Or, The Globe *said Wellesley College didn't even pay her and she was there, like, all the time.* My friends were happy to throw in details the articles missed. I assume it was Lindsey who made my dad's excessive travel and my mom's evening chardonnay common knowledge. And I heard Jake tell Noel that my parents had been fighting, a detail that had to come from John since they were bickering about a summer vacation the last time he was over.

I google *Rory Murray.* There are millions of hits, tech geniuses to porn stars. I narrow it down by adding a common word from the articles on my mother. *Tragic.* And there it is, Rory's misfortune for the world to read. I clutch my hand to my neck. The picture alone tells a story of what she lost: a good-looking man with his arm around a younger Rory as she holds up a newborn baby, beaming.

Holiday Tragedy, Avoidable Death of a Toddler

November 26, 2005
SAN DIEGO, CA, United States — A two-year-old child died today in a tragic traffic accident in the Gaslamp District on 6th Street. According to preliminary investigations, Steve O'Malley, 34, fell asleep behind the wheel of his 1998 Mitsubishi Montero, hitting Emma Murray, who was in a stroller pushed by her mother on the sidewalk.

The child was pronounced dead at the scene. The mother, Rory Murray, 29, was taken to the hospital suffering critical injuries, including a leg broken in four places.

According to sources in the department,

202

charges will be pressed against O'Malley, who had allegedly been on the road more than nine hours straight.

Everyone has a history. Sadness isn't mine alone. It only feels that way because my friends are too young to know the kind of pain that leaves you physically heavier than before. I wonder if there's a calculus equation for that? I look at the clock on the computer, surprised it's past four already.

I'm ten minutes late for round two of therapy. This time I picked a man. He's probably thirty years old, so his corduroy blazer with faux-leather elbow patches doesn't match his age. I can tell it's something he wears to look wise, but instead he looks dorky. After sharing the basics, I dig right in with my epiphany. "Everyone I go to school with will be devastated by something someday."

"That's an astute observation," Dr. Jahns says. "One that takes some a lifetime to figure out. Congratulations."

It's weird to be congratulated on understanding that everyone has a private hell to hide, but I accept the compliment. At least he didn't come back with *This too shall pass* or *You can't change what life brings, but you can chose what to do with it.* I'm tired of the feel-good shit.

I wait for Dr. Jahns's next question but get nothing. His practiced eye contact suggests this silence is a strategy of some sort. Won't he be disappointed to learn I'm in no hurry. We remain mute three minutes. I know it's three minutes exactly because there's a clock on the wall the size of an oven, probably to make sure weepy patients are aware when their session has ended. I fill the quiet time pretending we're in a staring competition. Dr. Jahns does pretty well considering he doesn't know we're playing.

He finally loses the chicken fight by asking me to describe my current state. "I don't know," I say, thrilled by the victory. "My mom did everything. I guess I'm afraid of how I'll get on without her."

"So you're scared for your well-being?"

"I didn't say scared," I correct.

"I'm sorry, you're right, you said afraid. Let me rephrase, are you afraid for your well-being?"

He succeeds at making me sound like a dumbass. Current score: 1-1. "Yeah, I guess," I say, looking at the clock. Forty-eight minutes until I can bail on talking doctors for good.

"Mmm. What about lonely? Do you feel lonely?"

"Duh."

"Tell me about that."

"Tell you the definition of *lonely*?" He folds his arms but says nothing. Another standoff. I don't want to sit through a round of silence, so I add, "We spent a lot of time together. Now she's gone. And it's not like anyone understands."

"So it sounds like *lonely* and *scared* are closely related emotions for you. You depended on your mom, so without her you've lost a key support. Losing that foundation would, quite understandably, make you feel isolated and unsure."

"Good summary," I reply in a voice my mom would call patronizing. It's fun to be a smart-ass with this guy. Maybe I'll come back just to mess with him.

"How did you feel about suicide prior to your mom's death?"

Is he for real? "Great. I loved it. I thought suicide was awesome."

He tips his head to the right. "Did my question irritate you?"

I tip my head to the left. "Yes."

"Because you found the answer obvious?"

"Because I found the question pointless."

"Huh. Okay. What should I have asked?"

I stop. That's actually a decent comeback. Another point for the talking doctor. "What you're really wondering."

"What am I really wondering?"

"If I know why she did it. If there's some big secret I'm hiding."

He raises his eyebrows like the thought hadn't crossed his mind. *As if.* "Is there?"

"No. I don't know. I-I thought she was happy." How did this get back to a serious conversation?

"So you didn't know your mom was having a tough time?"

"And for the second time — *no.*" He underlines something on his notepad. Hopefully it's the fact that I didn't know, so he'll fucking drop it.

"Right." He looks right at me. "So why did you think your mom *was* happy?"

He's got me there. Up until three months ago I thought everyone was more or less happy. "I mean . . . I like . . . assumed it, but then, I never asked her."

He puts the notepad down. "Asked her what?"

"Asked her anything. I mean, I asked if I could have stuff or if she could do stuff for me. You know, *Can you . . .* take me here, wash this, make that, buy these? I thought I was this great kid since I always said *please* and *thank you,* but I never asked how she was doing."

"I see," he says. That's doubtful. I don't think Dr. Jahns got out much in high school. I picture him as the mathlete in the *Star Wars* T-shirt eating lunch alone. I'm not saying that's a bad thing; I'm just saying he probably wasn't a very demanding kid. "And you feel badly about that?"

"Yeah. She constantly asked how I was doing, and it never crossed my mind to ask back. Isn't that sick? It's not like I held out to spite her. I really never thought, 'Huh. I wonder how Mom's doing.' "

"Sounds like you behaved the way every teenager in the world behaves."

"Well, that's screwed up. Who cares about clothes and curfews and prom dates? I feel so stupid I ever did. Like, even if she hadn't committed suicide, even if it'd been a car accident or something more normal, it was always a possibility I could lose her. My friends totally don't understand that they could come home one day to, like, a different world. And, I mean, I watch the news and stuff. I knew people died. I just never realized people *I* loved could die. That *my* mom could die." I start to cry. Waterproof mascara is a total sham.

He hands me a tissue, but presses on. "So now you feel like you understand more than your friends?"

"I know I do," I say, resting the back of my head on the couch. "They're all so totally clueless. Everyone thinks I'm depressed or whatever, but I'm not. I finally get it and they still don't. I can't pretend to give a shit that Lindsey gained five pounds, or Noel broke up with Katy when they were dating for, like, one freaking day." Snot streams from my nose. I grab another tissue. "I'm so pissed for not realizing how pointless all of it was sooner. Now she's gone and I missed my chance."

Dr. Jahns waits until my crying dies down. "Keep in mind that if you never answer the door, people will stop knocking." He sounds like my mom. The clock reads two minutes past five. I'm the weepy patient who needs to be reminded to leave. "Will you come back next week?" he asks, as I grab my bag.

I'm impressed he knows there's a chance I won't. "I think so," I say and he smiles.

"Oh, and Eve, we don't come into this world all-knowing. That's what life is for."

BRADY

No one knows who their partner will become after they marry. I once worked for a man who ran a ten-person finance team until he had a random dream where a crucifix floated above a box that had a ques-

208

tion mark seared to the side. He woke up certain the Lord was unhappy with his life. He quit his job to become a math teacher, gave up booze, and dropped out of our sporting pool, suddenly disgusted by gambling. Not long after, Maddy ran into his newly ex-wife at the supermarket. She said she got a divorce because finding the Lord made him boring as all get out, which was an unforgivable sin in her book. Thinking on it, I wonder if Maddy considered divorce as a possible alternative. I'd take joint custody at this point.

I proposed to the woman Maddy was in that exact moment. I married a phase and she did too. We changed. We adjusted to each other's changes. Those tweaks sparked further change and so on, to the point where it's impossible to unravel who I was before Maddy, what changed with her influence, and what my prevailing personal opinions are now that she's gone.

"If you can't articulate what's different since your wife passed, how about telling me what's stayed the same?" Dr. White asks.

It's an unmanageable task given our gnarled history. I'm terrified to untangle it; I don't know that I'll like the scraps tied solely to me. "*Christ* . . . I don't know. I'm still considered talented at my profession. I work out. I have Eve." He's visibly unimpressed. "What do you want me to say? I'm still a Republican allergic to penicillin?"

Dr. White scratches his head. I failed even the moron version. "I'm looking for something you enjoy already that you could do more with," he clarifies. "I'd like you to foster a passion. The Fourth of July is tomorrow. Have you thought about how you're going to spend it?"

"Probably at the office. Eve usually hangs out with friends."

One eyebrow lifts. "Are you sure Eve wants to be with friends tomorrow?"

I adjust my posture, embarrassed to admit I'm not. "I'll ask. I can't imagine she'll opt to spend the day with me."

"Ask, but either way, don't work. Maddy won't be here next Fourth of July either, and working every holiday is not a wholesome solution for a lifetime."

"So you're suggesting I host a barbecue for one? Set off sparklers alone in the driveway?"

He sighs the way I do when Eve takes something I say to an unreasonable degree. "*Nooo*. I'm saying if Eve is busy, work isn't your only option. You said you like to work out, so go for a long run. Maybe there's a holiday road race you could do. Rent a movie. Read a book. Relax for a change. But don't go to work. Your healthy new routine isn't at the office."

I wake up with a plan, as if my brain spent the night plotting while the rest of me slept.

Once I find the damn thing it's easy to get into a rhythm with the outdoor sweeper. It's nice to do something where the result is immediate, visible. Each time I extend the broom, dried leafs, sticks, and dead bugs move the hell out of my way. Cause and effect. I'm in a bit of a trance when Eve wanders outside searching for me.

"Look at you," she says, offering a mock round of applause. I unbend my shoulders to attention, happy the tennis court is almost clear. Her surprise is fair enough. Our fifty-thousand-dollar investment became an expensive lawn ornament once Eve started playing year-round at the country club.

"No time like the present," I say, more chipper than I feel. "You in?" I'll be pissed if she says no, but manage to hide my emotions more effectively than I did on her birthday.

"It's funny," she says. "I woke up craving a game too. Let me change."

Huh. That was easy.

Besides announcing the score, we don't speak the entire match. Eve fights hard; I fight hard. No freebies. It's a physical display of our current relationship: back and forth, control shifting almost every play. The final set runs eleven rallies before either of us earns a two-point lead.

"That was great," she says after winning match point.

"For the victor," I jest, looking at my watch. It's only noon. Even when I'm having some semblance of fun, time no longer flies. I hope I'm not one of those sorry bastards who live to a hundred. "Do you want to go to the festival in Natick after we clean up?"

"Oh boy, really?" she replies, dramatically clasping her hands together like an excited toddler. "Can I ride the Ferris wheel?" It's the same facetious reaction I had when Dr. White suggested I make plans alone, but relating doesn't assuage the sting of rejection. She can tell I'm wounded. "Let's just hang out," she counters. "Make burgers. Watch the fireworks from the back deck."

I look up, grateful. "Burgers might be tough." I point to the destroyed grill and charred patio. Once I find a new assistant, her first task will be hiring a contractor to take care of it.

"You're SO funny," Eve gibes. "We can cook things on the stove, you know."

"I don't think we have a choice, Julia Child."

"Who's Julia Child?" she asks, heading for the house before I have a chance to answer.

In the shower I brainstorm things for Eve and me to talk about. Our conversations are an effort. I enjoy time with my daughter, mostly, but I spend it petrified of screwing up. Fear consumes energy, so even when we're getting along, being with her is work.

An unsolicited thought crosses my mind: Maybe I should offer Eve a drink with dinner. Maddy would. She didn't believe naïveté was a good parenting quality. She'd argue Eve leaves for boarding school in two months, where I'll have no jurisdiction. There will be booze and worse at her disposal. Kids act the way they're treated, forbidden fruit and all that. Playing what I find to be a compelling devil's advocate, Eve got wasted at preprom and could've died. She's already proven herself reckless in this arena. No need to revisit it.

So you think she's never going to drink again? Maddy's voice shoots back in my consciousness.

No, but I also don't think I need to encourage it, I rebuke.

213

She needs to know you trust her.

If you wanted to be a part of these decisions you should've stuck around, I snap, ending the imaginary debate.

Full-blown make-believe conversations like this have been happening a lot lately. I appreciate that I'm not really some third-eye, spiritual intuitive talking to dead people. I'm a desperate, grief-stricken man telling myself what I want to hear, and since I know Maddy's two cents on everything, it isn't hard to re-create.

When we reconvene on the patio, I give in to Maddy's wish, as usual. Even in death she has a hold on me. "Can I get you something to drink?"

"Coke, please," Eve requests, giving me the perfect out.

"You can have a beer or glass of wine, if you want."

She eyes me suspiciously. *"Really?"*

"Yes, really. This isn't an after-school special." She laughs, but doesn't change her answer. "We're staying here tonight," I press. "You're leaving for boarding school soon. If you don't know how to handle yourself, we're in trouble either way."

What the hell? How did I go from not wanting to offer to begging her to have one?

Eve bites her bottom lip. "Sure, I'll have a

glass of chardonnay, please, with two ice cubes." I find the request comical, but withhold comment.

When I return with our glasses, Eve sees I put two ice cubes in mine too and smiles. "A hostess makes everyone feel comfortable," we recite in unison, bringing Maddy into the moment. If she'd died any other way it'd be a fond memory. We take a few sips in silence. The sun dips lower. I exhale what feels like more than a breath. I don't know if it's the wine or what, but without the usual anxiety, I ask Eve about "camp" starting next week and how math is going. She tells me math isn't so bad — she loves her tutor — and she's excited to work with kids. Then she reciprocates, asking about work: Have I found a replacement for Paula? Will I travel more after she leaves for school? Never once do we discuss logistics, finances, permissions, or punishments. She laughs at my jokes and I laugh at hers. We *listen* to each other. She's choosing to be with me instead of anyone else, and unlike the other times in my life when that was true, this time I appreciate it.

When the first firework erupts in the sky it brings a flash of serenity. Moving forward seems feasible. Not simple, not immediate, but possible. We'll be okay. I've said that to

Eve a hundred times since Maddy's death, but this is the first time I believe it.

CHAPTER NINE

MADELINE

Linda is dying. Rory leaves her brother a simple message. "Hi, Brian. Mom is at the hospital. Room 366B. It won't be long now."

She massages the veins on her mother's wrinkled hands and bloated feet, watching, whispering, "I love you. You're going to be okay." She notices the skin sagging from her mother's arms. Seeing her daily made the weight loss less evident, but today, this last day it seems, her mother's frailty is fully exposed — monitors humming, tubes delivering pain medication and hydration, eyelids remaining halfway down even while she's awake. When her heart fails they won't resuscitate; Linda's paperwork is clear. Rory is grateful for the formality of it, that it simply isn't her choice. Her mother's last gift.

"I'm so glad you've come," Linda says when she wakes, though Rory's been there all day. "I have something to tell you." It's exhilarating, for a moment, how engaged Linda appears, but she fades back to sleep before any telling takes place.

An hour later Linda wakes again and continues talking, as if the nap was only a pause. "You must forgive yourself, sweetie." Rory blinks, questioning her mom's lucidity. Forty-three years of motherhood enables Linda to read Rory's mind as well as I can. "I damn well remember who you were before that accident. You need to get back there."

"I will, Mom, I will," Rory soothes, holding back her tears for later.

"Don't you dare let my death be another excuse."

Rory nods. "Okay, Mom, I won't, you'll see."

Around noon, Linda's eyes jolt open. Rory continues running her hand down her mother's arm and asks if she needs anything. "No, nothing, my baby girl." Her breathing slows, but she clutches Rory's hand with startling strength. "Just promise you'll open your heart to love again."

"I promise," Rory whispers back.

Her spastic breathing and mild moans continue throughout the afternoon, but those are Linda's last words.

I try to keep this moment for Rory, but envy seeps in. I'm pretty sure I left the world screaming, *Oh shit.* Hollywood taught me that one's last seconds are spent looping through life's biggest moments, but all I remember is the wind carrying snot back up my face and thinking how disgusting it felt.

My own mother's death was no better. During our last conversation she called me a selfish martyr. Her mind was already going. I found it an amusing oxymoron, but later I uncovered a cruel truth in her words. Did I *need* to be needed? Did I use sacrifice to inflate my self-worth? My mother died the next day, alone and drunk. They found her covered in vomit. At the time I assumed she did it so Meg and I would regret the boundaries we set to protect our children from her drunken chaos, but later I came to see that was unfair, almost narcissistic. Her death had nothing to do with me. She just saw no reason to keep on keeping on.

Linda's death is exponentially more profound. She leaves in phases, willfully, as if someone is there, talking her through the steps. I didn't have that — no light, no escort, nothing. I was simply spit back into the atmosphere. I try to extract the guidance Linda receives for my own benefit, but the conversation is encrypted. Even before her last breath, life leaves her. I sense she's now nearer to me than Rory, not in the dimension I'm in, but closer, higher. I shudder at the idea I've been bypassed. I assume Linda is in heaven, so where the hell am I? As if in answer to that question, my spirit ascends, furthering the distance between the world I left and me faster than the times before. When the ride stops, I look down, terrified they won't still be there, but they are.

Brian arrives as they wheel away Linda's covered body. He sobs, the way guilty grievers do, hugging Rory almost violently.

She stands there, letting him pull strength from her. When he pauses to catch his breath, she gently moves away. "She was ready."

He's incredulous. "How can you say that? Why aren't you crying?"

She finds his audacity comical in that delirious way only very sad things can be to very tired people. She holds back the raw chuckle she feels. "I want Mom to be comfortable more than I want her here for me."

"But I didn't get to say good-bye."

Rory looks at her younger brother, deciding whether to let the comment slide. "No," she says, "you'd have to have been here for that."

"I came as soon as I could. You can't just bail on a court date."

Rory rests an arm around his shoulder, rubbing his back the way their mother would have. "Death doesn't wait to be convenient. And when you're older, you'll look back and see that life doesn't either."

He stiffens. "I have a great life."

"You have a busy life, where you make a lot of money and eat dinner alone." She hadn't meant to be so pointed. "I'm sorry, I'm exhausted. I'll call tonight so we can make arrangements."

I present Rory's subconscious with the hypocrisy of her words as she walks to her car. Rory doesn't make a lot of money, but she eats dinner alone. As her mother so eloquently pointed out, she, too, is closed to the world. If work is Brian's vice, grief is Rory's. I need her to recognize this as a flaw — the only one I've sussed after months of stalking — so she'll take her mother's parting advice seriously. Rory needs Eve and Brady as much as they need her. Our goals are colliding.

When she gets home it doesn't seem possible she's only been gone half a day. The twelve hours at the hospital spanned a week in her heart. Greta sits patiently on the couch, honored to be Linda's messenger. "Your mom gave me this weeks ago," she says, handing Rory an envelope.

Rory offers a wearied smile, unsurprised. Her mom was a schemer. "Thanks."

"Just so you know, honey" — Greta presses her hand against her heart — "your mom had a lot of clarity yesterday while you were tutoring. We talked about her childhood, her dancing, her labor with you. Did you know she picked Rory because it sounded powerful?"

"Yeah, she told me that."

"Well, yesterday, she called you her lion and I realized why she thought of Rory as a powerful name — Roar-y." Greta giggles. "Only your mom would think of that. She was quite a lady."

Rory embraces Greta with ostensible gratitude. "Thank you . . . so much, for, well, for everything."

"I'm going to miss her. And you. Stay in touch?"

Rory nods. Greta and Linda were the same age, both widows. They grew so close over the past few years that Rory had come to consider Greta part of the family. That she doesn't intend to disappear with her last paycheck is a relief to Rory.

Greta collects her things and goes. Rory sits on her mom's cot and opens the letter. There's no greeting, just Linda's distinctive script.

Don't put me in a coffin like your father. I have no desire to continue taking up space in this world (or to be consumed by maggots, for that matter). Have me cremated and buried in our plot. No wake . . . No death dress or makeup . . . No postfuneral potluck. I'm not beholden to any religious rules — I am myself a spiritual being. If you have a memorial, make it a celebration. This is not a tragic death. I'm ready.

And Rory, me leaving should give you time to focus on you. Enough already with the pain and guilt. You'll see Emma again, when the time is right. Until then, I'll watch over her. You're here with a purpose. Anaïs Nin wrote, "Life shrinks or expands in proportion to one's courage," or something like that, and she's right.

I'll be sending love, Mom

Rory's mind explodes with images and recollections. *The way she said "God bless you" right before you sneezed. Her hard laughter the day I put lines all over my body with permanent marker because I wanted to be a tiger. When she spoke at Emma's funeral and said that nothing will ever make sense again, but we still need to seek goodness wherever we go.*

She sits in the room her mom faded in, enjoying her scent, reading the note again and again, weeping. When she finishes, Rory dries her eyes with a lightness any mourner would covet. Rory did right by Linda; she won't suffer the way I did.

When I told Meg last Christmas I felt somewhat responsible for our mother's death, she laughed it off, saying, "Mom dug her grave one drink at a time."

True enough, but it wasn't always that way. I have three years on Meg; I remember things she doesn't. Before the zany jogging suits and hallway puke and everything else, she was a middle-class socialite, if there is such a thing. She attracted strong personalities like her friend Eve and my father. *The hostess with the mostess,* everyone agreed.

At eleven, I was the only one unimpressed.

I saw my mother as someone who let life happen to her. The cookbooks she loved, the clothes she wore, even mundane decisions like which flowers to plant each spring were all based on popular opinion. She'd rather be boring than risk ridicule. This fear was likely born from her own bad habit of calling out anyone who dared to differentiate. Though I was too young to know it, there's a strong correlation between judgment and insecurity.

I watched in awe as my mother's girlfriends broke the mold. I remember Eve stopping over after a court appearance, decked out in a smart suit, telling me about the time she led a band of ladies to a D.C. women's rally. "Can you believe it was 1972 and women still didn't have equal protection under the law?" I replied to my hero that, no, I couldn't believe it. She told me to hold on to my chair because here it was — 1982 — and fifteen states still hadn't ratified the Equal Rights Amendment, which was signed in both houses a few months after the rally Eve attended. I understood the legislation as historic, and in my naïveté, Eve played a major role. When I asked my mother if she went to D.C., she warned me to be careful what I wished for. "Equal rights? Sheesh. There's a lot your father does that I want no part of." I was disappointed. Women were demanding change, willing to serve in the military if that's what it took, and yet my mom seemed proud that she voted for whomever my father told her to.

By the time I was twelve her dependence repulsed me. Puberty kicked in. I scoffed when she offered up homemade cookies, saying obnoxious things like, "You do realize you wouldn't have to be on diets all the time if you stopped eating so many cookies, right?" Where the hell did I find the nerve? (Looking back, I have an idea where. She and my father had started to have a rocky go of it. I'd snicker alongside him as he berated her for letting any tiny household task slide. *I mean, really, Janine,* he'd say, leaning over the counter into her personal space, *what the hell were* you *doing all day*? How his disappointment became my anger is less clear. All I know is I let my aversion be known, and by my thirteenth birthday, my mother was drunk before noon. It was as if she turned into the useless character my father and I cast her as.)

If at first I was just a kid in need of proper discipline, once my mother morphed into a raging alcoholic I became a teenager with a vendetta. We were neglected — forgotten at practices, undersupervised, left to clean up bodily fluids that my mother was unable to contain — but I never examined how it got to that point. I never wondered *why* my mom self-medicated. We were too busy raising ourselves to question the reason we were raising ourselves.

My persecution was relentless. I took care to point out her flaws in front of an audience, so all would know I hadn't been infected with her same feeble nature. I poked and poked and poked.

The enormity of how I contributed to her backstory came crashing down on me last November. Brady and I were on a date night and happened into the same Thai restaurant my family went the night of my college graduation. It had been twenty-two years, but the ambiance was oddly preserved. When I spotted the booth we occupied, the scene rushed to my mind: over dinner, my mother declared in her scrambled speech that my next major milestone would be marriage. I looked at her with irreverence. "I don't need a husband to make milestones, Mom."

Her eyes widened. I assumed I'd upset her sensibilities, which had been my intent, but that night with Brady all those years later I had more context. I was, by then, a mother myself. Looking back on the scene, I saw her expression for what it was — not shock, but fear. My mother was *afraid* of me. She shook her head fiercely, swearing she only meant it'd be the next big celebration in my honor. My father, Meg, and I all rolled our eyes. There's no such thing as going from a drunk to a solid point. "I'm not a prize," I said, enunciating each word to highlight my mother's slur. "Women are honored for things besides marriage and children. I know that's hard for you to understand." I accentuated *you* to be sure the insult was clear, but there was no need. She'd been my tomato target for years.

After reliving that graduation memory, I analyzed our relationship in a way I hadn't thought to when we were both alive, and neglected to after her sudden death when there was a coffin to buy and awkward post-funeral party to host. During this unexpected slump, I dissected every fight we had with maternal goggles on, and came to see my mother wasn't out to get Meg and me. She just couldn't handle life. Perspective matured, I grew to view her addiction as almost predictable. She was a small-town girl who married her high-school sweetheart. My father had a strong, demanding personality. He controlled her highs and lows from the age of sixteen. They had no mortgage left on the three-bedroom house they bought in 1968. She didn't see what more one could want. Not upsetting the applecart, as she often preached, had served her well.

But society turned on her. What was once a woman's duty suddenly became passé. All her friends got jobs while my mom was busy swapping recipes with the grandmothers in our neighborhood. Imagine how stunned she must've been to realize the community no longer held her blind familial devotion in high esteem. Even my father wished he'd attached himself to someone more cosmopolitan, more worldly. And so he did — on the side. I envision my mother growing weak from abandonment and disrespect and finding strength, or at least solace, in Carlo Rossi's wine jugs, a man whose picture we saw so often Meg called him our grandfather.

So what came first? There's no doubt she was a shitty mom from twelve on, but did I send her on that course? During the family portion of what proved to be another failed rehab attempt, a doctor in a crisp lab coat explained the science behind the disease of alcoholism. It was all right there: my mother was genetically screwed. There were dozens of triggers — me, my dad, traffic — but only one person in control of the hand lifting that glass to her lips. And yet, the memory of how ungrateful and unpleasant I was gnawed at me. I started questioning my own evening chardonnay, my own loneliness.

Brady traveled a lot. Eve got her license. I was free, but I was lost. My mother was long gone, but her memory suddenly had a grip on my present.

Meg and Brady had no patience for it. *A drunk is a drunk because they like to get drunk,* they said. But I felt guilty. My role in it all haunted me. Brady will be alarmed when he reaches that part of my journal. It's a relief he's sticking to an entry a day. I have six more months of documented sanity.

For the first time, I wonder where my mother is. Perhaps Linda had a welcoming committee because the predeceased were excited for her arrival. Would I blame Mom for thinking she deserved death to herself? I can almost hear her encourage my father not to go to any trouble, that sometimes it's best to leave good enough alone.

Once again I find myself involuntarily elevating. Just the act of questioning my position relative to hers sparks the shift. My spirit hangs on a ladder and I just climbed several rungs.

I struggle to re-focus on Rory, the change instantly evident. My prowess is weakened. I can no longer make out thoughts as if there's a script to match. I need to sync the bits and pieces I extract with what I know and what I infer. *Tick, tock.* I've officially been put on notice that my time is running out.

Eve is defensive the next morning when Rory cancels their session. "Is this because of me?"

"You?"

"I know it was none of my business to ask all those questions the other day."

Rory senses the importance of setting the record straight. Here too is a girl with enough guilt on her hands. "No, no," she assures. "My mother passed away."

"Oh. My. God. She died? And you're calling me?"

The comment makes Rory self-conscious. "It was expected," she justifies. "She was ill."

"Yeah, but still. I'm sorry. I didn't, like, *know.*" Then, to Rory's astonishment, Eve starts to cry.

"It was her time," Rory says, before catching her mistake. Eve's cry goes an octave higher. For Eve, this isn't about Linda, it's about me, and it hadn't been my time. "Are you going to be okay, Eve? Is your dad home?"

"Don't ask about me! God. This is about *you.* I know that. I'm sorry, Rory. I'm so sorry I'm crying. I don't know why."

Rory does. Every new death brings back the full weight of those already gone. I don't need to be able to read every thought to know that memories of her daughter, Emma, have been flooding Rory since Linda's death, the same way that thoughts of my mother have been pestering me. "I shouldn't have told you all that. I just didn't want you to think it was about the other day."

"I'm fine," Eve manages, this time with a voice strong enough to convince Rory it's acceptable to hang up.

But Eve isn't fine. She curls up on her bed and howls, the way she did when she first learned of my death. My daughter truly believes she failed me. Her loss isn't pure like Rory's, it's layered thick like mine with *should have* and *could have* and *would have if only I'd known.* It's the worst kind of grief. I try to persuade her of her innocence, but Eve resists. I settle for focusing my energy on sending her warmth, hoping she feels my presence, my love. She coughs between sobs, choking on mucus. After an hour of this storming she falls asleep, raw from a running list of perceived failures.

If only there was a way to explain.

EVE

This is going to suck. I look at the other teenagers who were sentenced to community service. I'm the only girl. The oldest guy has a translator because he doesn't speak English (Dad will have a fun rant about taxpayers' dollars when he hears that). The youngest is covered in tattoos and has what looks to be a weapon of some sort wedged in his oversized jean pocket. The remaining two are chewing tobacco and spitting it in a shared empty Pepsi bottle. Camp Ray may want to rethink its recruiting pool.

"Thank you, everyone, for getting here early." As if the court gave us a choice. "I'm Robin Winters, director here at Camp Ray. After orientation this morning, arriving at quarter of eight will be fine." The other four delinquents grunt their relief. Seven a.m. competes with morning hangovers.

The director is right off the set of *The Parent Trap,* wide-rim safari hat and all. "Camp Ray is the only state-funded summer program available to special-needs children. The kids are between the ages of nine and twelve, with conditions ranging from deafness to cerebral palsy. Everyone alternates between drama, water sports, and crafts. Each station lasts an hour. There's an assigned aide for every three kids and a camp counselor in charge of each station."

She walks through our limited role, referencing her clipboard as if she couldn't possibly remember the three responsibilities entrusted to the delinquents: greet campers each morning, get them to their correct starting station based on group color, and assist between sessions with preparation and cleanup.

When she finishes we're all excused to the parking lot, except me. "Eve?" Robin says, tapping my shoulder.

"Yes, nice to meet you," I say, extending a hand.

"Hopefully you still feel that way in a minute. I need a favor." She looks down at her clipboard for moral support. I wonder what the top piece of paper actually says. "One of the counselors had to back out unexpectedly. I've been freaking out all morning, but when I saw you it was like a divine intervention. *Use Eve.* That's what my heart told me. I'd be so grateful if you'd step up and man the craft station."

I look at the rest of the involuntary volunteers and see why I've been singled out for the unpaid promotion. "Why not," I agree. I have to be here either way.

"Thank God. Well . . . I guess thank *you*

is more accurate. It's pretty basic." She shuffles through a stack of papers and hands me a catalog of choices. "Pick a craft, any craft. Get supplies from the storage shed first thing in the morning and instruct each group on the project as they come through."

"Got it," I say. With all the aides present, it shouldn't be a biggie. I walk to the shed and grab a bunch of Popsicle sticks and glue to make picture frames. When I return to the art station campers are arriving.

It's instantly clear there aren't enough aides. We're not talking about learning issues here — these kids have no-joke disabilities. Even a dedicated person for every single child wouldn't cover it. I do awkward things like stare a moment too long before wiping the drool off a boy's face and struggle to find an appropriate way to move the older kids in wheelchairs over to the bench. Then there's Hanna, a ten-year-old hooked up to a ventilator. I'm terrified to accidentally detach one of the tubes and go from an underage drinking violation to manslaughter.

Each second feels like an hour. When the five-minute-warning bell rings, I arrange the frames in a row to dry and work with the three aides to line everyone up. I lift Hanna, noticing midair that the bench is wet. I look down to see her soaking shorts in time to avoid mushing her pee into my T-shirt. "Oh my God," I shriek, knowing I sound like a spoiled brat. I hold the poor thing at arm's length with no idea what to do. It's not like I have a change of clothes. Hanna's aide rushes over, aggravated by my reaction. This is session one of day one — the idea that I have to live through twenty-nine more is totally overwhelming.

The second group includes Kathleen, who is blind. What the hell am I supposed to do with that? I can't exactly hand a blind girl a bottle of glue and say, "Make a rectangle." Maybe I should bail at the end of the day. I mean, legally, can I switch jobs? There were a ton of options that fulfilled the hours, the simplest filling ice trays at the senior center. It's not that I don't want to help, I do, I feel terrible for these kids, but I'm afraid I'll do more harm than good.

Kathleen sits at the freshly cleaned picnic table in total silence. "How old are you?" I ask.

"Twelve."

"Where do you live?"

"Framingham."

"Do you have any brothers or sisters?"

"Yes." *But apparently no interest in telling me about them. . . .*

I take the hint and leave her alone. I'd be pissed too, stuck at a camp where my only choice was to sit there. When Robin stops over to check in, I quietly suggest Kathleen stay at a different station twice since she can't really participate in art. Suddenly Kathleen is at my side, tugging my sleeve. How does she know where my arm is? "Excuse me, Miss Eve," she interrupts, "but this is my favorite activity."

I put a hand on her shoulder. "But you aren't able to do the project."

"I'm doing it with my imagination," she says. "I love art."

I'm such a freaking idiot. This whole time I've been interrupting her with pointless questions.

As the group files out of my station, I approach Kathleen. "I'm sorry about the confusion. Tomorrow I'll be sure to give you some peace and quiet while you think."

Her face lifts. "It's hard to know what to do with me sometimes. Thanks for apologizing. No one ever does that."

I smile. My mom would have. She was big into accountability. *Who makes mistakes?* she'd ask out of nowhere when I was a kid. *Everyone!* I'd shout, as she trained me to. *And what do you do when you realize you've made a mistake?* she'd ask, her voice getting louder. *Acknowledge! Apologize! Address!* I'd cheer.

I get home and take a nap without stopping for lunch. I'm too exhausted to even sneak some of my mom's journal. I'll deserve a trip to Paris by the time these two weeks are up.

I awake to a ringing phone and slobber on my pillow. Still groggy, I take a second to process that it's John's number. His thirty days in rehab are over. I'd be a giant ass to ignore this call.

"Hey," he says, pretending all is normal.

"Hey back," I play along.

Silence. There's no way to move the conversation forward without giving up the act. "We need to talk," he says. "Can you pick me up?"

"Sure." Better to get the breakup over with before he hooks up with someone and causes drama. I head to his house in sweats and no makeup, knowing this isn't a date that ends with a selfie.

When John gets in the car I notice he's lost weight and, for summer, is way pale. He's still completely hot, but it's like looking at a magazine photo; he doesn't feel like mine anymore.

"Was it horrible?" I ask.

"*Nah* . . . it wasn't that bad. It was crazy

to hear how messed up some people get. The circle would come to me and I was like the loser. Compared to those crack heads I haven't done shit."

"Sounds depressing."

He flings his chin my way. "Probably wasn't as bad as things have been for you. You holding up?"

I think of the night I just spent crying so hard I hyperventilated. "Yeah, I'm good." I wish we weren't in a car. It forces us to be so close.

"Jake and Noel said they haven't seen you around."

"Yeah, well, my dad's needed me, and I have the community-service thing."

He puts a leg up on my dashboard. "I hope you can forgive me for the accident, Eve. I know it's the last thing you needed."

The apology reminds me that he's a good guy. I hadn't been thinking he was a bad guy; I'd just stopped thinking about him altogether.

"Oh my God, John. I'm the whole reason we dragged ourselves to your car. It's my fault. I know your father blames me, like we were on some kind of death wish or something."

"My father blames a lot of people for a lot of things. I think it goes with being a judge."

"Well, I'm wicked sorry you got in so much trouble. Thank God no one got hurt."

"Yeah."

I know he has more to say because he flips his thumbs in circles without letting them touch, the way he did the first time he said he loved me. It's crazy to compare how much I cared then with how little I care now.

"Here's the thing though, I know my dad said we couldn't talk, but I was surprised you didn't send a letter or anything."

I look down at my lap. "I'm sorry. I suck. There's been a lot going on. Just constant shit."

"Stop apologizing. It's fine anyway; I'm only wondering if we are, you know, fine." His eyes are on me now, looking for clues.

"Is that what you want?" My voice can't hide my surprise.

"Of course that's what I want. I love you. I don't see why a car accident should change anything." He places a hand on my knee. I look at it. He loves me. *Huh.* I feel like I barely know him.

"Honestly though," I stall, "things were different before the accident."

"I know." He squeezes my knee to show that doesn't matter.

"I'm a totally different person now." Tears slide down my cheeks. "I think about everything more, you know? I question if I'm spending my time in, like, a meaningful way. No one really gets me right now."

"Do you think I get you?"

"*Pfft.* I don't know. I think you want to. I think you're the only one in our group who cares anymore."

"That's not fair. Everyone cares."

"No they —"

He puts a hand up. "In April, we didn't know how to respond. I admit that. But I've had a lot of time to think about it. A *lot* of time. I never should've dragged you to Lindsey's. Kara told me to skip it and she was right. That was shitty."

"Kara told you to skip it because she suddenly hates me. It's like my mom's death ruined her life."

"Forget Kara. She's been a freak to everyone, not just you. But the rest of us care. We just don't know how to show it."

I understand why John would fight to keep me. We're finally seniors. The bridge by the railroad track reads Class of 2016 for the next twelve months. He doesn't know how to separate me from his excitement. We lost our virginity together. We've been going out almost two years, the longest of any couple in our grade. People joke that we're the school mascot. I have to tell him I'm leaving. Telling him will end it for good.

"I'm going to Exeter in September," I whisper. "As a boarder."

He pulls his hand away, a relief. "Why?"

"You know why."

"I mean why didn't you tell me? How long have you known?"

"I dunno. Since May, I guess."

"So you knew before the accident, before I left?" I nod. He glares at me. "What the hell, Eve?"

The passion in his voice stuns me. How can two people view the same relationship so differently? "I-I guess I assumed no one would give a shit by the time I left anyway and-and I didn't want to get into a whole big conversation."

He throws both hands in the air. "What else can I possibly do to prove I love you?"

I turn the radio on instead of answering. Solid-gold oldies fill the car, making me think of my mom. If she were here she'd say, *Listen to this music. No wonder everyone was happy in the fifties.*

"How far away is Exeter?" he asks.

"A little over an hour."

"That's not too bad. You'll be back for weekends?"

"I have classes Saturday morning, but I'll be back after that unless there's a game or something."

He smirks. "Saturday classes? Sounds like an awesome time." I don't have a comeback, so he keeps talking. "Whatever. Weekends are what really matter, right?" His voice is desperate, like a wannabe's, which he's not.

It's tempting to join the world of the living with someone other than my father. I don't know what I'm going to say until I say it: "Wanna see a movie tonight?"

"Can't. My parents are having some lame welcome-home-even-though-we're-the-ones-who-sent-you-away-in-the-first-place dinner. Tomorrow?"

"I'm going to a funeral."

His eyes bug out, but I wave him off. "My tutor's mom. I never even met the lady. How about Thursday?"

"Great, but you'll have to pick me up. I can't drive till I'm nineteen." He winks to show there's no hard feelings, then leans in for a kiss good-bye. I turn so he'll catch my cheek. He settles for it.

I'm not worth his forgiveness, but he hasn't figured that out yet.

BRADY

It's tough to build on being a Republican businessman allergic to penicillin, so running is really my only option to Dr. White's

243

challenge of fostering a passion.

I'm training for the Boston Marathon next spring. To qualify, I need a time of less than three hours and twenty minutes at the race in Quebec. That's under an eight-minute mile for twenty-six consecutive miles. After a week and a half of training I ran a nine-minute mile for ten miles, so I have work to do. I've read several articles that say the type of training I need, in the five weeks I have to do it, can't be done. My confidence could use an impossible accomplishment right about now.

People often run in someone's memory or to promote a cause. I've been envisioning myself crossing the finish line with the tagline RUNNING FOR SUICIDE. Maddy laughs with me on that one. The sound is unmistakable, knocking against my skull, like she's running next to me. Keeping my eyes straight ahead, I indulge the fantasy that we're in this together, that after Quebec and Boston we'll travel the world running marathons.

Every day, about three miles in, I pass Wellesley College. I consider it penance. For two years I believed Maddy volunteered here to pass time and thrived, when really she came for fulfillment and failed. Usually I nod my head to pay respect, but today I veer off the sidewalk toward the library as though someone called my name. It's too late to stop Maddy, but I can stand in her final spot and beg her memory's forgiveness. How did I let work swallow me whole? If only I had been there, in that moment, to yell, "THIS CHOICE IS THE ONLY THING HAPPENING THAT IS PERMANENT. I CAN CHANGE."

A JAG#2 vanity plate brings me to a halt — Kara's dad's car. What the hell is Todd Anderson doing here? Compelled as I am to atone, I won't do it in the presence of a man who once questioned how three people manage to fit in a house that's *only* six thousand square feet. I turn back toward Route 9, but not before catching a glimpse of Todd with a woman I don't know. He presses low on the small of her back, guiding her to the passenger seat. I feel sorry for Christie, but not surprised. There've been long running rumors about the interesting interworkings of that marriage. Maddy never let Eve spend the night there. My general understanding is that faithfulness isn't revered by either spouse.

The rest of my run I'm overtaken by the possibility Maddy had an affair. That'd explain everything. There was a journal entry about a professor she met while having lunch on a bench overlooking the lake on campus. Maddy claimed she forced my name into the conversation early, as much to remind herself as enlighten him. That's not exactly a strong statement of loyalty. She went on and on about how marriage doesn't mean you'll never be attracted to another man, but rather that you respect your partner so much you'd never jeopardize what you built over such a fleeting inclination. She signed off claiming she'd take her lunch elsewhere moving forward, but who knows? Maybe it was the start of something.

By mile eight I have officially chucked Maddy in the same dirt pile as Todd Anderson, but by mile ten I acknowledge I'm being unfair. So she talked to someone intriguing . . . I can't pretend I've never had a conversation that left me wanting more. And Maddy wrote she was enthralled because the man asked so many questions. It's a fair stab. I only covered the basics. *What did you do today? How'd it go?*

It's amazing, really. My career — the entirety of my professional success — is founded on my ability to drill down, to understand every situation with specificity. My big claim to fame was precisely this sort of attention to detail. HT was about to buy a company that boasted twenty thousand customers. The client list was the primary motivation for the acquisition, so I asked random questions to multiple people during due-diligence meetings. How many customers bought additional software in the past twelve months? How many customers have you lost in that same period? Is it easy to find references? I uncovered a bleak picture: a base declining more rapidly than sales accounted for, no incremental business, and poor overall customer satisfaction. We avoided the train wreck. Our competitor did not. The acquisition ultimately brought both companies down, and Jack personally thanked me. It was the catalyst for my promotion to CFO. Why have I zipped that skill up in my briefcase before coming home at night?

I need to dig in more with Eve, but asking teenagers questions is a fine art. Ask too many and you're overbearing; ask the wrong ones and you don't get it; ask the right ones at the wrong time and you're annoying. It's like walking on the edge of a cliff that Eve occasionally elects to push me off. I never know what will set her off. Last night I tried to confirm she was certain about Exeter because the full tuition is due.

"You think I'm a flake?" she replied. It

was so hypersensitive that I laughed. "Is it funny when you offend people?" she snapped.

If I had a white flag I would've waved it. "Whoa there," I said.

"*Whoa there?* I'm not a horse, Dad."

"Sorry I asked," I said, uncertain why I was apologizing. "I'll mail the check." I left the room even though the show I'd been watching wasn't over.

How could Eve flip from the loving daughter I watched fireworks with to such a crazy lady? Maddy's voice popped into my head: *It's that time of month.* I have to give myself credit. For a man without a creative bone in his body, I have Maddy's phrasing and sense of humor down pat. Reconstructing my dead wife is the most inspired thing I've ever done.

Thirteen miles complete and I've come full circle. There's no other man to stick this mess on. Everything I provided Maddy was overshadowed by everything I held back. I thought it made good sense to treat work separate from home, but it meant my family only had access to half of me. I go inside to take a shower and wash off my shame.

CHAPTER TEN

MADELINE

Eve wears the same black dress she picked out with Meg for my funeral. I was as surprised to see her look up the time and location of Linda's memorial as Rory is when she arrives.

It's a simple burial led by the nursing-home minister. After some spiritual sayings about the circle of life, Rory stands, placing the urn into the plot next to her father's, and speaks softly to the thirty or so people in attendance. Eve expected to blend in with the crowd because her only point of reference was my service, which hundreds of people flocked to, in curiosity more than sorrow.

Rory's low volume commands attention and the group leans in to catch every word. She wears no makeup. There are faint lines on her forehead and around her mouth, but she still looks too young to lose a parent. I wonder where that leaves Eve.

"My mother was blessed with a lived life. She danced for the Rockettes at Radio City in her teens, fought for social justice in college, married her soul mate, bore two children in two different decades, and dutifully served our family for the remainder of her life.

"Linda Maureen Murray taught me to see the beauty in everyday things, what to wear on an interview, and who to trust secrets with — the people who don't tell you any. She believed mothers needed to keep a distinguishable life of their own, and she did. She ran a bridge group, headed up the first mentor program in New England, and rowed the Charles River daily until her body wouldn't allow it."

Sounds like I could have learned a lot from Linda. Keeping a distinguishable life of my own was my great life struggle. It made me feel greedy to long for more than I already had.

Rory continues speaking, but Eve's mind drifts to the eulogy Meg gave at my funeral. I can't follow her stream of consciousness exactly, I'm too high up, but for weeks after I died Eve read it before bed. She knows it verbatim and so do I.

Madeline loved to read. She was wise and often told her truths through quotations or storytelling. I don't know who originally said it, but her favorite words of wisdom were, "Everything will be okay in the end. If it isn't okay, it isn't the end." How I hope that proves true for all of us gathered here today in sadness.

When we were little, Maddy loved skinny-dipping and drinking ice cold, fresh-squeezed lemonade. If she were standing here now she'd laugh and say she still loves those things. As kids we watched the Muppets. Maddy could impersonate Miss Piggy to a T. She'd bob her head around and say in a mousy voice, "Beauty is in the eye of the beholder, and it may be necessary from time to time to give a stupid or misinformed beholder a black eye." She drank Shirley Temples long after she was of age to drink stronger. Her favorite fortune cookie read: *Simplicity of character is the natural result of profound thought.*

Although she was interested in many things, nothing competed with the respon-sibility and joy she found in motherhood. Eve was Maddy's life passion and true gift. She loved her family unequivocally, and wanted nothing more than for Eve and

Brady to be happy. That's why today is so damn confusing.

Meg's voice cracked with the last sentence and she stepped off the pulpit in tears. It was unclear to those in attendance if that was all she had to say, or if that was all she could get out. Paige was next up. She looked out at the faces that weren't mine and began to sob. She's lived in Wellesley twenty years and no one could ever remember seeing Paige so much as frazzled. There was total silence as her husband led her back to their pew. The memory arrests Eve and she forgets, for a second, where she is. She snaps back to the present when people begin to shuffle toward the parking lot. Eve follows, not wanting to burden Rory with her presence, when a man's voice shouts: "What the hell did you say?"

It's Brian. His words bring foot traffic to a standstill.

"I said I'm glad you could finally make it to see your mother," Greta hollers back.

"You're accosting me at my mother's funeral?"

"Yes, I am, young man," she says evenly.

"Young man? I'm twenty-six." Being on the offensive makes him sweat. He takes off his jacket, revealing his professional success

with a custom-tailored shirt and platinum
cuff links.

Rory intervenes. "Greta, Brian, *please,*
now is not the time."

"Oh, Rory, I'm sorry, honey. This jerk is
your brother, so you have to forgive him.
But I . . . I . . . don't." Greta points her
index finger in Brian's face. He's handsome,
the kind of man who looks athletic without
actually being so. "How dare you come here
today and cry like you lost something you
cherished."

Brian clenches his right hand into a fist,
the way Brady has so many times this summer. "How dare you, lady. You have no right
to make this spectacle. You're not even family."

She shakes off his words in that unflinch-
ing way only old people can. "Ask anyone
who works hospice and they'll tell you this
about family: it's made of the people who
show up. You don't know my name, do you?
I cared for your mother for *two years.* Two
beautiful years. I bathed her, dressed her,
fed her when her arthritis flared up . . . and-
and here you don't even know my name."

Brian's head is down now, in a look of surrender. "Good," she says. "At least you're
standing here, silent, looking as repentant
as you should feel. I'm Greta Robbins and I

have one last question. Do you have any idea how much the woman you ignored sacrificed for you and your self-absorbed life?"

It's been a drizzly day, and as though on cue, rain pours down in violent sheets. The weather breaks up the crowd. Eve walks away in shock.

Once in the privacy of the car, she pounds her head on the steering wheel, weighted by Greta's words. *Someone should have said that to me,* Eve thinks. *I was so selfish my mom killed herself.* Of all the thoughts to come through with great clarity, it seems cruel this had to be the one. It's torture to hear Eve give herself this undeserved lashing. I want to communicate the whole of my story to her, but it's layered and emotional. I tried pulling Brady into the fold during his run last week, got him to stand right in front of the problem, but he was distracted by Todd Anderson's car and tore off. Without context to draw from my story will never be told. *I love you,* I say instead, over and over. *I love you. I love you. I love you.*

It's not enough. Eve is hysterical. I find Rory. I hate to intrude during such a sensitive time, but I can't let Eve drive away in such a state. *Check on Eve,* I guide. *Check on Eve.*

She spots Eve's car and suddenly there she is, tapping on the window, motioning to let her in. "You look like you need a tissue, and I happen to have a pocket full," Rory says, helping herself to the passenger seat. "They're crumbled, not dirty."

"Thanks." Eve tries to get her breathing under control. "Listen, you don't have to, like, sit here with me. I'm fine. *God . . .* you're the one who should be consoled."

"My mother's death was different from yours." Rory looks to see if she offended Eve with the knowledge of my death, but Eve's expression doesn't change. She assumes everyone knows.

"I shouldn't have come," Eve says. "I wasn't trying to get your attention or anything. I-I was trying to worry about someone else, you know? But then that fight. What that woman said." Her voice turns to a mumble. "I treated my mom like garbage too."

"Eve, you're a teenager," Rory reasons. "Brian is a man."

"That's just an excuse."

Inside Rory melts at being needed in this maternal way. "No, it's not," she assures. "The day I turned thirteen my mom said, 'I

255

don't expect you to love me again until you're twenty.' And I didn't, or at least I didn't show it."

"Well, you weren't as bad as me because your mom stuck around."

Rory centers herself in Eve's vision. "Life is more complicated than that. Think of how many secrets you've kept from your parents. Think of all the things you haven't told them in only seventeen years. Now imagine everything you must not have known about your mother."

"Because I didn't ask."

"No. *No.* Because she didn't want to tell you. You don't always get to know what happened, or why things happened a certain way, but it always, *always,* goes deeper than any one thing. Every experience someone has contributes to their perspective, to their ability to handle their next experience." Eve looks up. I can't say she believes Rory, but she doesn't *not* believe her either. "I remember housing this tremendous guilt when my dad died because we'd never truly gotten to know each other. We had forty years of conversations consisting solely of weather and local sports. When his best friend gave a eulogy, he described my dad as an old-fashioned romantic who loved to waltz and earned a full scholarship to college playing the saxophone. And I thought, *what*? I never knew that. How did I not know that?"

"It was his past."

Rory nods in agreement. "Exactly. I went out the next day and signed up for ballroom-dance lessons. I needed something symbolic to feel closer to him."

Eve smiles, encouraged by the idea she can still get to know me. Rory will make a fine stand-in.

EVE

Mom had this way of making me and my friends feel important. Once when I was seven a girl in the neighborhood got caught French-kissing. All the older kids were talking about it, but none of my friends knew what it meant. Without much discussion we agreed to ask my mom. I wasn't nervous or embarrassed. Mom always preached that there's no harm asking and there's no point sitting around curious.

I marched in the kitchen and asked how the French kiss. She looked confused. I thought she didn't know the answer, but then my question registered. "Are you asking what it means to French-kiss?"

"Un-huh," I said, uncertain of the difference.

She casually stopped setting the table and

took a seat. "It's a more romantic kind of kissing, for when you're seriously dating or married, where your tongues touch. It's not just for French people, though. I know that's a weird name for it."

"Do you and Dad French-kiss?"

"Yep." The neighborhood girls couldn't believe it. My mom was our trusted advisor.

At camp, that's what I've become for Kathleen. Since borrowing my mom's line that there's no point being curious, Kathleen hasn't stopped asking questions. She practices braille by reading a weekly paper covering world news she's not old enough to understand, so there's no shortage of topics. She'll ask: "But how did AIDS start, I mean for the first person?" and "Why don't we use the actual votes to decide who is president?" and "Why do people care so much that Mexicans want to live here?" And on and on.

My answers are pathetic: "Maybe they're worried there's not enough space."

Her responses are smart: "But when there's not enough space, won't they stop wanting to come?" I usually have to admit I have no idea. It doesn't seem to bother her I'm clueless.

I pull into the parking lot and see Kathleen in the car with her mom, waiting. It's become routine for her to meet me early to help pick the daily project. I guide Kathleen to the sidewalk, waving at her mother as she drives away. A drop of rain hits my head. Then another. Then it's pouring. We run to a little shed off the lunch area as my cell rings. "Hi, Robin."

"*Oh.* Yes. Hi. I'm still surprised when people know it's me," the camp director says in her singsong voice. "It's 2015, and darn-it-all, I'm still not used to cell phones." It's work not to laugh. Robin is sweet, but she's the biggest dork I've ever met. I should set her up with Dr. Jahns. "*Any-hoo* . . . we're postponing an hour due to inclement weather."

"Okay," I say, seeing no reason to tell her I'm already here. I offer to take Kathleen home, but she asks if I mind staying. "The rain doesn't bother me if it doesn't bother you." It's not like there's somewhere else I need to be.

"I love rain," she says. "It's easy to picture."

She speaks so simply. I never wonder broadly the way Kathleen does. I read a headline and take it as fact. Kathleen reads a headline and it's the start of something. I have a hard time defending things I like with any detail. Everything in my life found me.

Kathleen understands herself intimately. She's certainly not going to pick friends based on some foolish formula that includes where people buy their clothes. I think I'm learning more from her than she from me.

The rain simmers to a drizzle, so we walk arm in arm to the playground. I smile. Knowing Kathleen can't see me, that there's no audience at all, makes the expression more genuine.

"Can I ask you something, Eve?"

This is how she starts every conversation. "Anything at all," I reply, how my mom always did.

"What do I look like?"

I stop. *I don't know* won't fly this time. "No one's told you?"

"No, people usually say pretty or beautiful, but no one has ever given any detail."

"There are worse things to be called."

She nods. "Yeah, but I want to know *exactly*. I want to be able to picture myself."

I set her on a swing, thinking about how best to respond. Kathleen is gorgeous, but how can I make her know it? "Well," I start, biting my nails with one hand and pushing her with the other, "you have flawless skin, especially for your age. I've heard people compare soft, clear skin like yours to milk. Every feature on your face is perfectly symmetrical, like you were drawn by an artist. Your chin is round, and when you smile it lifts up with your mouth in a way I've never seen on anyone else. But your best feature is your eyes."

"Huh. That's ironic." It seems like such a big word for a twelve-year-old.

"Yeah, I guess it is. They're blue and big and you have these incredible long eyelashes that curl up toward the sky. I put on mascara every day trying to get the look you have naturally with those eyelashes."

She latches an elbow around the side of the swing and touches her beautiful, useless eyes. "Keep going."

"Your cheekbones are high, and you have a beauty mark low on your right cheek like a famous model. You can probably feel it." She moves a fingertip down to the spot. "Your lips are tiny and defined. Your hair is perfectly straight and jet-black."

"The only color I know." Her eyes tear.

"I'm sorry," I soothe. "Please don't be upset."

"No. It's the opposite. I'm excited. You've given me a secret mirror."

Kathleen hears the cars arriving before I do. She wipes her eyes and, as I lead her up the hill, hugs me close. The kind of hug that makes you know you're necessary. "I'll always remember you," she whispers.

Being needed instead of needing is a new experience. I like it. A chill runs through me without the temperature changing. I swear it's my mom. This sounds crazy, but the sensation has her personality tied to it.

I go straight from camp to Dr. Jahns. I'm actually looking forward to his opinion on what to do about John, although I try not to show it.

As soon as I sit he digs in, knowing I'm not a fan of small talk. "So how was the movie?"

From his perspective, John is a dream come true. Who better than a high-school sweetheart to wash away a young girl's grief?

"Fine," I say. "I had to sort of dumb myself down to laugh at the right times, but it was good to get out."

"What do you mean 'dumb yourself down'?" He loves questions that include direct quotes. It drives me crazy.

"I don't know, it's hard to see the humor in anything."

He rubs the scruff on his chin. "I know all about human suffering, but I can't imagine a world without humor. It's one of the most important tools we have."

I arch my eyebrows. "If you're right, I'm

262

screwed. Nothing is funny to me anymore."

It's the first time I hear his laugh. He sounds feminine — I can see why he avoids it. "That's your grief talking. Someday you'll remember this conversation and know I'm right."

"I'm glad you're so confident today, because I have an ethical question for you." He straightens his posture, anticipating a breakthrough. "I don't love John," I say. "There's no version of my life where we stay together past August. So is it bad to, like, string him along for company until I don't need him anymore?" Paige thinks it's criminal, but she's biased since John plays soccer with her boys.

Dr. Jahns returns to a slouch. "It's selfish, but it's okay to be selfish sometimes, and, when you leave, I get the impression John will be fine."

Oh goody. Permission granted. I don't miss John, but I'm starting to miss sex.

BRADY

I read the journal entry again before my run. It kept me up last night. I don't know what the hell to do with it.

263

Brady's mother has been gone two years and I only just got around to sifting through her boxes. There's no excuse — she certainly wasn't a pack rat. Aside from the clothes, furniture, and books we gave to charity, movers fit her keepsakes into three cardboard boxes. After the funeral I tucked them on a shelf in the garage, overlooking their contents completely. But I was drawn to them today as I put out the trash. Next thing I knew I was elbow-deep in love letters from a man named Phillip Goldfarb, all dated before Bethany would've met Brady's dad. Love letters . . . stashed away by the least sentimental woman on the planet.

Phil was a soldier who had two children Bethany cared for. There was no mention of a wife or mother, but it was plain that Phil thought of Bethany as more than the kids' caretaker. He described her as "doting," "stunning," and "imaginative."

Bethany was a rigid, soap-in-your-mouth, entertain-yourself breed of mom to Brady. If they weren't among her things and addressed *Dear Bethany* (the same mother-in-law who told me Eve was a homely newborn), I wouldn't have believed it. The last letter was from December of 1959 and had an obituary paper-clipped to it. Phil died in Vietnam. He was survived by two children, Marie and Paul. The article made no mention of their mother. I wonder what happened to them.

My first instinct was to call Brady, but then I realized telling him would be a mistake. He won't notice if the boxes disappear and he'd likely overanalyze the letters. The woman Phil loved did not map to the mother he knew.

Bethany never said a word about what life was like before she married, but it's not as if I asked. I took her as someone who trudged through each day without looking for enjoyment. I figured she got pretty much what she put in. The idea that she was once passionate but was destroyed by grief is tragic.

I take off at a steady pace, questioning how well I've known any of the women in my life. *Left. Right. Left.* My feet sync with my breath. I've stopped taking music. Running has become my daily sounding board, a role Maddy once filled.

My parents married later than most in their day. I was an accident. Mom was forty-six when I was born and often reminded me she was too old and tired for any crap. She was stunning in her prime, but I can't think of a single memory where she was doting or imaginative. There aren't any, I'm sure. The day I got accepted to Harvard she said, "Good luck finding a way to pay for it." Maddy and I often joked that we learned what not to do from our families, but we'd have to figure out the rest on our own.

Everything about my childhood was aloof — no one was drunk all day, but no one tucked me in at night either. I know only the most basic facts about my mother. She deferred to God, even when parenting. She never explained the *why* of anything — whether something was unsafe or impolite or cruel — she just hoped I inherited her fear of the Lord. I remember her grabbing me by the arm on prom night and saying, "God will not forgive you if you get some poor girl pregnant." As if prom was the only night that was a possibility.

What bothers me now, though, as I ruminate, is that I know all my father's opinions from politics to the best fertilizer, but only the most rudimentary facts about my mother. She was a good cook; she liked to sew; she never complained. Never complaining, I recently learned, is different from having no complaints. For all the time I spent with her — eighteen years of daily conversations and another twenty in weekly contact — that's all I can come up with. In the argument over whether knowledge is power or ignorance is bliss, it seems I've always come down on the side of ignorance. And when that's the side you fall on, you don't realize it until it's too late. Maddy, Eve, my mother — the carousel of women I've disappointed. It's as if I'm running because they're chasing me.

I'm almost back to the house when Susan Dundel pops out in one of those skimpy, expensive Lulu-whatever outfits and starts running next to me like we'd arranged it. Maddy's laughter pops into my head and I grin. Susan misinterprets this as an encouraging sign.

"I could tell you wanted companionship out here," she says, matching her pace to mine. "You pass every night, and even sometimes again in the morning, and yesterday I thought, 'You know, there's no reason I couldn't change the time of my run to give poor Brady some company.' "

Poor Brady. My new, least-favorite popular phrase.

"Frankly, Susan, I don't." It's not difficult to shut her down, which says a lot considering I haven't been laid since April. "I'm training for a marathon next month, and I need to do these runs on my own." I say it with authority, but when I look her way to ensure the message was received all I see are her fake breasts flopping with each stride. I immediately lose all credibility.

She giggles. "I know, isn't it horrible? There's not a sports bra made that provides enough support for these things. My ex loved them though. Good for some things, but definitely not working out."

Eve drives by on her way home from therapy right as Susan makes an elaborate gesture to her chest. I shake my head at the bad timing. Susan giggles again. "It's hard for kids to see their parents moving on, but as you get out more, she'll come around. My son flipped the first time a man spent the night after the divorce, but now he's good about it. He'll eat breakfast with a smile on his face no matter who I bring home." She winks.

Her pride at that statement brings me to a halt. "Listen, I'm not moving on and I prefer to run alone." She jogs in place as I walk away.

When I get to the house, I brace myself

for a sassy comment about Susan, but it's immediately apparent Eve has her own agenda in mind. Something is up — the kitchen is too clean, Alicia Keys is playing, and I smell rack of lamb, my favorite, in the oven.

"Why don't you tell me what you want," I quip, "so we can enjoy dinner without me wondering how much it's gonna cost."

Eve gives an innocent smile. "I don't want anything."

"Sure you don't." I grab an ankle to stretch my quad. I'm up to fourteen miles on my long-distance days.

"Really, I just need to, um, tell you about something I did."

My stomach tightens. Money is a quick fix. There are plenty of teenage mistakes that don't have a fix at all. "What?"

"Time-out . . . first I have a question. Is there anything I could do that would result in you not paying for college?"

I run through the list of things that engulf parents' nightmares: drugs, stealing, eating disorders, pregnancy. I carefully word my response. "No, I've committed to that, but there are things that could delay going."

"Like what?"

"I don't know, Eve. Like if you need time to take responsibility for your actions. Or get help."

"I'm not pregnant, Dad," she says with a laugh.

"Jesus, Eve, this isn't a fun game. What already?"

"I got a tattoo," she blurts.

I hadn't considered that possibility. "*What*? When? Why would you —"

"Three days ago. 'Cause last week I was at Rory's mom's funeral, and Rory was saying how after her father died she did something symbolic to help her move on."

She crosses her arms as though that explains everything, when in fact it leaves me with more questions. I didn't know Eve left the house last weekend, or that she was close enough with her math tutor to attend a family funeral. But I'm not about to get distracted.

"Am I missing something? That doesn't equate to being seventeen and getting a tattoo. Is that even legal?"

"It's small."

"That's all you have to say? It's small? *Damn it,* Eve, it's permanent."

She tries again. "It's symbolic."

"So are lots of things that don't come with a lifetime commitment. *Christ.* Did you stop to think about what it will look like when you're my age? Or what you'll tell your grandchildren?"

Her head slumps to her chest. We wait to see who'll speak first. It's a game I usually lose, but not this time. I've given this day all I have to offer. A full minute passes.

"It's that quote you said Mom liked," she murmurs. "About learning from pain."

My daughter could earn a degree in surprising me. "You *tattooed* that quotation to your body? Where?"

"On the right side of my stomach, by my hip. I can hide it, even in a bathing suit, even in a bikini."

I have her show me. It's written in plain, black script. As tattoos go, it isn't that bad. I try to keep a stern face, hiding my relief, but my second thought makes me laugh.

"What's funny?"

"I'm picturing how it will balloon out unevenly when you're pregnant someday."

"*Huh.* I didn't think of that."

I point a finger at her. "That's why you should've involved me *before*hand."

She bites her lower lip. "Am I in trouble?"

I read the quotation plastered to my daughter's abdomen. *If we could learn to learn from pain even as it grasps us.* The answer comes to me. "No," I say. "You're the one that has to live with it. But don't go showing it off like it's cool. It's not. And don't do anything this over-the-top for a while. You've hit your reckless teenage behavior quota for the year."

Eve produces a closed-mouth smile she learned from Maddy. It was my wife's I-won-but-I'm-not-going-to-rub-it-in-since-you're-being-a-good-sport face.

"Did it hurt?" I ask.

"Like a bitch," she says, forgetting to filter. A hand flies to her mouth. "Sorry."

I think back to the drink on the Fourth of July and shake my head. Maddy can't kill herself and still make all the parenting decisions. "No, you know what, don't be. Swearing was your mother's battle, not mine."

"Really?"

I don't know why I chose to take a stand on this particular point. I backpedal slightly, "As long as it's used intelligently relative to the discussion, I'm fine with it."

"All right. I'll intelligently swear my ass off from now on."

I massage my temples. When will I learn to shut the hell up?

Chapter Eleven

MADELINE

Watching, always watching, I'm reminded of a conversation I had with Meg about whether to become a stay-at-homer. It was what Brady wanted. Of his buddies from Harvard, he was the only one with a working wife. I admired his brain while we dated; it wasn't until Eve arrived that I understood it was powerful enough to put me out of a job. I never intended to march in the footsteps of a mother I pitied at best, but Brady's success and Eve's neediness beat the ambition right out of me. I was certain I could avoid my mother's weaknesses. Depression never had a grip on me, and alcohol was like a fun cousin I visited once in a while but never planned a trip around. That its tentacles are often invisible until it's too late never crossed my mind.

Part of my hem and haw was that people counted on my effort to hit the annual number. Without me, my team wouldn't get a bonus. My sister in her I-can't-believe-I'm-younger-than-you voice said, "I find that arrogant, Maddy. Everyone is replaceable. People are, by nature, resourceful and resilient." She was right. I left Viking, and yet people still found their way to stores across New England to buy overpriced refrigerators and ovens.

I wish the truth of her wisdom would show itself once again, but replacing a sales manager is different from replacing a primary parent. Brady is a bulldozer; he sees only what's directly in front of him. For the past two months, with my persuasion, that's been Eve, but now he's craving a release, something of his own, and his attention has shifted to qualifying for the Boston Marathon. My ability to influence is waning. He's a man obsessed. He has retreated inward, at the expense of our daughter who was just starting to come around.

As he runs, he vacillates between being angry with me for abandoning the privileged life he provided and being at war with himself for not being more present while I was there. He's as astounded my priority wasn't ultimately them as he is horrified to realize his priority was never us. His internal battle is ironic because in death I have finally found clarity on the subject: Brady attempted to engage at home; I'm the one who pushed him away.

When we first married, Brady did little things to help like set the table, stop at the grocery store on his way home, or comically chop onions wearing sunglasses for protection. On several occasions he offered to cook, simple things like burgers or salad, but still, he offered. I always found fault in his approach. In my mind, I could have done it better, faster, cheaper, and so I did. Eventually, he settled for a few simple household duties like putting on music, taking out trash, and lighting winter fires. We joked they were safe chores. *Brady-proof*, he called them.

I encouraged this self-deprecation. I hadn't intended to be a stay-at-home-mom, but as soon as I walked down that path my domestic instincts took over. I bartered to only be a homemaker if I could be some kind of holy matriarch, the homemaker of homemakers. My mother had approached her days with the detachment of a minimum-wage employee denied overtime. I was going to prove motherhood was more than that. In my lofty execution of creating an emotionally sound, intellectually stimulating, health-conscious home, I left my husband very little room to prove himself. To an unwholesome degree, it was important to me he be inferior at home. He had enough to hang his hat on at the office. I needed a stage.

What I'm saying is, Brady had no training for the pool he's been tossed into. He's selfish because, as Eve got older, he became an outlier in the household. The two of us lovingly, but relentlessly, teased him. We didn't mean anything by it. He was a chief executive at a Fortune 500 company! He was living the life I'd sacrificed, or at least that's often how it felt. I didn't understand that our needling had worked its way into his core and convinced him of his domestic incompetence.

I continue trying to build his self-confidence with Eve through positive interactions, but that strategy is slow going and my surges upward continue. Time is limited. I need Rory to step in before I ascend too high to help.

It's Rory and Eve's first session since Linda's funeral, and chapter four looks to be as boring as chapters one through three. About halfway through they break for a soda. Rory notices the whiteboard Brady hastily hung to document phone calls and whereabouts after learning Eve attended a random funeral. Today it reads: *Insurance guy called to say our house is no longer covered and no one is returning his calls.* Brady read it on his way out this morning with a grunt. I managed that stuff. It was a detail I always threw out at holiday parties because his colleagues found it entertaining that the CFO didn't manage his own finances. From Brady's perspective, he dealt with that shit all day and deserved a break. From my perspective . . . *well* . . . no one ever asked my perspective, and once you take on an undesirable marital job it's yours till death do you part. A small part of me will enjoy watching him get quotes today. He'll have no idea whether we live in a flood zone, if the foundation is a slab, the year the house was built, or any of the other random tidbits he'll need. On certain matters I'll always be missed.

"Did you get to the practice problems?" Rory asks, recapturing my attention.

"Un-huh," Eve says. *Your tattoo,* I remind her. She takes a bag of chips from the pantry. "Oh, so I took your advice and did something symbolic to celebrate my mom."

Rory smiles. "Wonderful. What?"

"I got a tattoo."

Rory puts her Pepsi down (I love that she

277

doesn't drink diet) and studies Eve's expression to gauge whether she's serious. "Well, for heaven's sake, Eve, that's not what I meant."

"My mom didn't like ballroom dancing."

Rory snorts. "But she was into permanent body art?"

"The tattoo is symbolic of her. See?" Eve lifts the corner of her shirt. Rory reads her stomach, reluctantly fascinated.

"Hmm. That's a beautiful saying."

"Isn't it?" Eve's posture inflates with the compliment.

"Where did you come across it?"

"My mom," she says without further explanation.

Rory wonders if I wrote it in a suicide note. "That's going to inflate funny when you're pregnant," she points out.

"What is it with old people and obsessing about pregnancy?"

Rory laughs. "Gee, thanks. Can I ask what other 'old people' you're clumping me in with?"

"Just my dad."

She winces. "Oh, dear. What'd he say about the tattoo?"

"That a tattoo wasn't what you meant."

Rory's eyes expand. "You told your father *I* told you to do it?"

"No, of course not. You didn't. I just told him about our conversation, and-and that it . . . well . . . inspired me. Anyway, he called to say he's getting off work early, so he can finally meet you in person this afternoon."

Of course, after all my effort, it's Eve's tattoo that sparks their introduction.

"What?" Rory looks alarmed.

"He's not mad. I mean, he doesn't blame you or anything. I think he was a little weirded out I went to your mom's funeral, and I guess he wants to introduce himself since I talk about you sometimes."

Rory sighs, reaching back for the calculus book. "I haven't had to meet a parent who thinks I'm a bad influence in a long time. Could we at least finish this chapter so I can attempt to rebuild my reputation."

Brady arrives right before their time is up. Rory stands to greet him with a self-conscious wave. She's in lightweight jeans and a white V-neck cotton shirt with a braided belt. Her hair is pulled back with a pink and brown polka dot scarf revealing simple diamond studs on each ear. I'm not claiming love at first sight, but he definitely *notices* her.

"So you're the infamous Rory Murray."

Rory tucks her chin toward her shoulder,

mortified. "I had no intention of being *infa-mous*. Eve told me about her interpretation of our talk last week."

Brady chuckles with more levity than he feels. "Yes, well, what can you do?"

"Glad there's no hard feelings."

He shakes his head. "This sounds crazy, but you look familiar."

"I was so hoping you wouldn't piece it together," she says, laughing. "You saw me trip and fall at CVS a few months ago."

Brady smiles. "That's *right*! That was you."

"The one who falls always remembers the witnesses."

Brady runs a hand through his hair. "Can I admit something terrible?" *No,* I coach. *Don't.* But he's such a Boy Scout he can't help himself. "I'm the jackass who left the basket in the aisle."

Why? Why? Why? She never would've known. All my work and — *wait.* She's laughing. Hard. I would have been mad, but Rory is laughing.

"You totally pawned it off on someone else!" she says.

He slaps his palm to his chest. "I know. That was awful. It happened so fast and the words flew out of me and . . . honestly, I didn't think I'd ever see you again."

"But here we are."

280

"Here we are."

Eve is equal parts fascinated and horrified by what appears to be her father flirting. She hands Rory a check. While they confirm their next session, I question Brady on whether he knows enough about Rory given Eve's clear attachment. *Keep her close,* I coach, working my agenda. It isn't difficult to coerce him.

"Listen, I'm heading out for a run," he says, "but I'd love if you'd join us for dinner next Wednesday."

Rory steps back, put out by the idea that she's being asked on a date in front of Eve, but relaxes when I convey Brady's intent. He's a single parent. His daughter went to a random funeral for the mother of a woman he's never met, then got a tattoo based on her words of wisdom. It's not a date. It's an interview. Rory accepts the invitation.

Hopefully Brady takes this interview a little less formally than ones at the office. I'd like Rory to have a fighting chance and Brady to not come across as a complete ass, if that's at all possible. Rory seems to have a knack for bringing out his lighthearted side, a gift I never had.

EVE

My relationship with John is the equivalent of a brother and sister stuck on family vacation. Dad has more of a bond with my math tutor than I have with my boyfriend.

I made the mistake of telling John I sometimes sense my mother watching me. I meant it generally, but he thinks of it every time our clothes are off. Nothing like doing it with a guy who's totally wigged out. I tried to point out she wouldn't care anyway, but he stopped me mid-sentence, which was probably for the best.

I think John thought if we tortured each other a little longer we'd eventually end up back to normal. Or maybe he assumed he could bring me back to life, even though I wasn't interested in being revived. Either way, he was wrong and he knows it. If his father hadn't forbidden him to date me, he would've ended it already. Are there any parents out there who learned anything from *Romeo and Juliet*? Hello? Pay attention. Shakespeare knew his shit.

Every night starts the same freaking way. John says, "Do you want to go to the party at so-and-so's?" Tonight everyone is at Doug's.

I say, "No, but you can. We can get together tomorrow or whatever."

He turns on a pathetic voice. "I'm not going without you."

It's like dating a rash. "So I guess you're not gonna go, but I really don't mind if you do."

Eventually I pick him up at whatever friend's house is his cover story. My long wait in the driveway makes it obvious the short stint before I arrive is the highlight of his night. When he finally shows, I endure a full gossip rundown, as if I care. Tonight Jake dumping Kara is the headline.

"She's been showing up already wasted and ends every night bawling or puking. It's nasty."

"Oh."

"I don't blame Jake for being over her, but he was a dick about it. He's telling everyone if he wanted to date a lightweight he'd find a freshman."

"Oh."

"Kara's been a shit show, but she's obviously going through something."

I roll my eyes. "Whatever."

There's nothing Kara could possibly be going through that trumps what I'm going through. John is silenced by my indifference. I can't tell if he gets it or thinks I've turned into a raging bitch, but I know he's miserable, and I don't have space in my head or heart to care.

I wait until the movie ends and the TV is off to say, "I guess we should stop pretending this is working."

"Yeah." For the amount of emotion in the room I might as well have said, "Pass the Doritos."

"I know things changed when your mom died, but it doesn't have to stay different forever," he says after a minute.

I bite my lip. "I don't miss it the way you think I do. I'm not, like, sinking into depression. I just have different priorities."

"I wish I was one of them."

"Me too."

In some ways I mean it. There are times when I would return to my old self-absorbed existence if I could. It was easier being clueless. But I don't think a person can go back like that. Now that I see a bigger picture, how can I possibly hang out and stare at the little one?

John stands to leave and I remember I'm his ride. I've always sucked at timing. We drive with the radio loud to cover up the fact that there's nothing left to say. After getting out of the car, John hangs over the open door. "You know she loved you, right?" It takes me a second to process the pronoun — *she* not *I*. I can't speak without crying so I just sit there, looking straight ahead. "It wasn't your fault," he says before shutting the door.

I hold my breath until he turns toward his house, then I bawl. I might not be the reason she jumped, but I wasn't enough to keep her here. I was an afterthought to her, when she was my everything.

The bell dings for the third time of the day, marking the end of the last camp session.

It's weird to put words to, but I'm grateful the accident happened because it brought me to this place, where five hours a day I focused on other people's problems instead of my own. I'm probably the first person on the planet who'll miss mandatory community service.

Robin calls everyone to the parking lot to share a camp highlight. I make my way to Kathleen so we can walk together. "I smell you coming, Eve," she says.

"If anyone else said that, I'd take it as an insult." She laughs.

"Okey dokey," Robin says, once the wheelchairs and children have been maneuvered into a misshapen circle. "Who wants to kick things off?"

Kathleen's arm shoots in the air as she shouts, "Eve was the best part of camp this year!" A bunch of other kids nod and clap. My heart flutters. Maybe I'll be a teacher. I can almost picture it — reaching out to kids who are struggling, like Rory has to me. The thought freezes me: It's the first time I've considered a future without my mom in it.

The circle moves clockwise from Kathleen. The other four delinquents pass on sharing to Robin's visible relief. When it comes back around to me, I pause, thinking of all the things I wish I'd said to my mom when I had the chance. I don't want to keep living a life where I pass.

"I came here hoping I could be of help," I say, "but you all ended up helping me."

"What a perfect reflection to end our two weeks together," Robin says. "Time for a group hug."

That first day I would've been distracted by the kids' disabilities and assumed a group hug impossible, but now I link arms with Kathleen, and we fan out to the people on either side, me scooching down to Hanna's wheelchair, careful not to catch the ventilator tubes, and Kathleen linking arms with a boy using a walking brace.

The energy in the circle is indescribable — there is power in the act of us all leaning on each other. I can feel it.

An impatient parent beeps the horn, ending the moment. I herd the kids where they need to be, amazed that I know every parent by name.

Once the campers are gone, Robin jogs to me in the parking lot with her huge smile and famous clipboard. "Any interest in signing up for next year?"

"Sure thing." I write my name on the top line of an otherwise blank list.

"You surprised us all, Eve. The first day everyone was skeptical, but a voice in my head told me to stick it out, and you grew into it. Camp Ray needed help and you delivered."

"I needed Camp Ray too," I admit for a second time.

She puts her sacred clipboard on the ground and wraps an arm around my shoulder in a half hug. "I had a pretty crappy hand dealt to me too," she says. "Nothing cures a chip on the shoulder like giving back goodness."

I've wondered all summer if Robin knew my story; I guess that answers my question. We hug right there in the middle of the parking lot.

I can't stop thinking about my mother. If she loved Phillip so much, why didn't they marry? What happened to those kids? Why did she love them as her own when they weren't? Why couldn't she love me when I was? Her secrecy compels me to learn more about the story.

I let Eve in on it, forking over the journal entry about her grandmother's mysterious life. Maddy used to say the key to earning respect is vulnerability. "It's easier to admire people who put themselves out there," she explained. I didn't challenge her at the time, but in the business world you earn respect with killer execution. Now I see that while Maddy's strategy wouldn't work in an office setting, mine sure as hell doesn't work on Eve. So I put myself out there, hoping Eve will take comfort in the idea that my mom had skeletons too.

Her eyes illuminate with intrigue. I've been unwittingly living with a CIA agent. I laugh as she dives in, scanning a copy of the journal entry, saying she'll have "a lead" by the time I get back from my run. And she actually does, sort of. I return, dripping sweat, to a bombardment of questions.

"Where was Grandma born?"

"Virginia."

"And she lived there her whole life?"

"Far as I know." Which turns out isn't much . . .

"What year did your parents marry?"

My jaw slackens. "Let's see, Dad was twenty-eight, so that'd mean they were . . . married in . . . 1962."

"That was kind of slow for a CFO," she jokes.

"I'm not the one getting tutored in math."

She crosses her arms. "You say it like I'm getting tutored 'cause I failed a class. I'm getting tutored to get a year ahead in one summer."

"Touché," I concede. "Now what, Detective?"

"Well, there's a surprising number of Goldfarbs out there and we can't assume they're still in Virginia, but I found this site where you pay a fee to look up the U.S. Public Records Index. That's all the information we would need. Should I do it?"

"How much does it cost?"

"Two hundred dollars."

I whistle. "That's steep." Truthfully, I enjoy seeing her interested in something. As my running stamina improves, I have less and less time at the house, so we've barely spoken all week. "Do you think we should do it?"

"I do. I mean, Grandma was always so sad. I'd love to meet people who knew her differently." It's fascinating Eve remembers my mother as sad; Maddy and I always referred to her as cold. Kids are in a unique position to be perceptive — life hasn't muddied their take yet.

Eve keeps on her sales pitch. "And who knows? Maybe we'll connect with Marie and Paul. I mean, they're not really family, but beggars can't be choosers."

I try not to be offended. "Who's begging?"

"You know what I mean. Aside from Aunt Meg, Lucy, and Uncle Dan, it's just us. I always used to daydream about having a big family."

Her words punch me. "You did? Mom and I thought you'd hate sharing attention. It was one of the things that softened the blow of —" I hesitate to finish the sentence, but if I want a real relationship with Eve, I have to be real. She's seventeen. "You know, I don't think we ever told you this, but we couldn't have more kids."

The memory comes with a giant *what if* . . .

We wanted more. When Eve turned two, we started trying. When she was three, we went to a specialist — shot after shot, temperature-taking after testing after tears. It broke my heart each month when Maddy announced our failure, which she perceived as her failure. By the time we were ready to consider adoption, Eve was almost six and we were settled into our lifestyle. Maddy regretted that decision later. *Shortsighted,* she called it. I wonder how it would've changed things if we had an eleven-year-old right now. Would Maddy still be gone? Was there not enough keeping her here?

"Good thing it didn't work out," Eve says, answering my unspoken question. "Could you imagine if we were stuck raising a kid right now?" Talk about the devil's advocate. Does that make Eve a pessimist or a realist?

"Let's check into this thing, Dad. If nothing else, we'll learn more about Grandma."

"Okay." She takes my credit card and I head to the shower.

When I return to the kitchen for dinner, Eve has a match. Not right away, but by searching under different variations, she found an Anna Marie Watson born January 3, 1952, at Providence Hospital in Washington, D.C., to Sandra Watson and Phillip Goldfarb. Eve called information, but there was no one by that name in the greater D.C. area.

I think of Bobby. His brother is in the FBI. Maybe he could dig something up. I can tell Eve is pleased with my resourcefulness, so I call him right then, with her by my side. I'm racking up brownie points on this one.

"I've been meaning to call you, Brady," Bobby says after a quick hello. I can tell by the drag of his words that he's a few beers in.

"Oh, yeah?"

"Yeah, I'm a real asshole, you know that?"

"Yeah, Bobby, me too. Listen, I'm calling for a favor."

"Anything, man. You're my best friend. I never tell you that, but it's true. And I'm sorry about Madel—"

I cut him off with the reason for my call. He's confused why I care since we aren't biologically related, but agrees to look into it and get back to me. It doesn't sound promising, but Eve is happy, so I'm happy.

It hits me that she's probably been lonely. I've been neglecting her again. Maybe I can forgive myself for holding back in relationships with my mother and wife if I can salvage the one with my daughter. It's certainly better than going zero for three.

Chapter Twelve

Madeline

It's bizarre to watch Brady, Rory, and Eve seated at my dining-room table, the tableau of a happy family. I have to remind myself I wanted this.

Eve shows off by setting the table with linens and candlelight, serving baked salmon with a lemon caper sauce, and using random curse words in her stories. She's playing the part of the hostess, treating Rory as a peer now that she doesn't relate to her high-school friends. Both Brady and Rory allow the performance — Brady because there's a guest in the house and Rory because she understands why Eve is doing it.

I pester Brady's subconscious with carnal thoughts. I start simple, saying things like *She's beautiful* and *I wonder if she's attached,* but eventually my dark humor kicks in and I funnel down things like *Don't you want to see her naked?* and *Try not to get a hard-on in front of your daughter.* He's alarmed by this internal chatter, but chalks it up to not having sex in so long.

"So, how's calculus going?" Brady asks as everyone sits down. He looks sharp. I lured him into wearing his best-fitting dark jeans with a gray button-down shirt. He wouldn't remove his wedding ring, but he did brush the gel from his hair, giving him a softer, more casual air.

"Great," Rory answers when Eve doesn't. "I think we'll finish by the end of the month, which is no small task."

"Can we please not talk about it?" Eve sulks. "Sorry, but taking a class during the summer is a pain in the ass."

Brady isn't looking for a fight. "Fine," he agrees. "Rory, are you originally from the area?"

She smiles before answering and the whole room relaxes. Rory's smile is as contagious as a long yawn. "Yes. *Well* . . . Boston. But I went out west to Pepperdine for school, and lived there until about ten years ago."

The house phone rings. Brady gets up to answer it while Rory and Eve distribute food. They hear him going back and forth with whoever is on the line, but can't make

294

out any details until the end when, in a voice loud enough to infer he's talking over someone, Brady says, "Christie, I understand you're worried, but *of course* I'm sure. I'd know if Kara was at my house."

He reenters the dining room shaking his head. "Eve, you don't know where Kara Anderson is, right?"

Eve laughs — she hasn't seen Kara since the last day of school — but I worry. Given the circumstances of our last interaction, I momentarily ditch my family to make sure she's okay. I focus my energy until I find her alone on a dock at her aunt and uncle's cabin north of the city. There's a fifth of Captain Morgan propped against her side, but she's subdued. She won't do anything but pass out and be hunted by mosquitoes tonight. I leave her and return to the most important dinner party of my death.

Brady sends Eve a decisive look of warning in response to whatever happened during my absence. "Where were we?" he says, recharging the conversation. "Oh yeah, Pepperdine in southern California. Beautiful area, especially this time of year. Do you miss it?"

"Not so much."

Brady chuckles at her unexpected negativity. Rory is someone you expect to deliver only sunshine and roses. It's why I picked her. "I enjoyed it while I was there, but I'm a New Englander at heart. I came back to be closer to my family, and I'm thankful for the time I had with my parents. My brother is here too, so that's good. Well, mostly." She winks at Eve, who is happy to be in on the joke. "What about you, where are you from?"

Eve, looking for a way into the conversation, answers on Brady's behalf. "We've lived in Massachusetts my entire life. It gets duller every year. I plan to go away for college though. Maybe Texas."

Brady puts his fork down and looks at Eve, trying to gauge how serious she is. "I didn't know that," he says, unable to hide his disappointment.

"Well, you still have time to think about it," Rory intervenes. "Apply widely. That way you'll have choices. I remember wanting to go to Florida, but my mom convinced me the hurricanes would be a nightmare. When I got to California, I discovered earthquakes. There are advantages and disadvantages to every location."

"And Boston is rich with options," Brady says. "I don't know if you'd agree, Rory, but I was envious of people who were a car ride from home, especially on the weekends when I needed to do laundry." His obvious sales pitch gives Eve another opportunity to be controversial. She ignores my guidance to stand down.

"I'm surprised you're so totally emotional about the idea of Texas. I thought you'd enjoy the space. Then you could go for long runs with Mrs. Dundel or whatever."

Of all the times for Eve to bring up what she thought she saw three weeks ago, I cannot believe she picked tonight. It's sabotage. If only I had more recourses at my disposal. I wouldn't mind zapping her with a bout of explosive diarrhea to get Brady and Rory some time alone.

Brady takes the heat well, calmly wiping his mouth with his napkin. "I don't go for runs with Susan Dundel, first of all, and more importantly, I'm going to miss you a lot when you leave for New Hampshire in September, not to mention college next year." He tenses his lips to not tear up.

"I bet you didn't think you'd be saying that two months ago." Eve tries to pull it off as a joke, but her bitchy tone transmits hostility, making it easier for Brady to suppress his rising emotions. Our girl is on a mission to be memorable.

I've seen her this petulant only once before, about a year ago. She'd invited a handful of friends over after a tennis match, including two very popular seniors. They were hungry and wanted pizza, so Eve screamed for me from the kitchen. When I appeared — which I only did because I thought something was gravely wrong — she told me, with assumed authority, to "get your credit card because everyone is starving." I told her to meet me in the living room, alone. When she got there, without the comfort of her army present, she apologized before I even spoke. I had her send the friends home and go to her room. That was the end of that.

Brady responds more subtly to Eve's rebellion. "There certainly have been a lot of changes in our lives lately." He pauses to sip his wine. "I understand that's true for you too, Rory. I was sorry to hear about your recent loss." Rory offers a closed-mouth smile and quiet *thank you.* "Eve said it was a beautiful service."

"I hope so. My mother certainly deserved one. It was sweet of Eve to attend."

The conversation is too personal for a first-time dinner guest, so Brady defuses it by asking Rory what grade she teaches. He has an extraordinary talent for controlling conversations. He explained to me once that people mistakenly presume the person talking is in control. "It's the one asking the questions, Maddy. That's who's running the show."

The discussion rolls back to normal with Brady at the reins. He learns a little about Rory — she loves to read, swim, and eat Indian food — and *a lot* about his daughter. Continuing in her spirited frame of mind, Eve is uncharacteristically forthcoming. She tells them both about camp, how good it felt to be needed and how the experience changed her career aspirations. She talks about breaking up with John, which is news to Brady, declaring that they "no longer see the world from the same point of view." She then shares her excitement for school in the fall, claiming it "cannot come soon enough."

Rory registers Brady's hurt and graciously asks whether Eve plans to come home on the weekends. "Probably, to check up on my dad," she says. "I mean, I only got him to start eating dinner again like a month ago."

Brady is visibly injured by Eve's admission to the mere acquaintance sitting across from him. He's unable to rebound a fourth time. He stands. "Well, it's been a great night, ladies, but it's late."

Rory stands too. "I'm so glad we did this," she says, extending a hand. Their touch is soft, comfortable. "Thank you for having me." There's something playful about her, like she's too cute to be a grown-up.

"Thanks for coming." They lock eyes briefly before he turns to Eve. "Good night," he says, not hiding his agitation.

"Night," she replies, unabashed by her behavior. They both like Rory, but they didn't seem to like each other in her presence.

Rory stays to help with kitchen cleanup.

"Sorry about my dad," Eve says. "He bails a lot lately."

I nudge Rory to defend him. It doesn't take much; she respects Brady. "Your father did nothing wrong," she says, setting down the dishrag. She almost stops there, but I push her further. "The thing is, Eve, it's easy to see that it's wrong to be judgmental when you're the one being judged, but harder when you're sitting with the jury. Everyone grieves differently. Some want to be left alone, some want to be insanely busy, some gain weight, some lose weight, and some don't change their eating habits at all. It's not fair to critique people's reaction. I lost a lot by taking too long to learn that."

Eve can't catch the words before they're out. "You mean after your daughter died?"

Rory is surprised — it was a long time

ago on a different coast — but doesn't ask how Eve knows. "Yeah," she admits. "After Emma, I assumed my husband blamed me for what happened, but he didn't blame me. *I* blamed me. And I pushed him away. He just missed her, same as me, same as everyone, but I turned it into a personal attack. I've seen mourning bring people closer, but only when they both accept that on any given day the loss feels different."

Eve's posture relaxes. The teenage arrogance on display all night attenuates. "I guess I shouldn't have said that, about my dad's eating and stuff."

"If you wish you hadn't said it, you should tell him that," Rory says, turning to the door. Eve lights up at Rory's words, knowing it's the exact response I'd have offered. Ever since Paige handed her that Butterfinger, Eve is on the lookout for my messengers.

"Do you still miss Emma?" She wants so badly for Rory to say no, that time really has healed the wound. From Rory, Eve might believe it.

Rory knows what Eve is fishing for — she remembers asking more tenured grievers the same question — but she won't set a false expectation. "Every single day," she whispers. "It's there, and it hurts, but it

does become . . . I don't know . . . *familiar.*"
Rory slings her bag over her shoulder and
extends her arms in a timid hug. "Thanks
for tonight. You and your dad are wonderful
people."

EVE

Today would've been my mother's birthday.
The word *bittersweet* comes to mind.
There's a part of me, the part Dr. Jahns
refers to as exceptional, which can't help
but love August second. It's the day she arrived; the day her life was celebrated every
year; a day she looked forward to, at least
when she was younger. But there's another
part of me that resents the day and its
forgotten importance to most people. For
those who do remember, her birthday now
marks the end of her life instead of the
beginning. She died at forty-five. Every year
I'll think of it that way: *She would've been
forty-six or forty-seven or forty-eight today.*
Her birthday left with her.

What really makes me feel like shit is how
little we celebrated the years she was here.
Sick as it is, this is the most attention I've
ever given her birthday. Last year we went
out to dinner. I gave her a card I filled out
on the way there, literally behind her back,
as if she didn't know what I was doing. We

302

ate at Dad's favorite steakhouse where Mom always ordered whatever fish was the special. How did we miss that that meant she didn't care for anything on the menu? For a present I bought her one of those prepackaged spa baskets from the grocery store. She never used it, as I should've known she wouldn't, since she didn't like products with heavy fragrance. She never wore perfume, used only unscented deodorant, and bought fragrance-free laundry detergent. Yet damn-near-genius Eve Starling got her a basket full of peach extreme soaps, bubble bath, and lotion. My mom didn't even take baths. I only ever saw her use the tub to soak our dirty white laundry in bleach. The basket is still wrapped in cellophane, shoved in the back of her bathroom cabinet. How did she hide her disappointment?

I can't remember what I got her the year before that, but my father was out of town. I heard her crying that night. She'd told him the business trip was no big deal; work is work. But when the day came, she was bummed. Paige took her out to lunch because her twins share the same birthday, so that night it was just Mom and me. She made a simple soup, nothing fancy, and immediately after we ate she retreated to her room with a glass of wine. The next morning I noticed the bottle was gone. I didn't think to make a cake or anything. I never told my dad how sad she was, and he never asked. I wonder if he's as angry with himself for taking the business trip as I am for giving her a thoughtless card and crappy present, but we're avoiding each other. This is a day we'll suffer through alone.

As I think about everything I didn't do for her birthday, I'm reminded of everything she did do for mine. I had celebrations that took place everywhere from hibachi restaurants to amusement parks, and ended in slumber parties with like ten girls running around the house. I don't remember my dad being there, although I'm sure he was, but my mom is in every birthday memory I have. Taking pictures, cooking, cleaning, doing my hair, carrying presents, making gift lists for thank-you notes, picking up wrapping paper, finding batteries, driving kids home, ordering cakes, lighting candles, singing "Happy Birthday" . . .

And every year, on the day after my birthday, when all evidence of chaos was magically cleared away except for one or two helium balloons floating around the house, my mother would ask what I wished for. Once, I think after I turned ten, I said I wouldn't tell her because I wanted it to come true. "Whispering it only to me," she replied, "is your best chance." She winked as she said it, but I didn't get the joke until I recalled the conversation today. She was right; she made my wishes come true. And I got her a shitty peach extreme gift basket.

I've been making stupid mistakes all day, like squeezing body lotion onto my toothbrush and shutting off the car while it's still in drive. If I weren't so totally depressed I'd find it funny how your brain can completely shut down. When the phone rings, I stupidly answer without checking caller ID or processing the fact that I have no desire to talk to anyone. It's Aunt Meg. Of course. Our chats have been strained since my birthday, but she sounds grateful when I answer. "I've been thinking about you all day, sweetie. How are you holding up?"

"I don't know what to feel. I'm thinking about her death more than her life, and I hate myself for it."

I wait for a serving of unhelpful advice. *Take a run. Get a manicure. Have a friend over.* Something positive. Instead, she says, "I owe you an apology, Eve. Before, on the other calls and even when I was in town for the funeral, I wanted to make this better for you. Your mother could always do that for me. No matter what it was, she fixed it. I figured you'd be used to someone in that role, and I thought that someone could be me. I see now that I can't solve this for you, or me for that matter." She lets out a disturbed laugh. "You know what I did last week? I can't believe I'm telling you this, but whatever, something inside tells me you need to hear it . . . I intentionally rear-ended the car in front of me."

I can't believe she's telling me either. I ask the obvious question of why.

"It's not what I told the police — I said something about leaning to stretch my back and my foot slipping — but the truth is, I had an overwhelming urge to hit the damn thing. It looked at me like a target, like something that'd be great to smash." She sighs. "The horrible part is that it did feel great, for a couple seconds. I was in control, and you know how I love to be in control. And afterward, when the crazies wore off, I realized something: We all have to forge our own path in dealing with your mother's death. The path you take isn't, and probably shouldn't be, the same as mine. I mean, I certainly don't want you out there instigating traffic accidents." Her voice cracks. "I'm sorry it took me so long to figure that out."

I recall what Rory said the other night. *On*

any given day the loss feels different. "I'm sorry too, for my birthday. I know how close you guys were, and I had no right to say my pain was worse or whatever. It's just such a nightmare."

"It truly is."

Her confession and apology give me courage to ask a bold question. "Aunt Meg, do you feel appreciated?"

"Appreciated how?"

"By Uncle Dan and Lucy."

"Sure I do. We all love each other. You know that."

"Yeah, but knowing someone loves you and feeling appreciated are two different things, right? I've been thinking about it. My mom knew she was loved. I know it. So why'd she do it? That's the big, impossible question. But I'm beginning to think it had something to do with, like, the gap between being loved versus feeling appreciated, and I'm wondering if it's different for you since you have a job?"

The line goes so quiet I think she hung up. "Aunt Meg?"

She clears her throat. "These are tough questions, Eve, and my answer probably isn't as clear-cut as you're hoping for. First off, your mom had a bigger job than I have in a lot of ways. When things don't go

307

perfectly in our house, I'm more forgiving of myself because I can hide behind the to-do list of my career. Your mom . . . well . . . she didn't feel like she had an excuse for her household to be anything short of perfect.

"Now, do I feel like Dan and Lucy appreciate, or even comprehend, every thing I accomplish in a day? No, I don't. But I probably don't appreciate every thing they do either. And I don't need them to understand every sacrifice; neither did your mother. We talked about it a lot, actually. Your mom told me once that she gets enough nuggets. That's what she called them, *nuggets.* What she meant was, and I agree, we get these moments of validation from our family, and it's enough. I think —"

"But it wasn't enough. My dad shows me some of her journal, and there are whole sections where she talks about how no one noticed this or that, or no one asked her opinion. I'm telling you, she was *pissed.* A lot."

I'm taking a risk saying this. Dad never shows me anything negative. I don't even think he's read the ones where Mom questions whether she did enough to help Gram, or the creepy one where she imagines what her life would be like if she hadn't quit her job. But I think I'm safe because Dad and Aunt Meg haven't spoken since the funeral. It's like they both blame each other.

"*Pfft.* She was venting. Big deal. I'm sure your diary has all kinds of stuff about your mother that you didn't mean generally, stuff you wrote in the thick of it. I found a note last year in one of Lucy's pockets when I was doing the laundry. It said, 'My mom is such a bitch. She won't let me go Saturday because she gets some weird high off torturing me.' "

"Eek. What did Lucy say?"

"I didn't talk to her about it. Your mom advised me not to. She said, 'Come on, Meg, what do you expect Lucy to say to her friends? *My mom won't let me go because there's no parental supervision, and she loves me too much to put me in such a high-risk situation.* No. But that doesn't mean she doesn't know it's the truth.' And she was right. You have to take everything you read in that journal in the context of the moment she wrote it. She was writing for herself, so she could process things. She was an adult who spoke her mind. When things got pushed too far, when she felt squeezed or unappreciated, I guarantee she spoke up to your father."

For the second time this summer, I ask the obvious question. "Then why'd she do it?"

Aunt Meg lets out a deep exhale. "God. We don't get to know, honey. I've been writing out all the advice she gave me over the years, and it is becoming this mammoth list of truths. That's what I'm going to focus on instead of why she's gone — who I know she was."

Aunt Meg agrees to send a copy of the list when she finishes. I wonder how many pages I could fill if I wrote everything my mother ever taught me. It would be longer than the Bible. And just as sacred.

BRADY

On my run today even my sweat felt culpable. Right now I'm commemorating Maddy's life by getting drunk, and I'm doing a stand-up job. I'm at war with her birthday. I cannot remember what I got on her forty-fifth aside from the token flowers I sent every year. I think I had Paula make an appointment for a spa day, unless Meg or Paige had gotten her that. I know for sure Maddy went to the spa. Hell, maybe she booked it herself.

The gift wasn't the worst of it. We argued that night after dinner. Maddy thanked me again for the flowers, then casually asked what the note in the card said. It was a test I'd fail, so I led with a defense, asking why it mattered. Maddy combed her fingernails over her eyebrows, the way she did before deciding whether something was worth a fight. "It matters because I want to know if you picked up the goddamn phone to order me flowers with a nice note, or if you had Paula do it."

Like an idiot, I didn't back down. "What's the difference if I made the call? I remembered; I wanted you to have flowers."

"The difference is significant if you're me, and you might be the boob in that cliché movie scene where the assistant reminds her boss of his wife's birthday and he says, 'Send the usual.'"

"That's ridiculous, Maddy. No one had to remind me it was your birthday. *Yes. Fine.* I asked Paula to call the florist. So what? I was in meetings all day, trying to get everything done in time to take you and Eve out to dinner. And I was able to do it, with a little help."

"Well, tell Paula 'thank you' for me —"

"For making a phone call?" I interrupted. "I would, but that's her job. I work my ass off, and she helps me juggle everything. You have no concept of what my day-to-day is like."

"This isn't about the phone call," Maddy said flatly. "Thank Paula because it was the sweetest damn note I've gotten from you in a *long* time. Maybe ever. That's how I knew you didn't write it, Brady. Not because you were busy today and not because I'm some bumbling homemaker who has no memory of the working world. I knew you had nothing to do with it because the note was sweet. Too sweet. Sweeter than you actually are." She handed me the card. "When I blew out the candles tonight, I wished for my next birthday to not feel like such a goddamn chore to my immediate family. I would've rather been alone. *Again.*"

I threw my hands in the air, surrendering. "Maddy, look, I'm sorry you felt that way. I am. I thought we had fun. Jesus Christ, if I knew you wanted a card, I would've written a card. Why didn't you say so?"

She looked right at me and said, "I'd rather slit my wrist than have to tell you I want a card on my birthday."

She'd rather slit her wrist. That's what she said. I thought she was being dramatic.

After she left the room, I read the note:

Happy birthday, my Maddy! I look forward

to celebrating your life every year because you are the best thing that ever happened to me. You deserve the world for all you do for Eve and me. Cheers to another great year . . . Yours, Brady

I bowled over. This four-sentence card was the sweetest thing she'd gotten from me in years. But did I learn a lesson from that? *No.* No, I did not. Not one bit. All it did was leave me ticked at Paula. I didn't ask for a goddamn love letter, I asked for flowers.

Every year for my birthday Maddy did something special. Sometimes a party, sometimes a surprise weekend guest, twice a little getaway, but always something. She'd pair a beautiful card with a thoughtful gift — the kind you didn't know you wanted but afterward can't imagine living without. She had the windows of my car tinted because I always complained of the glare from the sun. She had my favorite leather briefcase repaired because she couldn't find a new one that had the same depth to the outside pockets. It never crossed my mind these were grievances I could address. Maddy was resourceful in a way that left other people scratching their heads.

I did make it up to her the following

Saturday while Eve was overnight at Lindsey's. I waited until Maddy left for the gym to get everything ready. When she got home, smelling of the coconut soap from the locker room, I was in a tux, pouring champagne. She laughed. "Someone wants to get laid after being a shithead, huh?"

"No," I said. "I'm hoping to close a deal, but not that one."

"What then?"

"Well, I believe I'm overdue in getting you to sign my five-year renewal."

The five-year renewal was a joke from our wedding day. As the story goes, right after Meg reached the altar and the bridal march began to play, Maddy whispered to her dad that she intended to stay committed to the marriage for five years. He broke into a stunned sweat, doing the math on how much the wedding would cost per year the marriage lasted. Then Maddy added that everyone should feel like they come up for renewal and I was on a five-year plan. Her father snorted and asked what plan I put Maddy on. "If he's as smart as I think he is," Maddy said, "it'll be monthly." They laughed the whole way down the aisle.

"I don't know if I'd be inquiring about that with your current status," Maddy warned. "You're still so far in the doghouse,

I should paint your name on it."

I directed her to the bedroom, where a black cocktail dress from Saks was laid on the bed. It was a sexy, perfect fit. She came out saying, "Just because I look amazing doesn't mean you're forgiven." I laughed, thinking we were making progress. She didn't join me.

She loosened up a bit when she noticed I not only remembered her favorite entrée but drove thirty minutes to the North End to get it. It was scallop risotto from the place she requested to go to on her birthday, but I failed to get a reservation in time. Just as her anger subsided, she asked whether Paula helped plan the evening. "I intend to live to my next birthday, Maddy, so no, Paula had nothing to do with this."

"Good," she said, finally offering a genuine smile. "At least it appears my message was received."

I raised my glass for a prepared toast. "You are my rock, Madeline Starling. I don't know what this world would look like without you by my side, and I hope I never find out. I'm sorry I made you feel like a chore. I promise, if you opt to renew for another five years, I will spend every day proving my devotion to you."

She balanced her hands back and forth

like a scale. "Okay, fine," she conceded, "I'll keep you. But Brady?"

"Yes?"

"Don't be such a prick ever again."

"Yes, dear."

The thing is, I was a prick again after that. And after that. And after that. I lost touch with our rich history. I forgot what made Maddy special. I assumed she'd be there to renew for another five years.

Chapter Thirteen

MADELINE

My vantage point continues to diminish. There is a cosmic hourglass counting down my time to have impact, and I intend to get the better of it.

The dinner served its purpose: Rory has my family on the brain. She thinks mostly about me, questioning what she's missing. The house, the good-looking husband, the smart kid, it all seems so perfect looking in. She can't figure out what I had to escape.

Rory gracefully transitions from downward dog to pigeon. Her mind is clear of activity, so I softly recite Brady's name. In the steady hum I've now mastered I say, *Brady . . . Brady . . . Brady.* I do it slowly, salaciously, trying to evoke the specific frame of mind I'm after. The image that pops into her consciousness is of Brady sipping his wine while maintaining deep, direct eye contact. There was something intimate about the exchange that she ignored at the time. Her cheeks blush with the recollection.

In her stretch pants and fitted tank, Rory's sex appeal multiplies. Gone is the childlike spunk she brings to the classroom. Her firm shape will be an upgrade for Brady; I was thin but soft. Rory is solid and sweats the perfect amount. After a hot yoga class I looked like I'd been put through the heavy towel cycle in the dryer. Rory looks like she's been sitting out by the pool on a hot day.

When class ends, Rory's effeminate yoga instructor asks if she wants to grab coffee sometime. "Thanks for the invitation," she demurs. "But I think we should stick to yoga."

His shoulders drop a bit. "Boyfriend?"

Rory bites her lip. Lying is the easiest way to end the conversation without offense and this is the only hot hatha flow class that works with her schedule. "Um hmm."

"Is it Frank? I notice you two always put your mats next to each other."

Rory wasn't expecting him to dig deeper. "Ah, nope. Not Frank. Definitely not Frank." Frank has nipple rings. "His name is Brady. You wouldn't know him."

Rory tells herself to shut the hell up and

offers a silent prayer that Brady doesn't have time for yoga. It's not exactly a common name and Wellesley is a small town. Once in the privacy of her car Rory sighs, wondering where that tall tale came from. I'll never tell.

Just as my capacity starts to dwindle, I'm getting good at being a ghost. I enlisted Meg to reach out to Brady about dating again, which wasn't easy since each message now takes a herculean effort to convey and she's against the idea of it. To Meg, Brady remaining abstinent for the rest of his life seems a reasonable consequence for missing my depression. I used Eve as bait, forcing my sister to admit she won't be Eve's go-to person in life. Meg manages a global department of a thousand people. She's on a plane more than she's in a car. Over time, Eve will be pushed down her to-do list along with dusting the fans. My message to Meg was that Brady needs someone so Eve has someone.

My sister couldn't bring herself to have the conversation outright, but she sent an email: *It's none of my business,* she began, *so there's no need to reply.* In fact she prayed he wouldn't. *But when Eve leaves for school this fall, no one would judge you for seeking companionship.* They both knew that's untrue; you can't change babysitters in Wellesley without being judged. *There will be times in life when Eve needs a woman she trusts. Maybe it will be Paige or me, we both hope so, but maybe we're too intertwined with Maddy. Maybe deep down Eve can't look at any of us without thinking we failed in some way. I appreciate you don't need permission but, for what it's worth, you have it.*

Brady read it once and deleted it, but the message served its purpose: the idea that my replacement will inherently be linked to Eve is floating around. Have you ever noticed what happens to your house the moment you consider moving? Suddenly the rooms turn claustrophobic, the kitchen cabinets look outdated, and sharing a bathroom sink with your spouse becomes intolerable. The power of suggestion is real, and I'm becoming a master at leveraging it.

I even got through to Brady's friend Bobby, who was so loaded when Brady called about tracking down Marie that he completely forgot to follow up with his brother. Eve keeps asking about it and I want Brady to get closure. It was wrong not to show him the letters when I found them. I thought I was saving him distress, but now I see it wasn't my call to make. I had a bad habit of protecting Brady and Eve from life, which has left them with unreasonable expectations and poor coping skills.

Although Bobby's brain isn't in overdrive like Brady's, his limited attention span made him a challenge. My first attempt was as a reminder: *Brady asked a favor.* He'd catch two words before being distracted by a billboard or good-looking passerby or the directions on a shampoo bottle. It doesn't take much to grab Bobby's eye.

My next tact was simpler: *Call your brother.* The hope was that Bobby would remember Brady's request when they connected. I got him to make the call, but Bobby started describing a NASCAR crash and then said, "Christ, I can't remember why I'm calling." His brother laughed and asked Bobby to hold on for a sec. I took the break to remind him: *Help Brady,* I said, again and again. *Help Brady.*

When his brother returned, Bobby enlisted his assistance and I did the equivalent of a ghost jig. Watch out, Casper, here I come.

EVE

I assess how the journal was left in the drawer so I know how to leave it when I'm done. I do this all the time; I don't know why it's making me nervous today. I check

321

the clock again. My father won't be home for two hours. I need to chill the hell out.

I've started drinking tea, like my mother. I like to sit at the kitchen table with a glass of sweetened rooibos and read her heavy script. I pretend she's in the chair next to mine and we're in a real conversation where she's choosing to share her deepest thoughts. Sometimes I swear I hear a voice-over like they do on soap operas when someone leaves a note before ditching town.

June 29, 2013

We had book club (aka wine and cheese club) tonight, and I was shocked to discover how often people sleep with their husbands. I was the one to start the conversation, saying how sad I found it that the heroine only had sex once a month. The conversation snowballed into everyone divulging their averages. Paige was the only one smart enough to remain silent. Christie Anderson claimed she couldn't possibly keep track. (There were a few giggles at that — she and Todd are believed to be swingers, although I can't imagine such a thing.) The lowest was Heidi, who said she and Grant were down to once a quarter, but the average of everyone's average was once or twice a month. Apparently, Brady and I are rabbits at once or twice a week. Who knew?

What started as a lighthearted conversation turned intense. People became insecure over what the number implied about the quality of their marriage. Including me. At one point, Mary asked how on earth Brady and I find the time and I reconsidered how long it takes us. I mean, how do we find twenty minutes, twice a week? It's not that hard. Is twenty minutes not normal? Maybe Heidi and Grant have three-hour sex marathons once a quarter. Is that normal? It was clear everyone's relationships had evolved differently. I got the hell out of there as fast as I could.

Holy shit. TMI. I could do without the twice a week visual for sure. I assumed a book club run by moms would stay pretty on task, but this makes it sound like books were a total afterthought. Where would they find time to analyze the author's intent between kinky comparisons on how much everyone on the block fucks? And I totally can't believe my saintly mother was in on the rumor that Kara's parents are swingers. The guys at school say it when they're going on about what a MILF Mrs. Anderson is, but I seriously thought it was wishful thinking. If it's true, I feel sorry for Kara. Having parents swapping lovers around town might actually be more shocking than a mother who commits suicide out of sheer boredom.

"What the hell are you doing?" Dad asks, slamming down his briefcase.

I look to either side as if the question might be directed at someone else, then put the journal on my lap like it isn't too late to hide it. "Wh-why are you home?"

"You have no rights," he says, yanking the journal from me and pressing it to his chest.

"She was my *mother.*"

"There are things in here . . . you-you have no business . . . I cannot even — go to your room."

His total failure to pick a sentence makes me nervous and somehow what comes out is laughter. "This is funny to you?" he shouts. "Get upstairs *now, Eve.*"

The delusion burns me. "Ahh, no, Dad, it's not funny that I don't have a mother, and it's not funny that this journal is, like, literally, the only way I have to get to know her."

"Don't pull that crap with me. This is a violation of your mother's privacy. Her

324

death does not give you the right to invade our bedroom and take something that isn't yours."

"*Our* bedroom?" I push. "Still? *Really?*"

He throws the journal against the kitchen wall. We both cringe as it hits the floor, a few pages detaching. Dad runs to it like a hurt child while I slip upstairs. He cares more about the damn journal than his own daughter.

I push through the door in a rage, and it's like I'm seeing my room for the first time. I'm repulsed by how childish it looks. Posters cover every inch of wall, mostly cutouts from magazines I spent hours gluing into collages; a colossal waste of time. Models, bands, Hollywood gossip headlines — maybe my father treats me like crap because I care about crap. I rip it all down as if it's my room's fault I got caught. When I get to the first store-bought poster, I pause. Mom would take these down carefully so she could donate them. She gave everything to charity. A couple years ago she dropped off my old skis at the Salvation Army. I ragged on her for it, questioning how skis would help people in need when they couldn't afford a ticket to get on the slopes. She goes, "You never know, Eve. On the news last week I heard about a homeless man who fended off attackers with a tennis racket. I'll bet he was glad he had it."

I take a last look at the three posters before tearing them in shreds. I can't spend my whole life copying my mother. Her plan obviously wasn't so hot in the end.

Eventually Dad knocks, then opens the door without waiting for a response. Why bother pretending to care about my privacy? How is barging into my room different from me barging into his? I almost point out the hypocrisy, but instead whisper, "I'm sorry." I don't know where the apology came from, but as soon as it's out there I wish I'd stuck to that line from the start.

"You should be." His eyes are distant. He doesn't acknowledge the state of emergency my room is in. I could have blood spewing from my wrists and all he'd care about is her journal. My life is a competition with a ghost. I'll never win.

"So, do you forgive me?" I ask.

I can't remember the last time he was up here. I think it was freshman year when he set up the desk I got for Christmas. He eyes the framed pictures on my bookshelf. They're mostly friends, but there's a few of Mom and me. None of my dad. Shitty time for him to notice.

"Sorry doesn't cut it, Eve."

"So, what then?"

"So nothing," he says, shaking his head at the impossibility of me ever making this right.

I collect trash from the floor, unsure what to say. He watches me, fists clenched. What the hell? What kind of parent says they won't forgive their kid?

"I'm heated," he finally says. "Even more than the journal, I'm disappointed in the things you said." He turns his back, but not before I see tears in his eyes. "I thought we were done with all that-that . . . blame. I'm considering canceling the trip to Paris. I haven't decided yet, but that's the way I'm leaning."

Oh my God. He's serious. It's the only thing he can take away that I care about. Car, cell phone, clothes, laptop, even the TV — it's all meaningless to me and he knows it. I bet he never even planned to go. He probably created the trip to have something to hang over my head.

"Please don't," I say, hating the desperation in my voice.

"After your performance downstairs . . . I don't see the point in spending all that money and missing work for a trip I'm no longer excited about."

"It's three weeks away. Don't you think

we will be past this?"

He walks to the door. "I don't know. Look, I'm not canceling anything tonight. Let's see how next week goes."

"Fine," I say, searching for a way to get the upper hand, "but it's not like you're a saint. People make mistakes. Mom said to practice love, compassion, and forgiveness."

His grip on the door handle is so tight his knuckles turn white. He leaves without responding.

My eyes water. It isn't only the trip. I'm down to one parent and I screwed it up. For what? Why didn't I just apologize, hand him the journal, and walk away?

The next morning I beat him downstairs and scrawl I'M SORRY across the whiteboard in huge letters. In small print underneath I add that I'm going to the library to study calculus. He's more of a pushover when I'm quote-unquote *prioritizing academics.* I might have to work for it, but I'm going to freaking Paris.

I pull into the library parking lot, recalling why I'd pushed back when Rory suggested we meet here for tutoring. I haven't stepped in a library since Mom died. I park the car but don't get out. Instead, I roll down the window and light a smoke, picturing my mother offering a mental farewell to her favorite books as she headed toward the roof. She always told me, "When the world gives you a hard time, pick up a book and join another." Why didn't she take her own advice that day?

After she died, people couldn't get over the fact that the building was only four stories. They questioned her intelligence and said terrible things within earshot like, "She could've just turned into a paraplegic — then she'd actually have a reason to be depressed." They were confused by her choice, but I understood. Of course she picked the library. She referred to the library, any library, as a sanctuary. She made a point of visiting them when we were on vacation, as though they were a common tourist attraction. The only time I ever heard her talk politics was when she found out Laura Bush was a librarian. She was so excited. "Think of how much funding they'll get," she gushed.

When I was little she took me to story time every week. "Isn't it amazing? All these books are at our disposal. Anyone can come in here and borrow them for free. It's the coolest thing the government has ever done, bar none." After story time, we'd pick new books for the week. My mom always approached the librarian for recommendations. She'd stand in line if she had to. Librarians carried celebrity status in her mind. "There's not enough time to read everything written," she'd whisper as we waited, "so it's important to be discerning."

She always spoke to me like an adult. People were wowed by my crazy vocabulary when I was a kid. My mom claimed it was all the books we read, but really, I had to learn big words if I wanted to know what the hell she was talking about. Language, expression, new ideas: these were things that made her heart race, and they all came to life at the library. So I get why it was her location of choice. If you're where you feel the most understood and still can't find peace, it's time to move on.

BRADY

I'd tucked away the mystery about my mom as another unknown on a mounting list of life unknowns when I got Bobby's call with Marie's phone number and address. She lives in Reston, Virginia. My next meeting isn't for forty minutes, so I dial the number. A woman with a heavy smoker's voice answers.

"Is Marie available?"

"If this is another goddamn telemarketer,

I'll report the number. I know my frigging rights." She sounds older than fifty-three. She sounds mean.

I think back to my first call with Rory where she too thought I was cold-calling — do I really sound that robotic? "It's not a telemarketer. Is this Marie?"

"Who the hell's asking?"

I glance to confirm my office door is closed. "This is Brady Starling, and I believe . . . well, I think you might've known —"

"Yeah. I know who you are."

I hold the phone from my ear. "Pardon?"

"Beth's son, right?"

I pause. "You know who I am?"

She lets out a villain laugh that leads into a coughing fit. It ends with the distinct sound of someone hocking a loogie. "That's what I said."

I consider the implications of being the only one not in the loop. "Did you know her well?"

"Beth? Course. She drove the foster families batty. Always checking on my condition, reporting the littlest things to the county." Marie makes her voice whinier to impersonate my mother. " 'Anna Marie had to take a cold shower today because there's too many people in that house.' Child services thought she was nuts."

Well, that describes my mother . . . not at all. I once went a year and a half with a spring popping out of my mattress. My mom said it wasn't rusty and my tetanus shot was up-to-date anyway, so I'd be fine if I just kept to the other side of the bed. It was a twin.

"What about Paul?" I ask.

"Yeah, sure, she was on his ass too, but Paul was adopted out of the system, so it was different. She still made sure we had each other, Paul and I. Always passing along our addresses and numbers. Setting it up so we'd be at the same park on the same day, that sort of thing." *Park?* My mother never took me to a park.

"I'd like to meet you," I say, though based on the call so far, I'm not sure that's true.

She clicks her tongue. "Why?"

The question catches me off guard, though I guess it shouldn't. If Marie wanted to meet me, she could've reached out at any time. "I'd like to learn more about my mother."

"*Ha!* Classic. The kid who was raised by the frigging woman wants to learn about her."

"I guess it does sound crazy, but it's the case."

"Well, if you're serious, you better hop to it because I have lung cancer. I ain't dying tomorrow, but I'm dying. And I'm not getting on a train or nothing either," she adds. "You want to meet me, you come here."

Cancer makes the situation more complicated. I'm not looking to be anyone's hero here. I have enough shit on my plate. "Lung cancer?" I repeat. "That's terrible. I'm sorry."

She expels more phlegm, hopefully into a tissue of some sort. "Don't be," she barks. "I'm not. I knew what I was getting into smoking two packs a day, even without the damn warning labels. Beth said it all the time and, anyways, there's no way you can smoke those things and think it's good for you. I don't care what no one says, that's horseshit."

I see no way around offering, so I ask if there's anything I can do to help. "Nope," she says to my relief. "Stopped treatment months ago. They took out a lung; I did the chemo thing; damn cells spread anyway. All chemo did was make me look and feel like shit. Now I'm just smoking in peace, waiting for my time." I ask if she has any children. "No, no kids. Never married. Neither did Paul."

I don't know where to take the conversation, and she doesn't reciprocate with questions. "Is next Monday too soon for me to come?" I have a firm policy of getting things I don't want to do over with as soon as possible. When I fire someone, it happens at eight in the morning. Unfortunately, I have vendor reviews this week, so Monday is the earliest I can swing.

"I gotta work at noon, so you'd have to come in the morning."

I'm genuinely curious where someone like Marie finds employment. "Okay. Where do you work?"

"I do customer service for the local telephone company."

I clamp down on my tongue to keep from laughing. Her voice is downright terrifying and she leaves the clear impression that customer satisfaction isn't a top priority.

"Okay. I'll arrive at nine."

"All right if Paul comes?"

It's the only hint of interest from her end. "That'd be great," I say. Maybe he's the communicator in the family.

"Great. Clock's ticking for me, but he'll still be around for sure."

She's so nonchalant about her pending death. She sounds almost excited. "Let me leave you my number in case —"

"Now, there's no need for that. I've got

nowhere to go, so I'll be here if you show, and if you don't that's fine too."

"All right then," I agree. "See you —"

The phone disconnects.

I'm tempted to screw it, but that feels too much like the path I've always taken, the one that got me to a point where I need to panhandle for details about the woman who raised me. I need to see this through.

I duck out of my office and ask my new assistant, Darlene, to book a flight and hotel before I overthink it. I've been well behaved with Darlene. The one time I barked, she said, "I'm not a mind reader, Brady. Feedback is appreciated, but please don't yell it at me." So I don't. There's no power high losing your temper when someone calls you out on it in an even tone.

The challenge of this impromptu trip will be hiding it from Eve. It's clear Marie isn't going to fill a familial hole. There are too many unknowns, and Eve doesn't need to meet someone with a death sentence right now. I'll put her off until I'm back. She knows Bobby's a flake; it shouldn't be too difficult. I'll need someone to stay overnight Sunday with her though. I'd call Paige, but she'd assume the right to ask a million questions. It'd be a work night for Meg, and an unreasonable commute. *Rory,* I think. Rory?

I don't know how someone I only recently met popped to mind, but it isn't a bad idea. Eve respects her and I-I . . . *well* . . . I find her relaxing. Unique. Certainly trustworthy.

She answers on the first ring. There's country music playing in the background. Maddy loved country. She said each song told a whole story, so it was like listening to a mini-audiobook. I hadn't pictured Rory as a country-music lover. Until this moment, I didn't realize I'd pictured her at all.

"This is Brady Starling," I say too formally. "Eve's father."

"You mean the guy I had dinner with last week?" Rory asks.

"Yes."

"And ran into at CVS?"

"Yes."

"That was a joke, Brady. I was being facetious." She accentuates *facetious* in a way that pokes fun at my seriousness and vocabulary and maybe even general approach to life.

"Right, right," I let out a forced chuckle. "I was calling for a favor."

"Sure."

I smile. "You don't know what the favor is yet."

"I'm not one to turn down favors." Is she flirting? I can't tell. Do I want her to be? I don't know.

"I've postponed most of my travel until Eve leaves in the fall, but a trip came up, only for a night, and I was hoping you'd stay at the house."

"Sure."

"I'll pay you, of course."

"When?" she asks, completely ignoring the compensation component.

"I'll leave Sunday night and be back Monday in time for dinner."

"Is cooking Monday's dinner part of the deal?"

This woman is completely uninhibited. Her brain isn't constrained by the same filter as mine. I wonder what it's like to say whatever comes to mind without worrying about long-term implications, risk, legalities. At least the joke is obvious this time. "Yes," I tease. "Everything from scratch, please." She laughs. "No, of course not. You can even leave Monday morning. I just don't want Eve alone overnight."

"We have tutoring Monday afternoon either way, so I'll be back then to make sure everything's all right."

"That'd be great. If you're still there when I get home, maybe we can all grab a bite or something."

Am I asking her on a date? With my daughter? I've officially lost it.

CHAPTER FOURTEEN

MADELINE

As the one influencing both ends of the call I know Rory and Brady weren't purposely flirting, but Rory questioned Brady's intentions with dinner Monday and Brady hung up wearing a boyish grin I haven't seen in a long time. I take it as a good sign they're exploring the possibility of each other's interest, especially given Rory's commitment to Eve. Rory craves the opportunity to mother someone as much as Eve needs to be mothered. It wasn't my plan, but Rory fell in love with Eve first, and I couldn't be more thrilled for that.

Eve doesn't stay away from my journal, but I'm certain she'll trust her instinct the next time I send a warning flare. And she's shrewder now. She washes her hands before picking it up and takes great care flipping the pages, cautious to prevent further damage to the binding. No matter how certain she is Brady won't come home, she no longer reads in common areas of the house. Instead, she goes to her bedroom, draws the shades, and locks the door. It's such a furtive process that it's a bit anticlimactic when everything is secure and she starts to read. Looking on, you'd expect her to shoot up heroin.

Unlike Brady, Eve doesn't read the entries in order. She leafs through the pages until a word catches her eye. Once she picks, she reads about my day over and over, considering every line, imagining where I sat while I wrote it, picturing what I wore that day. A woman's read. Then she writes in her journal, either directly about what I wrote or about what she thinks I secretly meant. She writes beautifully, searching for both my truth and hers. The journal is more potent to Eve than any drug.

I work to keep her away from the darker entries, though I'm not always watching at the right moment. I did my legacy a disservice leaving such a paper trail behind. I wrote honestly, but not all-inclusively, so Eve gathers insight into my anguish and imaginings, without any resolution or context. After a year of regurgitating the blah-blah details of my day, I tired of documenting the mundane. I challenged myself to dig deeper, to ask hard questions: *Where am I weak? What do I regret? How can I atone?* She's convinced the answer to my death lies between the lines. She's wrong, but I can't conceive a way to let her know it.

I watch as she flips through the pages, circling around an entry written while I was angry with her. Mega-angry. Questioning-where-I'd-gone-wrong-as-a-mother angry. Eve and her friends had been caught toilet-papering the home of a less popular girl in their class, Jenny. The reason for the attack was as heartless as Jenny having no friends. The poor thing was an easy target, and my daughter was complicit in taking advantage of that. It was the most trouble Eve ever landed in, a night she learned I take a hard stance on anything intentionally cruel. As punishment, I volunteered her services to public works for highway trash pickup the following four Saturdays. Eve had the audacity to fight back.

"That is *soooooo* unfair," she yelled, jutting her chin out defiantly. "Kara's mom grounded her Friday night. That's it."

"Have you met Kara's mother?" I railed. "Scratch that — have you met Kara? She's never been interested in anything she wasn't the star of in her entire life. She's a *meanie.* You can be friends with who you want, but don't expect me to skip along with the consequences. And since you feel compelled to talk back, your stint on trash duty is now five weekends."

"Mom, that doesn't even make sense. Who gets punished by, like, picking up trash?"

"I'll tell you who. Teenagers who live in this house and have the nerve to treat other people like garbage. How *dare* you hurt this poor girl's feelings. What the heck were you thinking?" I paused for an answer, but Eve just shook her head. "Do you really believe you're better than Jenny because you have a group of callous, bitchy friends by your side? You have every advantage in life, and this is how you behave? Honest to God, this sort of rebellion is my worst nightmare."

"It wasn't supposed to be a big deal," Eve grumbled, staring at the kitchen tile.

"Not a big deal to *whom,* Eve? To you? It wasn't supposed to be a big deal because you weren't supposed to get caught. Is that it? Because I talked to Jenny's mother and it was a tremendously big deal in their home. Jenny has been crying all day. She refuses to go to school tomorrow. She says she gets teased relentlessly by you girls."

"Not by me."

"Better not be you. I won't let this slide as typical teenage stuff. You have a head and a heart — I expect you to make choices that account for both. The next time I hear of your involvement with anything like this I will take away your car, your allowance, and your cell phone. *Permanently.* Don't experiment with people's hearts. Do you hear me?"

Eve nodded in agreement and retreated to her room, but I was still palpably mad as I wrote in my journal that night. In high school, good looks protected me from being an overt target, but my reading obsession made me a sidebar spectacle. I remember opening my science book one day to a picture of a giant penis taped on the inside cover. Sprawled across the top were the words *Have you ever seen one of these before?* My head jerked up in surprise; everyone howled with laughter. Worse than the shock and embarrassment was my secret fascination. I hadn't seen one, not up close. I blushed, upping the entertainment value. The idea that Eve, *my* Eve, had been involved in such terrorism horrified me. My journal that night used words like *disgusted, embarrassed,* and *furious.* I meant to describe what Eve had done, not her as a person, but I know she won't interpret it that way.

I attempt to intervene. *Flip the page.* I'm

now so high up that my messages often take more time than the situation affords. *Flip the page,* I say again. *Flip the page.* To my relief, she does, and I take in the cool rush of having impact. I'm not ready to give it up.

December 25, 2014
Christmas fell on a Thursday this year. We were about to leave for church when Eve said she thought it was stupid we only went on holidays.

"I feel more spiritual when I go for a long run than I ever have at church," she declared. "And what does it say about us that we pretend we go on days we know our neighbors will be there? We're not religious; we're, like, hypocrites."

I love when she takes a stance and articulates herself like that. Brady and I looked at each other — she had a point. So we made a pact to replace church days with mandatory family runs. It was a liberating moment.

Then tonight, Brady surprised me with the most beautiful diamond earrings. His note read, "May these earrings put some sparkle in your life, like you do in mine." Each one is probably a carat and a half. I didn't dare ask if Paula had anything to do with it because I feared my pride would be compromised if she picked them out and I still kept them.

Eve rubs her ears. She's been wearing the earrings. Brady said they look ridiculous on a girl her age, but Eve argued everyone assumes they're fake. The reality is no one sees them. With camp over, Eve's entire circle is Brady, Rory, Paige, Dr. Jahns, and a weekly call from my sister. She's wholly alone, and the only person who realizes it is me — the person who caused it. For all my good decisions and noble sacrifices it took only one moment, one bad call, to end it all.

Eve puts the forbidden journal away and heads to the kitchen that she already cleaned. She thinks back to the last time she changed her sheets. Yesterday. Brady is bringing takeout tonight, so there's no reason to cook. She's already done an hour of yoga and showered. She decides to paint her nails, but even using the full manicure set, feverishly setting about buffing and cuticle clipping, the whole process takes thirty minutes. A devilish thought sets in. She opens the fridge with the side of her palm, careful not to smudge the fresh paint, and scouts out an open bottle of wine. Brady now drinks a glass with dinner, postponing the strength of bourbon until they've said good night. A bottle lasts him three days; there's no way he'll notice a missing glass and Eve knows it. She looks at the microwave clock. It's three in the afternoon. *One glass,* she reasons, *no biggie.*

But I know better. Every alcoholic starts somewhere. There's always a first; one moment where the line of what's acceptable is crossed, motivated by trauma or boredom or both. For my mother I picture it happening after one of our vacations on the Jersey shore. We rented the same house for a week each June, when the prices were lower because the water was still freezing. Our cottage was a revolving door of visitors who'd come up to celebrate and relax, then pass out on the couch overnight. Each day had a theme and it started at lunch — Mai Tai Mondays, Tequila Tuesdays, Wildcard Wednesdays . . . it was the late seventies.

Eventually the week would end and we'd drive home. Dad went back to work. Meg and I walked to the YMCA for summer camp. Mom unpacked everything and did laundry. At some point I imagine it struck her that there was no reason *her* vacation had to end. So she rummaged through the

Walmart bag of leftover booze and mixed a screwdriver. Just one. Just to suck the monotony from her chores. That night no one noticed. So Mom adjusted the line of normalcy — one midday drink was okay. Then that line was tested, resulting in a new line. Then a new, new line. Within a year she was having a full-time affair with Carlo Rossi, all fueled by that first transgression.

I refuse for this to be Eve's moment. I know better than to lecture. My best bet is to offer an alternative. *Read,* I suggest. *Read.* Eve gave up reading for pleasure the day she got a cell phone. Something needed to be cut to account for the hundreds of texts and endless phone conversations that comprised her budding social life. I was devastated books took the hit. *Read.*

Eve stares at the bottle so long the refrigerator door beeps. *The last thing I need is to turn into a closet drunk like Kara,* she thinks, slamming it shut with such force that everything rattles. I don't know whether Eve came to that conclusion on her own or made out my faint protests until she marches toward the living room bookshelf. She ditched *The Celestine Prophecy* after only thirty pages because her grief was too raw for anything offering answers. It likely still is. Lesson learned. I zip through titles, looking for a book that will swallow her so completely Brady will have to physically take it when he wants her attention. If I succeed, this will be the beginning. I'll create a lifetime reader, something I failed to accomplish when I was alive.

I see it — Gregory Maguire's *Wicked* — a book so phantasmagorical that you forget the boundaries of reality. An escape book, exactly what Eve needs. *Wicked,* I prompt. *Wicked. Wicked.* She receives my message and continues the search until her fingers pass the binding. She's captivated before the end of the first paragraph: *They seemed oblivious of their fate. But it was not up to the Witch to enlighten them.* I hadn't considered the possibility Eve would see me in the witch, but if it helps her get through this without afternoon cocktails, I'll gladly take one for the team.

EVE

I hand Dad a snack bag for the plane like Mom always did before long road trips. "Thanks, Bean," he says. He hasn't called me Bean since our fight over prom-dress shopping. This time I'm grateful. He's been distant since the journal incident.

Something's up with this business trip. He called me to his room to confirm the outfit he packed "looked okay" and got a haircut out of his sacred four-week cycle. Maybe his job is on the line. He's been getting home at seven to be with me and hasn't traveled for work in months. HT could be fed up with his new fatherly duties.

"Damn it," he mutters, staring at an unoccupied hook in the closet.

"Everything okay?"

"Do you know where my umbrella is?"

"It's in the mudroom. But seriously, Dad, is something wrong?"

"No, why?"

"I dunno. You're acting like a weirdo. Is this business trip wicked important?"

"Ah, yeah."

The doorbell rings. Rory's here. I told him I'm too old for a babysitter, not that he'd listen to me. I leave to answer it.

"Wait. Bean?" I turn. "I want you to know I'm looking forward to Paris. I'm not going to cancel. We both deserve a vacation."

I have no idea which part of my ass-kissing earned his forgiveness or why he's acting like such a freak, but if we're still going to Paris he's probably not getting canned.

Dad follows me out with his roller bag and a handful of papers. "Hi, Rory," he says, reaching out to shake her hand.

"Oh, okay, hi," Rory replies with a giggle,

amused by his formality.

"Here's Eve's insurance information and a waiver for you to make emergency medical decisions in my absence for the next thirty-six hours."

Rory glances my way to confirm he sounds crazy. I nod. "Thanks, Brady. Hopefully it won't come to that." My father isn't good at being laughed at, so we're received with a silence that makes the room uncomfortable.

"If you need anything, or have any questions, you have my cell."

"Yep, and if you aren't available, I can always ask your seventeen-year-old daughter." I laugh. Dad doesn't. "Really, Brady, we got this," she assures. "Go do whatever it is you do."

"All right. Make yourself at home. Please sleep in my bed. I mean, I, ah —" Rory looks startled. I try not to laugh again. Dad attempts to move the conversation forward by pointing out that he put clean sheets on it, but ends up implying he's done her some sort of favor, so then he spits out, "The master bedroom is ready for your stay."

He sounds like a bellhop. Rory teases him by saying so, but my dad has had enough as the butt of our jokes. He gives me an efficient hug and leaves.

I decide to pretend that didn't happen.

"Want pizza?"

"Yes. Extra cheese please."

I set the table in the front garden, which Dad's new assistant recently arranged to have renovated after the fire damage. It now looks like the outdoor kitchen my mother had been begging for, which breaks my heart. When the pizza arrives, my elaborate table setting looks ridiculous next to the cardboard box. Rory ignores the knife and fork and digs right in, so I do the same. She's supercasual. It's refreshing, especially now that I appreciate how much effort it took my mom to be traditional. Everything in our house looked perfect, which was awesome when I thought everything *was* perfect, but disturbing now that I know the truth. It's like we lived on a stage.

What the hell will Rory and I talk about for the next twenty-four hours? Just as I start to panic that this will be totally awkward she says, "You know, there are a lot of famous people who graduated from Exeter."

I shrug. "I honestly don't know much about the school."

"Franklin Pierce, John Irving, Mark Zuckerberg . . ."

"I'm over Facebook. I think it's only fun when you feel a little better than everyone else, and I don't anymore." She laughs.

There's something about Rory that draws me out. "But I like John Irving. My mom made me read *A Prayer for Owen Meany*. It was her favorite."

"I loved that book," Rory says, putting a hand over her heart. "Actually, I thought about it a lot after Brian's graduation. The speaker went through the meaning of everything in Latin on the school seal. The central quotation was interpreted as 'The end depends upon the beginning.'" She pauses to see if I understand. I don't see the connection. "You know how at the end it becomes clear Owen was preparing for his ultimate destiny his whole life?" I nod. "Well, 'The end depends upon the beginning' is telling, right? John Irving must've heard that saying a million times while he was at Exeter."

"Huh. Yeah."

The end depends upon the beginning.

Maybe it's as simple as that. Maybe Mom jumped because of her shitty childhood. It's obvious, even to me, that she had nothing to do with instigating Gram's drinking problem. Seriously, she was like ten years old. How could her little remarks provoke a jug of wine a day? But imagine the damage from *believing* you'd caused something so horrible from such a young age; imagine the burden of thinking you ruined your mother's life. The thought stops me — I guess it's not a far leap in my case. So my mom carried the same guilt I now carry. Playing it out, I can see how her mind turned on her, how reflecting pulled her into weeds that weren't really there. I need to break that cycle. *The end depends upon the beginning.*

I like talking to Rory. She's philosophical without being condescending. She's softer than Paige, and more real than Aunt Meg. I feel older around her, smarter. "What else do you remember about the campus?" I ask.

Rory licks sauce off the side of her lip. She's a messy eater. "Let's see. I remember Brian telling me that everyone called skipping class *dicking,* which I thought was a riot. And everyone referred to the cafeteria as the fishbowl. But I guess that makes sense when you're in it." She looks to me for confirmation.

"Wouldn't know. I haven't been on campus yet."

Rory plops the pizza on her plate. "You're kidding. Why not?"

"My dad's boss is an alumni, so he did the interview from here. We never really had a reason to make the trip."

"Ahhh — so you can see the place you're

going to *live*?"

I didn't find it at all strange until she repeated the situation back to me. "*Well,* when you say it like that . . ."

"It's only an hour and a half away. Don't you want to see the campus before you arrive with everyone else?"

"I guess, but it'll be fine. It's not like I can change my mind at this point."

Rory scoots her chair closer to mine. "Never box yourself in like that. You have options. If you give it a fair shot and you're unhappy, do something about it. I guarantee you and your dad can figure out a Plan B."

She waits for acknowledgement. "Okay," I agree. I won't back out, but it's sweet she cares.

"You need to learn your way around before the first day of class. You're taking on enough unfamiliar faces and new routines; you can't afford to be disoriented on top of it." Just as her lecture starts to freak me out, she smiles. "I vote tomorrow we skip math and go to Exeter."

"Sounds good to me." We both grab another slice.

"Are you nervous about going?"

"Tomorrow?"

She flaps her napkin at me. "No, you goof, when school starts."

"Oh, no. I'd be more nervous if I was staying." I see no reason to sugarcoat it. "Or not nervous, but like, depressed. I can't move on in Wellesley. I can't show up my senior year a completely different person and expect everyone to accept it. They all feel sorry for me. It's this constant reminder I'm supposed to be sad." I look up at the clouds to keep from getting weepy. "I don't know. It's like you said the other night: something will always be missing, but I don't want to wear it as a badge. Yanno?"

Rory looks proud. "That's good," she says. "I'm glad you aren't blindly running away. There's no distance where you won't miss her. A fresh start I can support."

I find a smile. This is the first time I've talked about leaving and been happy afterward. Everyone else is burdened by *why* I'm going instead of *that* I'm going.

BRADY

I don't totally understand what I'm out to accomplish with this trip, and not having a set goal leaves me anxious. My gut tells me to dig deeper, but my mind wants to return on the next flight to Boston. Envisioning the first moment of our interaction doesn't help. To hug or not to hug? Bring a gift? Coffee and doughnuts?

It's not in a trailer park, but the house would best be described as a double-wide. When Marie answers the door, it's obvious there will be no hug, and I feel silly handing her fresh flowers. She laughs in my face, something women seem to do a lot lately. "We going on a date I don't know about?"

"I didn't want to come empty-handed."

Marie is fat and loud, exactly what I pictured from our call. Paul is thin, quiet, and positioned in a spot that blocks me from entering. I extend an arm for a handshake. He reciprocates, which I appreciate because the marine tattoos snaking up both his arms are intimidating, even on a senior citizen.

It's possible Marie is drunk. Between her odd sense of humor, coughing fits, and half-angry, half-pleased bursts of laughter, it's hard to know how to respond.

Paul and I sit on the couch, and Marie follows us in with a lawn chair. "I'll sit on this," she says. "Never anyone here but me and Paul, so the love seat's usually enough." I offer up my spot on the couch, and not just to be polite — I'm not at all convinced the lawn chair can support all Marie has to offer. "Huh, a gentleman. How about that? Paul never would've switched."

"You're right 'bout that," Paul says. He

mumbles such that his words are almost indecipherable.

I direct my first question to Marie. "Can you tell me about your father?"

"I can tell you he was a hell of a lot better than the SOB that raised you."

I choke on my coffee. "You knew my dad?"

"Only from what Beth'd say."

"How often did you two talk?"

"Oh, she hunted me down as much as she could, least once a week until I graduated high school."

So while hiding their existence from me, she advertised my existence to them. I don't know which of us should be more offended.

"What did she say about my father?"

"She was trapped. I was eleven when Dad died and we became the state's problem. She bawled like a baby in a wet diaper. Got married about two years after that. Things got worse over time. I know that for sure. Our dad was encouraging of Beth's free spirit. But yours — what's-his-name, Bob? — he had a set place for a wife."

My hands stiffen on my lap. "I wouldn't say that." *Would I?* It's not as if she wore sunglasses from the lessons Dad taught her. My parents walked around each other, the way Eve and I do sometimes. They didn't fight; it was more like there was no affiliation between them whatsoever. When my father got home, my mother went quiet. Things stayed perfectly still until he left for work the next day.

Marie brushes my reaction aside. "Who knows? Maybe she carried on about him so we'd feel sorry for her. But she hadda sneak out of the house while he was working to see us because Bob didn't allow it. We weren't his problem, far as he could see. Can't say I disagree there. Never did get why Beth kept on us. I'll say though, hearing everything she went through with your dad was one of the reasons I never married."

I have a hard time picturing anyone asking Marie for her hand in marriage, but keep that observation to myself. "When did you see her last?"

"Sheesh. Let's see. I reckon the last time we saw Beth was two, maybe three years before she died. Right, Paul?" Paul starts to say something but gets cut off by another of Marie's coughing fits. She waves her hand to move us along like it's nothing, but it would be like talking over a blow-dryer. When the hacking subsides, the three of us stare at one another in a moment of silence I spend grateful Marie didn't just drop dead. Then I ask if my mom and Phil were publicly dating.

"Oh sure, they were the real deal. Lot of good that did us. If only they'd married. Then our life would've been different."

We have that in common, to opposite ends. Marie and Paul would've had a home growing up, whereas I would've been erased completely. "Why didn't they?"

"Couldn't. Wouldn't. Depends how you see it. He was Jewish. No shocker there with the last name Goldfarb. His folks were rich, so Dad kept on the right side of them, figuring the inheritance'd be worth it someday. Beth said they called her everything from a street whore to a gold digger. She couldn't talk about those people without raising her fists like the fight was still going on."

"Did you get the inheritance?"

Marie scoffs. "You think my fat ass would be planted in this plastic chair if the answer to that was yes? We were bastards in their eyes. My dad never married our mother either. The man never fell in love with a girl from the right goddamn religion. Those crotchety pieces of shit left everything to the synagogue."

A hostile laugh escapes before Marie's next cough. The visit will end as soon as I stop asking questions, so I plug along. "Do you know how they met?"

"Beth was our caretaker after Mom died. She was always at the house, cooking, cleaning, hovering over us."

I'm rapt. Marie is describing a complete stranger. "Can you share a memory?"

"I have a good one," Paul volunteers more audibly than before. "She bought me a guitar for my fifteenth birthday. First I thought she'd stolen it because she didn't have that kind of money, but it turned out she'd been taking a couple dollars out of her grocery money every week." Paul looks down at his lap with a distinct frown. "It was the nicest gift I ever got. Probably still have that thing somewheres."

Marie smacks her knee. "I'll be damned. She never got me nothing. That's Paul for you. Don't hear a peep out of him all morning, then he comes out with that sweet story. Didn't know that one myself." She rises from the lawn chair, careful to pry the armrests from her sides so the chair doesn't come with her. "Well, it's been real nice meeting you, but I have to get off to work soon." I know it's an excuse. Her shift doesn't start for two hours.

I stand. "Thanks for agreeing to meet." There won't be a second rendezvous and all three of us know it.

"Uh huh." She guides me to the door.

"Listen, Marie, if there's anything I can do to make you more comfortable, or just anything you need, here's my business card." For whatever reason, my mother cherished these people. Helping them would be a way to honor her memory.

"We don't need your money, Bradley, but thanks."

"It's Brady," I correct, embarrassing us both.

"Right, right, Brady. That's what I was thinking just not what I said."

"I didn't mean to imply you needed money. I just know you're ill. That was all I meant."

She looks annoyed. Meeting me wasn't on Marie's bucket list. "Okay, that's fine. You travel safe now." The door shuts.

So that's how the divorcées feel when I slam the door in their face. I stand there like a complete dipshit. The case is closed, only it's not. The disappointing fact is that my mother showered two random kids with attention instead of me, my wife jumped off a building to avoid our happily-ever-after, and my daughter enrolled herself in boarding school to get out of one more year in my company. I'm a finance guy. Three women opting out of spending time with the same man is statistically relevant. It's a trend. Trends are the result of a catalyst, and the only common denominator here is me.

I don't want to be bitter, but that's the taste in my mouth as I board the plane. By the time I land in Boston, I'm mentally drained and dreading dinner with Rory and Eve. I conjure up a few excuses to bail on the drive back, but the effort proves unnecessary. I return to an empty house and a note on the counter.

Hi Dad,
We went to Exeter to see the campus this afternoon. We may be back a little bit after you. I hope your big business trip was a success ☺

Love, Bean

I have spent a lifetime misreading women.

CHAPTER FIFTEEN

MADELINE

I'm mortified by my first reaction to this Paris trip. It was very Christie Anderson. Their lives are not about me anymore and I need to get over it.

Brady had his new assistant fill every minute of the itinerary, sparing no expense. I thought Darlene would be irritated to work on something so personal, but she can't wait to have him out of the office for a week. I think she'd have bought the tickets herself. They're having lunch at Le Jules Verne, taking a boat cruise down the Seine, spending a day at the vineyards of Champagne, and attending a private Louvre exhibition. To account for Eve's time while he trains for the marathon, Brady booked her an afternoon at the hotel spa and an appointment with a personal shopper at Galeries Lafayette. He bought first-class tickets, a first for Eve and a stab at me. I considered first class an excessive perk for a child, so when Eve was with us we took over a row in coach: me in the middle, Brady on the aisle, Eve at the window. Apparently, it was my battle alone; Brady didn't hesitate to take the upgrade.

If all three of us were going we'd have gotten one room with two queens, but Brady found the idea of sharing a room with his daughter in Paris depressing, so he booked them each their own. It's ironic; they're down one person but somehow more than doubling the cost.

The prospect of spending eight days alone with Eve has Brady tense. He spends half an hour looking for our vacation luggage, only to spend another half hour staring at his closet trying to determine what to bring. Brady never packed for anything that wasn't work-related. Since getting him to agree to vacation at all was such an effort, I took on any burden associated with the actual trip. I don't even think he registered that someone packed his luggage until this very moment. Now, flabbergasted, he says aloud, "Another hidden talent, huh, Maddy?"

The doorbell rings. "I'll get it," Eve calls.

"Happy leave-for-Paris day," Paige says when the door opens.

"Thanks." Her excitement is tangled with

apprehension around how she and Brady will get along, and a deep sadness that I won't be there for the adventure.

"Sooo . . . I couldn't refrain . . . after you said you loved *Wicked* I had to pick up some vacation books for you." She hands Eve a bag from Wellesley Books that leaves me nostalgic for the afternoons I wasted an hour perusing their rows and rows of shelves for the perfect next read.

"Sweet."

Eve has been devouring our bookshelf. She'll stay up until one in the morning reading, then curse herself for it the next day, the same way I used to.

"In the interest of full disclosure, I'm hoping you'll become my book buddy. I can't go back to book club. Not without —" Paige shakes off the urge to cry.

"I'd love to," Eve cuts in, looking at the clock on her cell. She has to finish packing.

"Great," Paige says. "And one last thing." Eve sighs, bracing for a *be careful* speech, but that's not the mission I sent Paige on. "Try to surprise yourself on the trip. Step outside your comfort zone."

Eve grins. "What are we talking about here — shoplifting? Skydiving? A nose ring?"

Paige raised five kids and knows how to handle wisecracks. "Yes, all those things for sure," she says, "but also, be kind to your-self. Make the trip about you. If an hour passes where you don't think of Her, that's okay." Eve steps back, physically distancing herself from the thought. "Really, honey. It can't be all mourning, all day, every day. Living doesn't mean you're over it or selfish or cold; it just means you're still here, and she's not."

The words pierce Eve's most private thoughts. "I'll try," she whispers.

Back in her room, she mulls over Paige's words. *The end depends upon the beginning, I remind her. The hourglass counting down my time is low on sand. I need Eve to feel empowered to move forward.*

She checks the weather in Paris and picks a nail polish and lipstick to go with each outfit. Once the suitcase is stuffed enough to be at risk of bursting open, she decides to call Lindsey and tell her about the trip. It's the first outbound call she's made to a friend in months. When Lindsey doesn't answer, she settles for Kara. All she's look-ing for is a sliver of normalcy, a quick chat with a friend to prove she still knows how to communicate. Unfortunately, Christie answers Kara's cell.

I've often wondered if the age of your soul correlates with the pitch of your voice;

women who screech like Christie tend to come across as newbies. "Oh, Eve, it's you," she squeals. "Perfect. Before I grab Kara, give me the quick skinny on whatever's going on."

"Going on?"

"With Kara."

Eve already regrets the call. "I have no idea."

"*Yes,* you do. She's up and down with a bout of PMS that won't end." Christie laughs, feeling clever.

"Mrs. Anderson, I wouldn't know. Really. Kara and I haven't spoken since tennis ended."

"Ya. I'm very aware of that. You and everyone else. Why has my daughter been blackballed?"

"Blackballed?"

Christie lets out a haughty scoff. "Eve, *dear,* cut the act. I want to help Kara through this, but I can't if I don't know what happened."

I wish I had the power to kill the phone line, but I do the next best thing and guide Eve to hang up. "I should go," Eve says. "I'll call back another time." After disconnecting, Eve stares at the receiver unsure what that was about. I wish there was a way to share what I know, but the only one who can tell the story now is Kara, which, of course, will never happen. It's too complicated to convey a few words at a time without any context.

The phone is still in Eve's hand when Lindsey calls back. Eve plays back her weird conversation with Christie.

"Blackballed?" Lindsey repeats. "Who even says that? I mean, Kara's been a spaz lately, but it's not like anyone's excluding her. The girl seriously needs to learn to handle her liquor."

Eve wishes she'd kept her mouth shut. "Well, maybe give her a call in case something really is wrong," she suggests. "I would, but my dad and I leave tonight for Paris."

"Oh. My. God. Serious? That's awesome. He definitely wouldn't have taken you on a trip like that before."

Before; a haunting word. "I've got to go."

"Umm, you called me," Lindsey says, in a masterfully rehearsed teenage voice.

Eve's teenage voice is out of practice. "Yeah, I did, but now I have to go." She sounds older than Lindsey, and more noteworthy, she knows it.

"Whatever, Eve. Maybe you should worry about yourself instead of Kara. I swear my two closest friends are going to end up institutionalized."

This time Eve needs no prompting to hang up. *It's time to get the hell out of here,* she thinks. It is a larger notion than she appreciates, meaning immediately for the impending trip, and permanently, with boarding school and college and the rest of her life. I focus my energy so it runs through her, a virtual hug. And then, to my wonderment, I find myself on the receiving end of something similar. Eve's sentiment echoes back to me as a suggestion from a higher place: *It's time to get the hell out of here.* I'm not ready. *How?* I ask. No response, but a vibration stirs underneath me. It's weak at first but grows stronger and stronger. When it's as if my spirit is fully resting on its source, I begin to soar straight up at an alarming pace. It's exhilarating and full of promise until I worry this is it, I'll never see Eve or Brady again, and with that thought the ride stops as unexpectedly as it began. I look down, nervous, but life's movie is still there to view. I just inherited a really crappy seat.

Eve and Brady are on an evening flight. The driver arrives at five, but Eve can't find her headphones. Brady attempts a breathing exercise Dr. White taught him, but doesn't make it through a full inhale/exhale cycle before screaming, "Come down or I'm leaving without you."

"Keep your pants on," Eve yells back. "I'll be down in two secs."

They're quiet on the drive to Logan airport and remain so as they trounce through security to their gate. The silence worries them both. Brady's been in a funk since D.C. and, since he hasn't told Eve about Marie and Paul, she's worried his rut either is caused by their trip to Paris or will be ruined by it.

Momentum shifts in their favor on the plane. Eve flips out when she takes her seat. First class to Paris isn't your typical oversized leather seat with extra incline — it's a personal pod that extends to a flat bed. Hers faces Brady's with a low divider so they can see each other. Eve scrolls through the "free" movies, showering Brady with choices. A flight attendant appears, offering them champagne. Eve looks gingerly to Brady, who gives her a nod. There's a chance she'll enjoy the flight more than the actual trip. As they take off, she hands Brady a poem she wrote titled "Typical Teenager," adding that her contribution to the trip is promising not to be one.

That's not the right answer.
You didn't ask the right question.
Will you please give an answer?
I'm afraid of rejection.
So make sure you're right.
You'll find a correction.
I won't say a word.
I don't need your protection!
So you refuse to answer?
Could you rephrase the question?

Brady folds the paper and slides it into his carry-on. "Now I know you know," he says smugly.

"Know what?"

"When you're talking in circles like that all the time, frustrating me. It's intentional, huh?" He smiles. "You just let the cat out of the bag."

"That's okay," Eve says. "I'm not a typical teenager anymore, so anything you think you now know is history." They smile, comforted their conversation isn't strained. Perhaps all the time I sat in the middle, considering myself the liaison between them, I was really a barrier. Perhaps we all offer what we can, until we can't, and then our loved ones step up or have others step in. Perhaps death exists to challenge the people left behind.

371

Brady has a drink to unwind. When he falls asleep Eve pulls out her journal, dating it the way I did mine. She sips champagne and considers her words, looking substantially older than seventeen.

August 19, 2015
I feel like this trip is the beginning of something important. It's our first attempt at creating a memory without Her. The Fourth of July and all of our other nice talks have been indirectly related to her death — a conversation we were settling on because she wasn't here. This trip is <u>ours.</u>
  I've never been so hopeful for a good time, which is funny because good times used to find me. I hope it won't seem forced, and I hope I won't be disappointed.

Me too, Eve. Me too.

EVE

My father is on a sixteen-mile run, the longest he'll do before the qualifier in Quebec next week. We agreed to meet in the lobby at six for dinner, leaving me three hours to roam Paris.

I find a little café with outdoor seating and pull out my book, *To Kill a Mockingbird.*

Rory recommended it. She said she couldn't wait to laugh about passing the damn ham, whatever that means. She couldn't believe it hadn't been required reading at school. I was too embarrassed to admit that not recalling the story doesn't mean it was never assigned. Rory doesn't come across as someone with an appreciation for Cliffs-Notes. My mom certainly wasn't. I hid those yellow booklets as carefully as I hid condoms.

I flip a page every once in a while in case anyone's watching, but I'm too distracted by how I appear to the outside world — sipping cappuccino; wearing big, black sunglasses and a new couture shirtdress; a young American in Paris — to actually take in the story. Do people walking by think I'm famous? Rich? Over twenty?

When he approaches, I act like it's totally routine, like men hit on me all the time. "What is your name?" he asks.

"Charlotte," I say, because I want to and I can. *Charlotte* sounds chic and fun, and I desperately want to be both.

"Charlotte," he repeats, "I am Dameon. May I sit with you?"

"I have a better idea." His deep-set eyes lift in anticipation. "Take me for a walk around Le Bois de Boulogne. I'm dying to see it." It's an outrageous request to a total stranger, but I feel so bold I stand to leave even before he answers.

"Parlez-vous français?"

"No."

"Oh. You have the accent for the park name perfect."

I haven't completely lost my mind. It's only a couple blocks away, all crowded streets. I can bolt at any time.

As we walk, I refuse to think about my mother. Each time her presence seeps in, I shut it down. I'm just a girl in Paris. Dameon isn't spending time with me out of pity. He's not avoiding topics like family or death, and he's not constantly darting his eyes my way to check whether he inadvertently reminded me of Her. He doesn't even know She existed. Shedding my backstory is intoxicating.

He has no idea how old I am. I'd guess he's twenty-five, but don't dare ask. We share a cigarette and walk along the park, arms linked. I smoke sometimes, but this is different. We're not out to prove anything or rebel against anyone. We're simply enjoying a sunny afternoon. "The land was made a park by Napoleon the Third," he says, sharing the history of the things we pass in a way I could never pull off with a visitor back home. "In this way, we all still benefit from his time exiled in London. They say a lot of the streams and landscaping was inspired by his love of Hyde Park."

I've never paid much attention to my surroundings, to why things are the way they are and how long they've been that way. I picture myself showing Dameon around Boston, limited to places where I eat and shop. How quickly I'd run out of things to say. I lean in closer. Each time he calls me Charlotte I slip more into character, pretending I really am this cosmopolitan woman. The act illuminates everything. I become theatrical, drunk off how unfamiliar and inviting life appears. I see a baby and feel maternal. I see a child rolling on the grass and have an urge to be a kid again. I see a couple kissing and crave romance. Even my laugh sounds different because, to Charlotte who has no worries, everything is entertaining.

After two hours a chill sets in and Dameon drapes his khaki coat over my shoulders. I pull it snug, acting as though it's the most natural thing in the world. I'm careful about the time though. At half past five I tell Dameon I have to go. He asks if we can meet for dinner. I say no, that I'm catching a flight home in two hours. The lie slips out like all the others. He nods and takes me in, his hand centered on the small of my back. "It was a perfect afternoon, no?"

"Oui." He lifts my chin with his other hand and kisses me.

The sensation is so different with a man. John never had that kind of patience. When Dameon lets go, my whole body wants more. The kiss belongs on a defining-moment time line of my life. It just happened and yet it's already changed me.

Dameon squeezes my hand and says, "I wish you well, Charlotte." I sigh and turn toward the hotel. Part of me wishes I got his number or tried to make plans for tomorrow, but I don't want to be a tourist fuck. I speed back to meet my dad, delirious over the fact that I French-kissed a Frenchman in France. I guess I'm not that mature after all.

Dad eyes me suspiciously at dinner. I know I'm beaming but can't shut it off. It's been forever since I had fun. He asks three times exactly what I did while he was on the run. I'm out of ways to say I just walked around.

Without reason, his eyes tear. "What is it?" I ask, relieved for the spotlight to shift.

"Mom would've loved seeing you so happy. Even more than Paris, and she would've enjoyed this trip immensely, she'd love this moment with you." His words send a bullet of shame to my heart — I spent the last three hours desperate to forget Her.

I can't come up with a response, so I nod and butter my bread. When the moment passes, I ask whether we're rich. "Officially I guess it depends which party is in office," he says, "but by most people's standards we are, yes."

"I guess I never realized it until this trip."

I don't expect the wary look he gives. He takes an aggressive cut into his steak. "You've lived a very privileged life, Eve, and if you didn't realize it before now, that's disconcerting."

I wave my hand in the air to cool him off. "Oh, calm down. I knew we were well off. I mean, everyone in Wellesley is, pretty much. It's more like . . . this past week — staying at such an outrageous hotel, going to the spa all day, ordering fancy champagne at dinner — it seems *different*. I mean, I'd never even heard of a personal shopper. You have to admit, Dad, we never went on a trip like this when Mom was alive."

Even before I finish the sentence I wish there was a way to take it back. My big mouth is no better than Lindsey's and Mrs. Anderson's and everyone else's back home.

I suck in my breath, terrified I've ruined an otherwise perfect week.

Dad looks back at me with a calm and knowing bob of his head. When did he get so Zen? I swear, the longer he runs a day, the nicer he is. "No, we didn't, at least not as a family, and I regret it. Your mother and I went on some long weekends here and there where we splurged, but I never gave us the time or permission to do it all together. I see that now. I see so many things differently." He takes a slow sip of champagne, then reaches across the table to squeeze my hand. Two months ago I'd have pulled away, but somehow this seems natural, like it would've coming from Mom. "This week would have made your mother so happy."

"She's here," I say, "watching us. I know it." As I say the words I sense her affirming them.

"Yeah, I guess I do too. Mostly, I hear her laughter when something is funny, particularly if the joke is on me and I'm not amused."

"She had the best sense of humor." I blot a napkin to my tears, checking the linen for mascara.

"She did. And an enormous heart." We never talk like this. It's hard to celebrate how wonderful she was without getting weighed down by how she died.

The waiter refills our water glasses. I can tell he's curious about our relationship. In Wellesley my dad and I are a known tragedy, here we're a curiosity. Based on our age difference, father and daughter is the most logical, but without a mother at the table people check us out. Rich guy with a young lover? Sleazeball and his escort?

When we're alone again, I say, "Thank you for this trip." I know he understands I don't mean the hotel or the clothes or the facial — or I do, but only partly — it's mostly a thank-you for proving there are good times to be had.

"You're welcome." He shifts his chair closer to me and scratches his neck, suddenly uncomfortable. "Listen, I actually have some news on that odd journal about Grandma."

I blink to catch up. "What kind of news?"

He tells me about finding Marie and Paul and his trip to Reston. I'm hurt. "You should've told me. Even if you didn't want me to go. I've asked like a million times if you heard back from Bobby."

His expression offers some sympathy, but he doesn't apologize. "I needed to go alone."

"She was my grandma."

He nods. "Yep. She was. But I'm sure you can appreciate that it's a sensitive situation for me."

I raise my eyebrows. "You're the one always saying we only have each other. We can't afford to have secrets."

Half his mouth winds up in a teasing smile. "So you don't keep *any* secrets from me?"

I think about Dameon's kiss and the journal and my recent struggle to see the point of life, then say, "Well, for the most part, I don't."

"I don't, for the most part, either." We grin at the fuzzy middle ground. My dad is funny. Well, maybe not funny, but not as serious as I thought either.

"So what were they like?"

He grunts. "They're whacked."

"Dad! I can't believe you just said that."

"It's the truth. They're eccentric, and I did not receive a warm welcome." He must sense my pity because his voice turns upbeat. "It's for the best. I don't need any more on my plate."

"Were they mean to you?"

"Nah. They just weren't nice. But the trip wasn't a waste. I learned a lot. With Mom gone, and everything I've uncovered about my own mother, I've come to terms with the fact that I've missed something with the women in my life, maybe even something about life in general, and I refuse to make the same mistake with you."

I'm honored. It's like winning a grand prize in a raffle I never knew I entered.

And there it is, the tender shiver of my mother crawling up my spine, cheering us on.

BRADY

I had no idea my daughter was a young woman, subject to the seductive glances of men and envious glares of less-blessed females, until this trip. I never even recognized her as beautiful, beyond the way I assume most fathers think of their offspring as good-looking. But Eve is what the current generation refers to as hot. Her complexion is clear and she adds a hint of blush to each cheek, so she always looks like she just returned from grabbing fresh air. She walks with her shoulders back in a confident posture and when she laughs, which has to be earned, her whole body moves with the sound, how it did with her mother. It's strange to put words to, but I'm getting to know my daughter and I like her. I mean obviously I love her, but I am discovering that I also enjoy her company. She's sarcastic as all hell, but she's fearless.

Her appeal sits with me now like something I can't quite digest. It'd help if this hot-air-balloon guide would stop staring at her breasts. I ignore him, knowing Eve will be annoyed if I make a stink. "I think that's the vineyard we ate lunch at yesterday," I say, pointing.

"Yeah, there's the stone patio. This is amazing. I feel closer to Mom up here."

Before I can respond, the guide says, "I do too. It's why I took this job."

Eve rolls her eyes at him and whispers, "He feels closer to *my* mom?"

Although this dipshit just ruined a moment I'm paying nine hundred dollars for, it's a relief to see her respond to the predator with authority. Still, the revelation makes me less certain about the boarding-school decision. It was one thing for Eve to leave when I thought of her as a child under the supervision of adults, but quite another if she's a young lady, capable of making adult-sized mistakes.

When we step out of the basket, my feet wobble to find their place on the ground. "You okay there, old man?" Eve teases.

The guide lets out a belly laugh disproportionate to the humor provided. I take advantage of the only offensive move I have and leave without offering a tip. He can ogle his heart out, but he's not having a drink on me tonight for the privilege.

We sit for lunch, both famished, having gotten up at four this morning. Eve replays how cool it was to float through the sky, but I'm distracted. She stops talking mid-sentence and says, "Hello? Dad. You there?"

I cannot hold back my observation. It's time for one of Maddy's serious talks. "Sorry. It's just . . . *well.*" My palms start sweating. "I've noticed . . ."

"Sp-sp-sp-spit it out," Eve says with a laugh.

She's right. I can't go through life afraid of her. "Okay, fine: I've noticed how much older you look, and how many men look at you with interest, and-and I want to make sure you're aware of it also, so you don't land in a precarious situation."

"Precarious situation?"

"It means —"

She puts a hand up. "I know what it means, Dad. Stop worrying. I think that's just how the French, like, are."

How can I explain that she's too beautiful not to worry without me turning into the inappropriate one? "Well, I do worry, Eve. You're at the age where people don't know if you're seventeen or out of college, and

383

I'm not stupid enough to believe your admirers only exist in this country. It's a problem."

"A problem?" Her arms cross. I'm losing her.

"Well, it could be a problem if you don't carry yourself in a conservative way. You have to send a clear message."

"What if I disagree?"

"You'd be wrong. I'm a man. I know about this stuff."

She looks me over with a questioning eye, struggling with the assertion that I represent a typical guy. "So what, Dad? Should I yell at people when they look at me?" She rolls her eyes like she did at the pervert guide. It infuriates me, but I want this discussion to be constructive, so I don't call her out on it.

"I just want you to be aware that as you grow up and look . . . older . . . people's intentions change. That's all."

"Okay, fine. I get it —"

"And," I pause to collect the thought that just revealed itself. "I'd like you to take a self-defense class when we get back."

"You've lost it."

"There are courses that take a day. Your mom took one once, and it's the least you can do for your poor father who's just re-alized that his little girl is a young woman."

"Oh, Jesus, here we go." Her expression is now playful. On some level, she's enjoying this.

"I'm serious, Eve. I'm really freaking out over here. Please take the damn class." Of everything I said, this is the line that endears me to her.

"Let's make a deal," she offers. "I'll take the class if you go on a date."

I'm still working on accepting her knack for catching me off guard. I take a sip of wine to buy time. "This isn't a negotiation, but why do you want me to go on a date?"

"I don't care if you do or not, but I've been looking for a way to let you know it's okay with me. You know, if you ever want to go on a date, I'm fine with that."

Her and Meg both. *Huh.* "I haven't wanted to go on a date."

What I want is sex. You never hear widows voice the sentiment, but I could stave off companionship indefinitely. Sex, not so much.

"Well, if you ever do, you'll know I'm fine with it, so you won't feel like you need my permission."

"I appreciate that," I say. And, surprisingly, I mean it.

That night I lie alone in the hotel bed, circling around Meg's and Eve's consent. I wouldn't know where to begin in the dating world. I might have been a subpar husband, but I was a faithful subpar husband. I don't even have a type. I mean, where the hell would I meet someone? I wouldn't mind getting laid, but can't picture marching a woman into the house Maddy decorated. And, really, how would I broach my past? I envision the conversation:

"Are you divorced?"

"No, a widow." With no other information the sympathy produced would likely be to my benefit, but then she'd carefully inquire how Maddy passed, assuming cancer. Curiosity killed the cat, as they say.

"Suicide," I'd confess.

Date over.

Even if I found someone who respected all I've been through, I can't imagine trusting happiness again. I think of Rory. She's a pleaser, like Maddy. The doubt would be torture. I'd drive us both insane relentlessly asking if she was content. And even if she swore she was, how could I be certain?

Loving a person doesn't make them who you desire; it makes you vulnerable to their reality.

CHAPTER SIXTEEN

MADELINE

Meg finished compiling the advice I gave her over the years and, as promised, sent a copy to Eve. It's matted professionally in a wooden frame with a gray border, the words carefully penned in her script. Despite each thought occurring during different phases of my life — high school through motherhood — Meg wrote it as prose. It looks like one of those old Irish blessings that gets passed through generations and eventually ends up hanging on a bathroom wall where people have time to read it.

Eve opens the card before unwrapping the frame. I'm grateful Meg took the time to preface my sentiments; many of the statements now deemed sage advice are questionable at best. Death glorified the profoundness of my thoughts.

Dear Eve,

Your mother didn't believe in each of these things with equal passion, but in the moment she spoke the words they were true to her. I'm not gifted with her self-awareness. I relied on my big sister for guidance as I set my course, and more often than not, I relied on her to gently point out when I lost my way. If I were to summarize her words of wisdom, I'd say this: the most important approval to earn in this life is your own.

Your mother was a philosopher in her own way, and so, I see now, are you.

Enjoy, Aunt Meg

MADDY'S TRUTHS

Make room for who you are by knowing who you're not. Smile all the time, at everyone, without exception: when you're happy it will be contagious, and when you're angry it will drive the person you're mad at bonkers. Blow-dry before lipstick. Counters before sweeping. Water before dinner. To hell with what everyone thinks about your life, but you should know what you think about it. Don't stay out past one

---

a.m. — nobody is proud of the stories born later than that. Plans contingent on perfection fail. It's dangerous to fight who you are. The stupidest thing you can do is believe your own bullshit, but you probably will every once in a while. Flowery perfume smells like a cover-up. Don't have a room your kids can't play in or a couch your kids can't sit on; it's their house too. If you don't know what to say, say, "I don't know what to say." If you mess up, say, "I messed up." If you need help, say, "I need help." Never count on any one thing. Don't confuse wanting to have sex and rent movies with someone for wanting to marry him. Never buy button-fly jeans — they aren't flattering on anyone ever. Practice love, compassion, and forgiveness. Try not to speak consecutively for more than two minutes; it's hard to be a good listener longer than that. It's good to have one friend who still smokes a lot of pot. It's important to speak up even if no one will stand behind you. A home is something you create. Gatorade and greasy food cure hangovers. The impression you have of someone is most likely the impression they have of you (that's why I'm so self-conscious around annoying people). Give yourself a break, but not a free pass. Never become a prize, possession, puppet, or toy — it's no fun hanging on someone's wall for any substantial amount of time. When someone gives you the creeps, don't worry about their feelings or apologize, just get the hell away. Constantly earn the hearts of your friends and family, and expect them to earn yours back. Ask questions. Don't give out answers you don't have. Think before you speak. Sometimes you'll lie, but have a person who knows both your truths and the lies you've told; pick someone who won't judge you. Don't give up on reading before you find a favorite book, and even then I don't recommend it. At the end of each day, acknowledge the things you wish you'd done differently so that tomorrow you will. We're given the gift of life with the consequence of death.

I remember saying all of it at one time or another, some repeated over and over and some thrown out only once, not knowing I had such an attentive audience. But I specifically remember telling Meg that final sentence at her home on the Cape, bundled up by the bonfire. It was almost Halloween. The air was crisp, mosquitoes had died off, and the stars were showing off more than usual.

Everyone else had gone in for the night when Meg confided that she had severe anxiety about death. "Common enough," I said, "but we'll all die."

"Well, yeah Maddy, I didn't say I was stupid, just anxious."

We laughed. Look, "you can obsess that our time is limited, ranking your memories on some giant scorecard, or you can truck on. I bet the people trucking on end up with the best scorecard."

"Wow. That's deep," she said. "Maybe I was wrong about you."

I slapped her arm, but then looked in her eyes and saw someone other than my little sister. Meg was a complicated woman, a peer, a mother in her own right. The insight helped me find the words she needed to hear. "Mock me all you want, but I've been thinking about mortality a lot too; maybe that's the age we're at. And the best I can come up with is this: we're given the gift of life with the consequence of death. I think it'd be a mistake to focus on the consequence instead of the gift."

That night when we hugged before bed, Meg said, "I'm glad I don't have to be the big sister. It must be such a burden to figure out everything first."

Her words inflated me. My life wasn't what I'd imagined. I envisioned commanding a larger sphere of influence. In my twenties I felt certain I'd be a CEO someday; in my thirties I came to believe that my contribution to the world was whatever Eve delivered (leveraging skills from her kick-ass mom); in my forties I realized Eve could cure cancer, but bragging about your awesome kid isn't enough to sail you through four more decades. It gnawed at me. Eve graduating would conclude my daily purpose if I didn't turn up a new beginning. Already the to-do list was thinning. Eve could drive. She no longer needed to talk through every unpleasant social interaction, and she certainly didn't need my help with homework. If it wasn't for volunteering at the library, I'd already have gone crazy. I became fearful of what happened to matriarchs after everyone grew up. Meg's words provided solace. My world turned out to be small, but damn it, my sister needed me, and so did Eve and Brady. Happiness is an every man for himself endeavor. To three people, I was everything, and that turned out to be enough.

Eve reads Meg's list as though she'll be tested on it. Most of the lines she'd heard me say before, but some are revelations. I was not, for example, planning to be so cavalier about sleeping with people and smoking pot. Meg believed my essence could only be captured with an unedited version. She's been on a mission to find her authentic self.

Brady is also surprised by Meg's openness. Months ago he'd have been angry, but now, with his increased comfort in Eve's capacity, he lets the perceived infraction slide. When Eve heads back upstairs, Brady touches the frame and calls Meg. " 'Don't feel pressure to use chopsticks,' " he says when she answers. " 'The fork is functionally superior.' " They both laugh for a moment, but Meg's end of the line quickly turns to weeping.

They haven't spoken since the funeral. It's hard to be around people whose loss matches your own. It's almost competitive. "I miss her, Brady," my little sister mourns. "I miss her so much."

"I know, Meg. Me too." He pauses. "Listen, I should have called sooner, but —"

"I have a phone. I know."

Brady resists his rising emotions. "You and Dan have been my family for twenty years. There's no one left on my side, for Eve and me. I don't want to lose you." He sucks the snot back into his nose at one last attempt to ward off tears. It doesn't work.

"You haven't lost us. Dan and I should've reached out. It's intense still. It's hard to imagine talking about anything other than the person missing. But we'll get there."

Brady's voice lowers to a whisper. "I was afraid you blamed me." He feels completely naked saying so. "I figured you thought something horrible must've been happening behind closed doors. Hell, maybe it did, but I certainly didn't know about it."

"No, Brady. Never. It didn't even cross my mind." She's lying; of course it crossed her mind. But Meg had the hardest time picturing me in trouble and not raising my hand for help. "I don't know what happened," she says, "but whatever it was, we both missed it." Her words, while not completely exonerating him, succeed in spreading the blame across more than one conscience.

There's silence as they pull themselves together. Brady is the first to speak. "So Eve said she called about staying there next weekend."

Meg takes one last emotional breath. "Yep. We're set. It's too bad you didn't make it to the Cape this summer, but it's pretty amazing you're running a marathon. The McManns are impressed. Dan said he'll eat a hot dog in your honor on Saturday."

"Don't be too awestruck. I have a lot of guilt to run off."

My sister lets out an uneasy laugh. "I'm thinking of quitting work, Brady."

"Why?"

"Same reason you started running, it sounds like."

Brady sighs. "You have nothing to feel guilty about, Meg."

"I don't know about that. I was never a giver like Maddy. I always took up more oxygen than her, and I feel horribly in the wrong about that now."

"No. *No.* You've always been someone who makes things happen. Maddy admired that about you."

Meg sniffles. "So, you vote for not quitting?"

"No, *Maddy and I* vote for not quitting. It's dangerous to fight who you are, right?" It's the first time Brady is positive that the voice he hears is truly mine. My power is fading, but his mounting openness makes up for it.

"Oh, Brady, bless you. I still need my big sister's advice, you know?"

Thank you, I pass down to Brady. Meg would make everyone miserable as a stay-at-home mom, herself included. Having an alcoholic mother from such a tender age left her craving structure. She needs an outlet for her competitive nature to avoid competing with Dan or, worse, Lucy. She's capable of immense love, but only when she feels needed and secure. Work is her anchor. Family is her safety net.

At least my sister is settled before my view dissipates completely. It's ironic though: the person I haven't been helping is the first to find her way.

EVE

Rory joins me for the self-defense course my father mandated. Our first assignment is to share why we registered. I say, "My father made me," and Rory says, "Her father made her." Everyone cracks up, especially the instructor, Eddie, who blatantly eyes Rory's left hand for a wedding ring.

Once we start doing drills it's clear Rory is a pro. She expertly completes every exercise, comfortably handling the oversized safety pads and showing me side moves. At lunch, Eddie uses his observation skills —

the number-one tool in self-defense — as an opening.

"Where did you train?" he asks, sitting at the picnic table as if we asked him to join us.

"I started when I was a kid and got my black belt in college." She takes a huge bite of her turkey sandwich. A little mayo squirts out the other side onto her cheek. Eddie ignores it. I pass Rory a napkin.

"Which discipline?"

"Kung fu. Shaolin."

"What?" I say. "Why the hell did you agree to do a beginner class with me?"

She ignores my language as usual. "Everyone can use a refresher, and I agree with your father that you should do this before you leave."

"You're her mother?"

"No," Rory says. "We're friends." I smile. That's how I've come to think of us too.

"That makes more sense. You're way too young to be her mother." I try to make eye contact with Rory about how obvious he's being, but she seems into him. Their expressions go a little gaga. "Any chance we could have dinner one night this week?" he asks.

Rory agrees. "At least I know I'll be safe," she jokes when he's gone. "That's more than I can say for most dates I've been on."

My dad pops to mind. He and Rory are about the same age. She's so genuine. And funny. Of course, he'd probably be an ass at some point and then things would be weird between Rory and me. I dismiss the thought. Better to stay out of it.

When we get home, Rory and my dad have a little celebration to mark my completion of precalculus. I'm curious whose idea it was. Rory made a chocolate cake and Dad got fancy takeout from the city. We stand in a circle, glasses raised. "Stubborn, but smart," my father toasts, clinking his glass to ours.

"Wonder where I get that from," I reply. We're so similar, my dad and me. I'm starting to realize that our problem was never not liking each other, it was that we *are* each other. And ours is a personality that needs watering down by a third party.

We chat for ten minutes or so, reliving events from the summer. When my tattoo becomes the topic of conversation I excuse myself to the restroom. I don't intend to eavesdrop, but they're talking about me when I come back, so I stop short of the doorframe. My father is trying to "square up" for the Sunday Rory stayed over and today's self-defense class. "I don't want any money for that," Rory says, refilling her glass, "but thanks for offering."

I catch a glimpse of my dad reaching his glass out for more too. "That's crazy," he says as he pours. "You've done so much for us this summer."

"I appreciate that, but it wasn't work. I'm not a saint. I took your money for tutoring because calculus was rough, and trust me, if I felt I was owed for more I wouldn't be shy. But I haven't been babysitting Eve. She's been there for me too. I wouldn't feel right being paid for my time." Knowing I wasn't intended to hear the compliment makes it that much more meaningful.

The truth is, if Dad were paying Rory he'd owe for more than today and his trip to D.C. I don't think he realizes how much we've been together this past month. The day we went to Exeter, we were gone eight hours. She got my class schedule and a campus map and walked me to each building. When the doors were unlocked, we went all the way to the classroom. Most had desks arranged as open horseshoes, some with as few as ten chairs. I freaked at how small the class sizes were, but Rory calmed me down, saying the only students who need to worry about small classes are the ones who don't do their work. Then she talked a janitor into letting us see my dorm so we could figure out how much space I had to work with. This week we went shopping. I wouldn't have known to get cinder blocks to raise my bed for storage space or sandals to wear in the shower. Warts were never a concern at my house.

After dinner I walk Rory to her car. "Thank you for all your help this summer. Not just calculus, but everything. Really."

"You have no idea how nice it is to have a young woman I can offer random advice to."

"And you have no idea how nice it is to get it."

She grins. "I'll never take responsibility for the tattoo, though. Fifteen years from now, when you have an inquiring child and you're trying to pin that decision on someone, I'll still declare my innocence." We laugh at her joke, but I'm more excited by the implication that our friendship won't end when I leave.

I replay the conversation to Dr. Jahns the next day, but he says I shouldn't count on the relationship continuing. "As you grow up, Eve, you'll see that sometimes adults make commitments because they don't want to let young people down. Rory might not realize she's doing it, but in the fall, when school starts back up, it'll be hard for her to keep in touch. I don't want you to be devastated if that happens."

I sit there and think about what it would take, now, to devastate me. After losing my mother, anything less than death is bearable.

This realization is still with me when I sneak in a journal entry before my dad gets home from work. I somehow pick one where my mom seems to be agreeing.

November 11, 2014
It's midterms for the Wellesley girls this week, so the library is packed. Their pure panic brings their immaturity to the front stage. With all I know now it's hard to believe the difference between an *A* and *B* ever seemed significant. I want to put a sign on the checkout desk that reads, "A year after you graduate, this will mean nothing to you."

Real things will happen to these ladies. Great things. Atrocious things. They will be faced with tests of character bearing much higher stakes than tests of intelligence. They'll look back at this finals-induced hysteria with perspective and have a good laugh at their own expense. Or the lucky ones will. The unlucky ones will never learn.

What I wish for my daughter more than anything is the gift of perspective at a young age. Perspective makes you asshole-proof. The two are mutually exclusive. And as long as you're not an asshole, you can find people to love you, and as long as you're loved, you can be happy.

Which means I should be happy. I need to get out of my current funk. I wish I could connect my sudden self-doubt to early menopause or thyroid changes, but I know my core is infected with regret. I am, right now, living the life I stole from my mother. The one I taught her to be ashamed of wanting.

Maybe I need to see a shrink.

I tear up at the idea of her hidden sadness. I was still catty and stuck-up at the time she wrote that, but I gained perspective with her death. It's hard to be arrogant when your mom decides that a terrifying death is more appealing than returning home to finish raising you. I might've been a disappointment to her when she was alive, but I'll do right by her wish now. I'll be strong and open and kind and, above all, not an asshole.

Seven minutes short. I failed to qualify. I ran twenty-six-point-two goddamn miles to come up seven minutes short. I look around for a ledge or a curb, anything to sit on.

A lady standing next to me flails a finger at a friend. "No. I'm telling you, your qualifying time is based on the age you'll be at the Boston Marathon. You're a September birthday, right?"

In my depleted state, it takes a second to process that I'll also be a year older by then, which means three hours and twenty-seven minutes is good enough. I do a little fist pump that does not go unnoticed. "I'm glad I sat here," I explain when the women look my way. "I didn't think I'd made it."

The runner smiles. "Me neither. And I would have been pissed." Her words are more aggressive than you'd expect given her petite frame. "Pamela," she says.

"Brady." We exchange basic pleasantries as the crowd ebbs. It's refreshing to converse with someone who assumes your life is normal. She owns her own commercial real-estate business in Boston. This was her first marathon. She's a Patriots fan too.

I don't know if it's delirium from the run or if I'm just up for celebrating, but I ask Pamela to dinner. Her friend giggles and politely looks the other way, pretending to be distracted by someone in the crowd.

Pamela scowls at my wedding ring. "I don't think so," she says coldly, wiping a new layer of sweat from her forehead with the back of her hand. "Your wife deserves a little more respect, don't you think?"

I clam up, unable to respond, as though I've been justly busted. I look around for an exit strategy, but people are everywhere. Pamela continues her lecture. "I've been on the receiving end of a husband like you before. Worst decision I ever made." She mutters something with the word *asshole* in it and turns back to her friend.

I look to the pavement, ashamed. Suddenly, the sounds of the city and crowd merge together into an unintelligible din that clouds my ability to think. As if there's an earthquake, my footing becomes unstable. My heart pounds more than it did during the race. I can't make sense of what's happening, but this-this *force* that has taken me hostage shouts at Pamela's back, "Maddy is gone. *Dead.* She died. And I wasn't there to stop her." My legs buckle beneath me and I fall to the ground. I look ridiculous, and I know it, but I'm not in control. All the tears I replaced with temper tantrums and expensive bourbon pour out now, a sprung leak.

Newly finished runners swarm me. Some are jovial, slapping my back, saying things like "It's all over buddy!" or "You did it, man!" I lay there, blanketed in sweat, sobbing.

There's a soft kick at my side. Pamela stands over me, arms extended. I reach for them and she pulls me up. "Where are you staying?" she asks. I point down the street to the Hyatt. "Okay, okay, I'll get you there. Walk with me."

She props her small frame under my shoulder, leading me through the maze of people. Her height is misleading; the woman is solid muscle. I lean on her in a complete haze, emotionally and physically spent.

She brings me all the way to my room. I collapse on the hotel comforter that Maddy always took off right away because you never knew what foul things had taken place on it, and fall asleep.

It's dark when I wake. The humiliation of my finish line debacle wakes with me. A thick film covers my body like a wet suit. My eyes are swollen, my head is throbbing, but mostly, I'm thirsty. Savagely thirsty. Kill-a-man thirsty. I drink both of the four-dollar waters on the dresser, then hit the minibar for apple juice, orange juice, pineapple juice, and iced tea. When I finish, about forty dollars later, I enjoy the primal sense of survival. I stretch, smelling myself with disgust, and head to the bathroom for a shower.

The water has an almost spiritual quality. It's roasting hot and I welcome the burn. I soap and then soap again, scrubbing away the memory of my mental breakdown. I can picture Dr. White correcting me at my next session: "Brady, what you're describing is a break*through,* not a breakdown. Your core is finally admitting the magnitude of its loss. That's progress."

I stand under the scalding water so long my body acclimates to it. *Is it progress?* I'm mortified by my lack of composure, but damn it, I do feel lighter having gotten that out. When I finally call it and turn off the shower, the steam is so thick it seeped underneath the bathroom door into the bedroom.

Refreshed and donning only a towel, I call Eve at the Cape. She picks up on the first ring, worried I hadn't called sooner. As soon as I tell her my time qualified, she forgets her anxiety and cheers with genuine excitement. "I'm so proud of you, Dad. You worked so hard." I might be the only man to ever hear those words from his seventeen-year-old daughter.

"Thanks, Bean. I'm sort of proud of me too. How's the Cape?"

"Good. We miss you. Uncle Dan says there's too much estrogen in the house, and if I ever come without you again, he's staying home."

"Tell him I can only imagine. I won't let it happen twice." I have no intention of sharing my "breakthrough," so after I hear about their gorgeous beach day we say good night.

I'm starving.

The lobby bar is hopping with runners. I'm eager to blend in with the crowd and knock back a few celebratory drinks, until I see her. Apparently, escorting me to the Hyatt wasn't out of Pamela's way. I try to duck out, but she taps my shoulder as I turn to leave. "I was about to call and check on you. I'm glad you came down."

I want to disappear. I'd banked on the fact that, statistically, I'd never see this woman again. Yet here we are, five hours later. I improvise, determined not to lose any more credibility. "Um, I'm actually getting room service. I'm here to snag a menu because there wasn't one in my room."

She smiles and I remember why I was initially attracted to her. "Well, I'm glad you seem to be feeling better. And congratulations on qualifying."

"You too. Listen," I start, but what can I say? Sorry I completely lost my shit earlier? I clear my throat. "About before, I don't know what came over me." I grab a menu off the bar with the intent to excuse myself.

"No, I'm sorry. I have a big, fat mouth and it gets me in trouble sometimes."

"You couldn't have known. I don't know why I still wear the ring."

Pamela adjusts the clasp on her necklace. "I only wish I could take back my reaction. It's the last thing you needed." A nice, simple response. I let it sink over me.

"It felt good to let it out, actually." I tell myself to stop talking, to get upstairs, to jump off the bar mezzanine, anything to end the embarrassment of putting such raw vulnerability on display. But there's nothing waiting for me in my room or anywhere else. And that smile.

"Let me buy you an appetizer," I suggest, "as payment for your courier service. I'm not a light load."

"Great. Anything without shellfish. I'm allergic."

I flag down the bartender and order two martinis, chicken wings, and a nacho, then turn back to Pamela. "So where in Boston do you live?"

Three martinis later the crowd has faded and Pamela gets the courage to ask about Maddy. "Was it cancer?"

"No," I say, shaking my head. "I wish. God, that sounds terrible." I slug back the rest of my drink. It's none of her business, and yet I want to confess, to get it over with so she can plan her exit. "She took her own life." I look her right in the eyes as I say it, shocked to find only compassion.

"I'm so sorry."

The only reason she hasn't bolted is because she doesn't understand. "It was my . . ." I can't say fault. I didn't suggest it. I didn't push her. "I was working too much, traveling all the time, and I think — I don't know — I can be cold, distant."

Pamela leans in and speaks softly. "For depression to take your wife to such an extreme, she had to be trapped inside her own thoughts to a point where she couldn't perceive the ripple effect of her decision." I look up. It's the first time anyone has attempted to understand Maddy's frame of mind. "Brady: she wasn't leaving *you;* she was leaving *her.*"

My senses flood. *Is it possible?* I have a sudden compulsion to read Maddy's last journal entry. If Pamela's right, the answer will be there. I flag the bartender. "Put it all on my tab." He nods.

"I'm sorry to leave like this, I am, but this day —"

"Go," she says. "Think and cry and sleep. We'll catch each other in Boston sometime."

I bolt for the elevators Cinderella style, grateful for Pamela's ability to read the situation so well. Once in the safety of my room, I retrieve the journal and flip to the last page. I've been a coward, putting it off for so long. It's the equivalent of a suicide note. If Pamela is right, it'll show in Maddy's words.

April 13, 2015

Easter kind of gives me the creeps. Rising from the dead? The story allows the idea of the afterlife to function as a sort of insurance policy. It makes it too easy to never face fears or regrets. I don't think the universe should hand out free passes. Combing through the weeds of my childhood with a therapist allowed me to find compassion for my mother, which freed the chip from my shoulder. I'm fortunate for the autonomy in my life. I was able to have a hiccup and get help without Eve and Brady even knowing.

I believe there's a higher power. There has to be. Science can't rationalize it all.

To our understanding, there's no such thing as nothing, which means there's always been something, which means there is a divine force at work.

I'm excited for our family run on Easter Sunday so I can ask Brady and Eve what they think about these things. It is, hands down, my favorite of our family traditions. Meg says we're a sacrilege, and maybe we are, but Easter doesn't make any more spiritual sense to me than a long family jog where we all take the time to connect. I'm finally at an age where I no longer have an intense need to be understood. I just want to learn from the past and move on.

I read the entry thirty times, thrown. She saw a therapist about her mother, but she doesn't sound caged by depression. Or angered by my flawed priorities. Or saddened by Eve's independence. She wasn't in love with someone else or drinking too much or tired by the banality of suburban life.

Why the hell did she leave us?

CHAPTER SEVENTEEN

MADELINE

A fog has set in. It won't be long now; I can only faintly make out the scenes unfolding below. I keep expecting a glimpse of my final destination but the openness above appears infinite.

I take note of the oak tree we planted out front when Eve was in kindergarten. It was Earth Day and every child came home with a sapling. I had no hope — I couldn't conceive how such a puny, flimsy thing could defend itself from New England's nor'easters — but I let Eve take care in picking a spot. *It needs sunlight,* she said, *and lots of space.* I assumed Eve's interest would wane when she woke up the next morning and there wasn't yet a branch to swing from, but I was mistaken. She watered that thing every day. When she noticed a deer sniffing nearby, she chased it away. *We have to protect it,* she begged. *It's our tree.* I googled "protecting oak saplings" and — of course — there was a wiki page and YouTube video that made it look easy enough. Twelve years later, and it's the size of Eve. The memory supports many truths: plant yourself in a place that gives you room to grow; let the light in; everyone needs help to survive; have patience.

The philosophical thought turns dark; the damn tree outlived me. I should be there ten years from now, when Eve is full-grown and her tree towers over us all as a reminder of the impact we can have. I wasn't patient that night. I didn't give myself enough space. When a decision had to be made, I thought of my mother. My *mother,* of all people! If I'd thought of Eve and Brady, everything would be different now, but I thought of my mother and how I hadn't done enough. I'd failed her, and she took her life, and this was the universe giving me a chance to make it right. I was so certain.

I spend what I assume to be my last moments telling Eve I love her. I repeat it over and over like waves lapping the shore. I remember thinking I'd found true love with Brady, but when Eve arrived I discovered love has tiers and motherhood is the pinnacle. I wasn't much of a scorekeeper, but parenting was the only relationship where

413

the idea of keeping score was preposterous. Eve and I were on the same team, united. When she won, I won, and when she lost — even when the lesson learned was valuable — I ached for her. Unlike with Brady, it was a simple love. I wanted nothing in return.

Well, that's not true. I wanted time. I wanted so much more time.

My musings continue as I watch Kara pull down our driveway. Even so far removed, the Andersons' neon-yellow Jag stands out. An obnoxious car for obnoxious people. I don't process what it means until I sense Kara's panic and shame.

"Stay away," she warned that night, her eyes frantic. But my mother's face flashed before me and I knew I couldn't turn my back on someone so desperate. Not again. Not a child. I replayed Brady's lectures on having boundaries and saying no even as I nuzzled my way so far into the Andersons' problem that it became my problem instead. I liked my life, loved it even, and Kara must be here to tell my family that. *Thank you,* I say now. *Thank you.* How brave of her to come forward. I honestly never thought she would. Of all the girls, Kara's was a callousness I assumed incurable. I wonder what broke her down?

I linger briefly on the idea that I spared
Christie the unnatural grief of burying her
own. The thought warms me with pleasure
and my spirit climbs higher still. I can't
make out Eve's expression as she answers
the door, but I'm no longer afraid. I have
finally pieced together the corollary: they
will find their way without me. My presence
might expedite fate, but in loitering I give
up whatever's next for me. I'm inflated with
the understanding that I wasn't sentenced
to this purgatory; I opted in, unready to
leave my family. With the appreciation that
their lives aren't waiting on me I'm free to
move on, but first, I pass one final message
to Eve. *Forgive her,* I beg. *Practice love,
compassion and forgiveness.* Anger is nothing but an anchor that keeps you from moving forward.

The peace surrounding me intensifies, and
the vibration returns, creating a soft hum.
I'm transforming. The light I craved as I fell
finds me now, welcoming me toward it. It's
easy to identify the energy seeping in: it is
love. I'm ready to be loved again. I have no
duty to serve my past life, except every once
in a while to offer a warm shiver of praise
to my daughter or the sound of my laughter
joining Brady's for an inside joke.

EVE

I'm unloading groceries when the doorbell chimes. It's Kara, only without her usual makeup and smug look on her face. She's in a hoodie and reeks of rum. We stare at each other for a second.

"What happened to you?" I ask, but even as I say it I suspect it's really me something happened to.

"Can I come in?" She looks behind her shoulder like she might've been followed.

"Are you drunk?"

"Does it matter?"

Given her paranoia she's probably drunk and stoned. This should be a fun chat. I open the door. Kara stays standing, her eyes darting around the room as if she's looking for something. "I was there," she whispers. "Your mom didn't jump."

I'm still registering her words when I realize that she plans to bail, as if the movie is over, as if the movie has even started. I pull her down to the couch by the elbow, my nails digging into her skin. She waits for me to say something, which is crazy because I can't even breathe. If Mom didn't jump then *how*? *Why*? What could Kara possibly know about it? I stare at her, searching for my voice, until she gets that I can't speak and starts talking. "So I used my dad's

416

laptop to get directions and his email was up. He was having an affair wi—"

"There's no way in hell my mom —"

"Shut up and listen," Kara snaps. "It was some slutty professor — Courtney Lawrence, Courtney Lawrence, Courtney Lawrence — there must've been forty emails all right there. I was so pissed off and I saw she had a Wellesley College email so I looked her up. A professor of psychology. Her bio said she enjoys mountain climbing with her gay-looking husband so I was, like, perfect, and after practice the next day I drank a three-hundred-dollar bottle of pinot noir my gigolo of a father had been saving for the perfect fucking occasion, and went to Wellesley to put the bitch in her place."

For months I've practiced drowning Kara out; she's such a fast talker it was easy to do. Now I'm desperate to catch every word. I read her lips to follow along. "Her office was in the library so I busted in and was all, 'You better back off my dad or I'll tell your husband what's going on,' and the trampy bitch looked at me like I was a little pathetic kid she felt sorry for and said, 'I don't think you understand the situation.' " Kara pulls a flask out of her hoodie, takes a sip, then grunts. "So I was like, 'Pretty sure I got it

— you're a skank and you're sleeping with my father and if you don't stop I'm going to ruin your life.' And she just looked at me with this shit-eating grin. I was totally confused. Then she goes, 'You should talk to your parents.' Talk to my *parents*? So I go, 'WHAT THE FUCK?' "

I jump in my seat. Kara laughs, mumbles something more about Courtney Lawrence, and takes another swig.

My thoughts are frozen. I can't see how this story and my mom collide, but they must. *She didn't jump.* That's what she said. And if she didn't jump, then she didn't want to leave me, and if she didn't want to leave me, then I shouldn't be alone. I grab the flask from Kara's hand. She raises her eyebrows, daring me to hear more, like there's anything she could say that'd be worse than what she hasn't said all these months. "You're cut off," I say. "Keep talking."

She rolls her eyes. "I stared at the ho. When she saw I wasn't leaving I guess she figured *what the hell* and goes, 'Do you know what an open marriage is?' And I didn't, not really, but as soon as she said it I did. And I said no, *no way,* and that skinny bitch just smiled and said yep. YEP. An open marriage meant it went both ways. It was such a mind fuck.

"I ran from her office, I needed to get the hell away, but then I didn't know where the fuck to go. And then it was like, *duh,* oh my fucking god, all these things clicked. Like Coach Wilkins picking my mom up one night and the weird dinner we had with my old babysitter and her boyfriend from college and the time I called my parents' hotel on vacation and the receptionist asked which of their rooms I wanted. It was this cracked-out list that kept growing and growing. I felt wicked sick. I ran to the bathroom to puke and as I was heaving I thought — it could be worse — at least no one else knows."

She grabs the flask from my hand and tips it back, laughing when some of it misses her mouth. "It's as close as I've ever been to a real live retard. EVERYONE KNEW. I mean, you knew, right?"

She's so totally out of it. I'm afraid I'll lose her if I give the wrong answer. "I just want to know what happened to my mom," I whisper.

"You *knew.* I can tell you knew. Everyone fucking knew." She looks at me, disgusted. "Right there on the bathroom floor I saw it so clearly — Mike's jabs after I slept with Doug when I was dating Noel; the football guys laughing their asses off when I got on the swing after homecoming; making varsity this year even though I totally suck. I'm the only loser who didn't fucking see it."

Her body starts to teeter. She can't pass out, not yet, not *here.* I hold her up. "Tell me about my mom."

"I laid on the nasty bathroom floor and played this whacked-out game of connect-the-dots. My parents were whores. People must joke about us all the time. They do, don't they? DON'T THEY?"

The moment doesn't seem real, but I slow my brain down enough to understand that Kara won't go on without an answer. "Yeah," I admit. "People joke."

Kara lets out a stink-bomb burp. I back away. She cracks up. She's legit insane. "I'm SCREWED," she shouts. "Do you get it, Eve? My parents fucked all the people that'd have them in this little piece-of-shit town and now I'm branded for life."

She starts to cry, but all I hear is what she hasn't said. I shake my head. "Who cares about your parents' fucking soap opera? At least you *have* parents." Calm and steady is not getting her attention. I nudge her. Hard. "What happened to my mother?"

"Augh. God! You're like that bitch who follows me fucking everywhere. This wasn't my fault! I went to leave, but then I saw through a glass wall that the door to the roof was propped open with a vacuum. It was like a sign or something. I couldn't imagine going home and facing them. Or going back to school. Or living at all with such a fucked-up family. Who marries a girl with swingers for parents? I might as well have a big fucking scar across my face. So I ran up the staircase. She must have seen me — right? — because as soon as I swung my legs over the barrier I heard your mom. I couldn't believe my bad fucking luck. She was yelling from the other side of the ledge but there was machinery and shit so I couldn't hear. I needed to jump before she had time to get help. And, *fuck me,* I don't know . . . maybe she knew that was my plan because instead of running downstairs she came right over the barrier and stood next to me." She stops for a second to stare at me. "Your mom was such a damn do-gooder."

Tears gush from my eyes fast enough to carry the current right over the hand that grips my neck. My mother wanted to live. Of course she did. How did I ever believe otherwise? I look at Kara, graduating from shock to relief to *rage.* I'm having a conversation with the person responsible for her death. I want her out of my house, but not as badly as I want every detail. "Tell me what she said," I yell. "Or did you push her?"

She shakes her head no. "I didn't. I *swear*. I liked your prissy mom. I'd rather sixteen years with her than a lifetime with mine."

I stand, towering over her. "Sixteen years is all I got." Wasted as she is, Kara looks scared. Good. She tries to get up but I take my hand to her shoulder and force her back down. I'm taller and stronger. "Tell me what she said." Kara doesn't deserve to be the only one who knows my mother's last words.

She blows her nose right into her hoodie. "She said there's a reason for everything, that the reason no one else could volunteer that afternoon was so she could be there for me. I didn't say anything but she kept going on about how life is hard but worth it, that we all need to suffer so we can appreciate when things are good, that she'd been feeling sad too earlier this year so she got help and now she's stronger. I told her about Courtney Lawrence and she said, 'So what? Who cares? You don't have to make the same choices your parents make.' "

My tears have stopped. I've moved to hatred. Absolute hatred beyond anything

I've ever felt before. If only Kara had jumped right away. Then the rest of this story wouldn't matter. I want her dead.

"Then what?" I want every detail. I need to be there with my mom.

"I don't *know,* okay? I don't . . . she was looking right at me, right in my eyes, and everything went all slo-mo. I went back over the barrier. I took a step toward the door, assuming she'd follow. I guess maybe she started to but slipped. Or something. I didn't see it. But I heard the scream. Fucking awful."

I lunge at Kara, shoving her chest against the back of the couch with everything I have. But then I hear my mom. *Forgive her.* I laugh. I actually laugh. But I hear her again. *Forgive her. Practice love, compassion, and forgiveness.* That was Mom's big mantra. She preached that love, compassion, and forgiveness are capacities you have to actively engage because experiences will strip you of them if you aren't careful.

I feel none of those things, but her words calm me enough to consider what more I need to know from Kara. "Why didn't you help her?"

"By the time I looked, it was over. She must have slipped, right? She had on these high-heeled boots and —"

The detail infuriates me. "I know what shoes she was wearing. Don't talk to me like I don't know what shoes she wore that goddamn day!" Kara takes the opportunity to move to my right and stand to leave, but she's staggering enough for me to get ahead before the door and block her exit. "If it was an accident why didn't you tell someone? Why didn't you get help?" My eyes beg her to fix it now, to change the ending.

She shrugs. "Your mom was dead. It's not like it really mattered how she got there."

I drop to the floor, disgusted, shocked. But I shouldn't be. Every time Kara did something horrible my mom would ask why I was surprised. *Kara has always been in it for Kara.* She must've warned me a million times.

"Why tell me now?" I call to her back as she walks to the car.

Kara shudders, again looking around like there's an audience. "Because I'm haunted. I swear it." She tries to take another swig from her flask but remembers it's empty and drops it on the driveway instead. "I can't sleep because the second I do she crawls into my dreams and lets out that scream. And I can't focus because she talks over whatever else is happening. *Tell Evie. Tell Evie. Tell Evie.* She's obsessed. It's like having a song loop in my fucking brain. I wish I'd just jumped that night. So fuck it. She wins." Kara twirls around shouting, "Are you happy now? My parents are sex fiends and Mrs. Starling didn't kill herself. So now can you leave me the fuck alone?"

It's over. There's nothing more to say. Kara steps over the flask and gets in her car, mumbling that it's my turn to ruin her life, and peels out of the driveway.

Kara's ghost was Gram. It had to be. I only saw her once a year until I was eight and she died, but Gram is the *only* person who ever called me Evie. It drove my mom crazy — "If I wanted to name you Evie, I would've named you Evie," she always said.

I remain collapsed on the tile, unable to shut the front door. My mom loved me. And we were happy. Her words come back to me again. *Practice love, compassion, and forgiveness.* Only now, I'm certain the voice is real. It's Her. If Gram can get in Kara's head then Mom can get in mine. She wouldn't have harassed Kara, my mother didn't have it in her to torture someone like that, but she'd definitely sing me lyrical lessons and pass down wisdom and comfort.

I close my eyes and picture her on that ledge, feeling victorious as Kara moved to safety, her mind already plotting what to do next. The image is so clear it's as if I'm there, as if the memory is now mine. She turns and reaches for the top of the barrier, but misses. She looks at her hand like it failed her. Realizing she's off balance, then her foot slips. She reaches both arms toward the ledge but gravity has already won.

My breathing slows. She died terrified. She had no time to think of me or Dad or her garden or the book she'd never read the end of. I cry, but this time I cry for *her*. Not me. Her. For all *she* lost. Her death *was* a sacrifice. A sacrifice for Kara.

I lift myself up. Of course she hadn't left Kara alone that night. My mom wasn't a shirker. If she was in a position to help, she'd see it as her duty. She'd see it through to the end.

My mom was a hero.

BRADY

I'm not even through the door when Eve says it wasn't suicide. Her face is serene — the contradiction between what was said and her expression baffle me.

"Kara came here."

"Kara Anderson?"

"Yeah. She's the one who went out on the ledge. Mom talked her back inside."

"What?"

"She fell, Dad. It was an accident."

I slide my back down the wall and onto the floor. It doesn't make sense. "Why was she there?" I ask. "Why didn't she say anything?"

Eve shakes her head. "It was *messed up*. Kara found out her parents are total nymphos and got wasted and just, like, snapped. Mom calmed her down, but then fell."

I take off my tie. The veins in my forehead drum against my skull. I can see Eve is relieved — at least Maddy's death doesn't betray our memory of who she was — and I am too, only relief sits second to my anger. A far second. I get up and grab the portable phone. "I'm calling the police."

"To say what?"

My voice gets louder as I speak. "To say my wife was a goddamn saint. That she wasn't depressed. That Kara fucking Anderson decided it was okay to screw with us all. I'm going to demand the state press charges."

Eve squeezes her eyes shut. "What's the point, Dad? I get what you're saying, but we can't change what happened."

I back away as if Eve might infect me with her ability to forgive. "So it's okay with you that Kara let everyone think your mother was unhappy? She let everyone believe

Mom took her own life. That's okay with you?"

Eve throws her hands in the air. "No, it's not *okay*. But it is what it is. At least we know, Dad. At least she told us. It could be worse. Think about what Mom would —"

"No." I cut her off. I see what she's saying but can't match it. There's a certificate that lists my wife's cause of death as suicide. It's disrespectful to Madeline, disrespectful to our life together.

Eve endures thirty minutes of questioning at the police station.

"Did Kara indicate she asked or otherwise coerced your mom to step out on the ledge?"

"No. She said her instinct was to jump before my mother could get help."

"Did Kara in any way indicate her movements on the ledge caused your mom to fall?"

"No. She said she was already headed toward the door."

"But she knew your mom fell?"

"Yeah, she heard her scream."

I listen in awe. Eve's recall is impeccable. She rationally delivers this sensitive material in a way I never could've at her age. Or now. Imagine what this afternoon was like for my daughter: she consumed facts that are, at most lenient, emotional and, at most accurate, life altering. Then she thought about them, independently, and developed her position. And now she's here supporting me, even though we disagree. Seventeen going on thirty.

The detectives stand. "What now?" I ask.

"We question Kara."

Eve and I wait in silence. After a few minutes she reaches over and squeezes my hand twice. A simple gesture of backing. She's telling me we're a team. No matter what.

Neither officer makes eye contact when they return. "Kara's story was consistent," the older one says, "although harder to understand because she's still quite intoxicated."

They exchange glances to determine, without speaking, who will break the news. The rookie loses the silent argument. "We talked to the D.A. and there's really no action for us to take at this point. Miss Anderson did not commit a criminal act."

"How is that possible?" I sneer. "She knew it wasn't suicide and failed to come forward. How is that not illegal?" Eve stays mute, willing me to drop it, but I can't be the bigger person here. Maddy believed in showing love, compassion, and forgiveness, but some things are unpardonable.

"The fact is, Madeline's death was an accident. The only possible argument for liability would be that she created a perilous situation for your wife, and then failed to make an effort to protect her."

"That's true. That's what happened."

He scratches his cheek. "It's a stretch. She only really created a perilous situation for herself. Your wife stepped into it voluntarily."

"Can't you argue that by going out on a ledge, you're creating danger for anyone that finds you? Obviously if someone notices you're there, they're going to try to help."

"Even if we could prove that, your wife slipped. There's nothing the state could argue Kara could've done to save her. For a charge to stick, she needs to have failed to take action."

I shake my head defiantly. "She killed my wife."

The older officer sighs. "Because of her your wife is dead, no one is arguing that, but she didn't *kill* her."

"What about the fact that she didn't report it? Isn't that negligence or accessory or something?"

"There's no law in Massachusetts that you

have to report a crime. Not to mention that we just concluded there was no crime. And keep in mind that she's a kid. She was probably scared to come forward."

I need to conjure up an angle that puts Kara in a position to pay.

I catch Eve's eye. She looks so much like Maddy, sitting there, waiting for me to come to my senses. A wave of oxygen courses through me. *That's it.* That's why Eve is so serene. She's thinking of it the way Maddy would have: everything happens for a reason. So what's the reason Eve sees that I'm missing?

It's a fact that we learned more from Maddy's death because we thought it was a suicide. If I'd known it was an accident, I would've been angry at the world and retreated to work. I wouldn't have questioned my life, my priorities. And if I hadn't done that, I wouldn't have worked so hard to find common ground with Eve. And if I hadn't done that, I would've become a bitter workaholic with an estranged daughter. Kara's cover-up was to my benefit. The epiphany calms me.

Eve and I stand to leave as though on cue. I put my arm around her and she clasps into my side, our physical closeness no longer uncomfortable. We leave the officers confused by what transpired during the silence. As we walk away, the older one calls out, "We'll get that death certificate changed, though."

EPILOGUE

Ten Years Later

EVE

I'm the matron of honor in Rory's wedding.

Robert is even crunchier than she is. He's such a passionate advocate for natural beauty that Rory grew out her roots as a wedding present. She's only fifty, but she prances around with silver hair and an AARP card, saying things like "When I grow old I shall wear purple." I joked that Madeline will think her auntie is the Fairy Godmother.

"Fairy *Grand* mother is more like it," she said with a snort.

Brian agrees with his sister that her hair makes her look older. Change is hard for him, but eventually, he gets there.

Rory was the maid of honor at our wedding three years ago. For her speech she said: *I'd take credit for my dear friend and younger brother falling in love, but they did that on their own. A lawyer and a writer might seem an unlikely match, but what better combination is there than confidence and curiosity?*

We connected one night when Brian picked up Rory at my apartment in the North End. I knew him only from the piercing memory of their mother's funeral. When I opened the door my image softened. He'd changed; life had beaten him down to a more honorable perspective. Rory said it was Greta who sparked it. He still takes her to lunch once a month, not only to atone, but to get to know his mother through her dear friend. It's amazing what can happen when someone learns to learn from pain.

We were clumsy in our introductions that night; neither of us intended it to be more than a standard pickup/drop-off scenario. "Aren't you coming to dinner?" he asked, feigning surprise when I said I wasn't. "I'd like you to," he pushed, to Rory's surprise. "And it's my birthday. I'm just saying."

By the end of dinner I knew I'd be tied to Brian forever. He still has a slight arrogance, but there's something soothing about it, something that brings out a more assured version of myself. He reminds me of my father. The next day two dozen roses arrived with a note that read: *Your presence was the perfect present.*

I worried Dad would be put off by our age difference, but he just shrugged and said, "You've been older than your time for a while now. He makes sense to me, if he makes sense to you." His acceptance didn't stop him from joking though. He refers to our nine-year age gap as *the delta.* Whenever he starts in, Brian gives it right back to him. "I might've robbed the cradle," he'll quip in front of Pamela, "but at least I made an honest woman out of her."

Pamela jumps to her own defense. "I'm a hell of a lot more honest than any attorney."

Though her aggressiveness is occasionally at my expense, Pamela has been a blessing for my dad. He wasn't looking to replace my mom. He knew that wasn't possible. He was looking for the person you'd pick to be stranded on an island with. I'd probably pick Pamela for that too — she's a modern-day warrior.

Their relationship allowed me to go to California for college without worrying about my dad. The West Coast is where I discovered myself as a writer and where I learned to enjoy people again, to laugh despite loss. Some are offended by the idea that there's beauty in mourning, but I can't afford to be swayed by them. For a long time, my loss was all I had. I've trained myself to appreciate the independence and knowledge that accompanies pain. So my tattoo did serve a purpose, though Dad and Rory were right — it looked hideous during my third trimester carrying Madeline.

It was an Exeter alumni connection that ultimately got my first poem published in *Underground,* a literary magazine that only people in the industry are familiar with. I can hardly remember my state of mind when I wrote it, but I embrace the words as a part of my history.

DISSOLVING

I am everywhere God is
Encompassing a truth
A truth that does encourage compassion
And this startles me
But from this vintage view
I can distinguish the universal difference:
Truth the drought that drains the terrain
Just there, just is, no justice
It does not cater to reality as compassion
   does
Molding structure into an eroded tomb of
   bias
It does not seek it with fury

As its destination is always right where you
  are
Going where you're going
And from these eyes I've borrowed brilliant
  power
Compassion surrendering
Dissolving like the sugar in my iced tea
Not sweet though —
Bitter.

Rory still has a framed copy on her mantle. "I don't totally get it," she admitted over the phone, "but it came from you, so I love it."

Aunt Meg read more into it. "I only wonder if it means you're healing or still raw from her death?"

"Healing," I assured. "At least this way I've put my pain out there. At least I'm not afraid of it."

"You're just like your mother," she said. A compliment of the highest order.

After school I found California crowded, and the mild season changes made it hard to keep track of time, but mostly, I came back to be closer to Dad. He and Pamela live in the same house I grew up in. It doesn't appear they'll ever marry. "You get married for the kid's sake," Pamela confided once after a couple glasses of wine, "or for money. But my kids are grown and I'm rich as all hell, so if your dad doesn't want to wear rings that's fine with me."

They came to Rory and Robert's wedding, cheering on little Madeline as she crawled down the aisle. Rory is the only person clever enough to dress up the flower girl as an actual flower because she's too young to walk. I can't wait to see the pictures. Madeline has my mother's eyes and full cheeks. More painful than my loss is knowing she'll never meet her namesake, and vice versa.

Brian squeezes my knee under the table. It's my turn. I stand, one hand to my heart, and hold up a glass. "To watch the person who found your happiness find happiness is a beautiful thing. The day I knew Rory would always be a mentor, she said, 'You don't always get to know what happened, or why things happened a certain way, but it always, *always,* goes deeper than any one thing.' I look at her life, and all she's done for others — her students, her family, her friends . . . *me* — and then I think about Robert entering the picture, and giving all that love back, and I realize Rory is right. Their love brings me a sense of justice, something I've struggled to find for a long time. They'll be happy because they found each other at a point in their lives when they know what a gift it is. Please raise your glass for my mentor and best friend, and her lovely husband, to toast the blessing that happened on this day."

When I lean down to hug Rory I whisper, "Sometimes I feel like you were sent by my mother."

SHOUT-OUTS

Okay, raise your glasses! A toast:

To my husband, Kevin Wittnebert, for absolutely everything.

To my sister, Sarah Byrnes, for being my first reader and pro bono therapist, and to her husband, Matty, for his complimentary legal advice on the ending.

To agent Elizabeth Winick Rubinstein — it's not just her name that's badass.

To the entire team at St. Martin's Press — Jennifer Weis, Sylvan Creekmore, Katie Bassel, Karen Masnica, Brant Janeway, and everyone in editing and subrights that I don't interact with directly — for taking a risk on an unknown.

To author Lisa Daily for her Friday dose of hope accompanied by a slice of cheesecake.

To Emily Anderson for sharing the wisdom that family is made of the people who show up, and then showing up for me.

To Vala Afshar for reminding me what charisma looks like.

To Crystal Walker for teaching me the art of +1.

To Gabriela Lessa, whom I've never met, for her candid feedback. It made me cry a little, but saved this manuscript from the rejection pile.

To Richard Sachse, a.k.a. Mr. Wonderful, for his honesty, and his wife, Lynne, for encouraging me to practice love, compassion, and forgiveness.

To my cuz, Ezra Ace Caraeff, for his twelve-year-old wisdom on raging hormones, and the insight that people think of you what you think of them.

To Stephen King for offering *On Writing* to the world, and Professor Carolyn Megan for making me read it.

To Sara Bareilles: *Brave* cures my writer's block.

To Rachel Platten: *Fight Song* brought me back to life after I got sick.

To the writing community: I'm in awe of how you band together to support newbies.

To the dozens of readers who marked up drafts over the years I puttered on this while working full-time . . . y'all kept me going.